I0653410

Immigrant Hearts

a novel

by Catherine Gigante-Brown

Cover & Interior design by Vinnie Corbo
Author photo by Anne Coleman

Published by Volossal Publishing
www.volossal.com

Copyright © 2025
ISBN 978-1-963359-20-6

TABLE OF CONTENTS

Publisher's Note

Immigrant Hearts is a work of fiction. Names of characters, places, and incidents are products of the author's imagination or are used fictitiously. Any resemblance to actual events, locales, or persons, living or dead, is entirely coincidental.

For my grandparents,
Antonio and Luisa De Muccio

Part One
1919

CHAPTER ONE

Antonio

Antonio DeMarco was born in a small village in the province of Cosenza called San Vincenzo La Costa. Situated in the boot of Italy, San Vincenzo was located above the toe, in the part of the shoe known as the "vamp." The vamp is a rather unremarkable component of footwear. Not nearly as exciting as, say, the heel or the shaft. And this is the way Antonio felt about San Vincenzo: it was a rather unremarkable part of Italy. Not nearly as exciting as, say, Rome or Florence.

As far back as he could remember, Antonio wanted to escape the town of his birth. He felt as though he didn't really belong there. His younger brother Francisco (more commonly known as "Franco") seemed more content, accepted more, questioned less. But not Antonio. He could not be satisfied with the whitewashed houses on the stony hillsides. He could not find beauty in the smoky mountains nor in the crooked streets.

Although there was a glimmer of grace in the piercing, forlorn eyes of Santa Maria Della Neve as she stared at Antonio from the church's cupola. Her beauty was fleeting, however. It was there one moment, then gone the next. Was the Madonna of the Snow silently judging him? Voicing her disappointment without a voice, just in the gaze of her downcast eyes? These questions kept Antonio away from church.

He was drafted into a war he didn't understand, and promptly tried to forget soon after he was discharged. Because a Bosnian Serb took the life of an Archduke, the world was turned onto its ear. Antonio's world as well. He unceremoniously gave his manhood to a woman in Udine whose name he never bothered to learn, a woman whose body he bought for a few short moments on the evening of his eighteenth birthday, April 16, 1917.

Because Antonio was competent with a needle and thread, he never saw active combat. Instead, he was deployed sewing uniforms, mending socks and affixing patches to rough khaki fabric. There was even the occasional bullet hole or knife slash to repair. Scouring out bloodstains was left to another set of workers.

Some might consider being excused from battle a blessing, but not Antonio. He considered his unadorned chest a failure, though he did cut a dashing figure in his single-breasted tunic, knee wraps and short boots. His high collar, decorated with two stars, choked him. But he came out of the war alive. That was a lucky break, yes?

Antonio's family thought it fortunate that Gennaro Pucci, the local tailor, had taken him on as an apprentice before the war. So, Pucci gladly took him back in peacetime. Antonio's relatives joked that he was far too refined to dirty his hands with farm work as his father Giovanni did and as his grandfather before him had done. Antonio simply went along with his bestowed-upon career in tailoring as he did most things: quietly, affably, questioning nothing outwardly. But on the inside, Antonio was teeming, mutely roiling. He felt out of place, out of sorts. He knew he needed to leave San Vincenzo. But how? And where would he go?

CHAPTER TWO

Luisa

'There are so many of them,' Luisa thought. At first, it was almost as though her mother's womb had gone on strike when they left Italy. But after five years, Serafino and Dominic came, one year after the other. There were three already, not counting the child that was on the way. And not counting the one the family was forced to leave behind in Italy. (They were forbidden to even speak the girl's name.)

'If I let you take her, I'll never see you again,' Luisa's grandmother had supposedly told Luisa's mother Assunta. 'If I let you take her, you will never come back to Longobucco.'

The only reason the old *strega* didn't force her daughter to abandon Luisa was because the child was still nursing. The crone's prophecy turned out to be true. Since the Tozzis left Italy in 1909, Assunta had never once returned to Longobucco, not even when her daughter died from Spanish Influenza in 1918.

Since her sister's death a year earlier, Luisa could detect a new sadness in her mother, deeper, more profound than her usual melancholy. It was different than the sorrow that possessed Assunta after she'd popped out Luisa's brothers Sam and Dom onto bloody bedsheets, barely a year apart. And here Assunta was, fat with child

yet again, always tired, always mad, never enough love to
go around. Especially for Luisa.

'Why doesn't she learn English better?' Luisa
wondered as she bartered with the greengrocer about the
price of eggplant. *'Non pagare più di un centesimo a testa,'*
her mother had warned before Luisa left the cold-water
flat that was too small for five, let alone the sixth who
would arrive soon. The last time Luisa was tasked with
procuring eggplant, she paid two cents apiece. When she
got home, Assunta had pinched and twisted the skin on
Luisa's arm so hard her eyes watered and it left a mark.
But she didn't cry. Luisa refused to cry in front of her
mother. Or anyone.

'Why doesn't she cook anymore?' Luisa asked herself
as she fried the sliced, breaded eggplant in sizzling olive
oil. She had to stand on a footstool to reach the burners
on the cast-iron stove. At ten, Luisa was strong and
stocky but shorter than most girls her age. She attributed
her diminutive height to her mother's inferior breastmilk,
which had probably been tainted with sadness. Sadness
from being coerced to leave her firstborn behind in
Longobucco. Beatrice. There, Luisa said her name. Well,
she thought it at least.

A tongue of oil leapt from the pan and spat onto
Luisa's hand, as if to admonish her. She licked the
spot to soothe it, but that made it burn even more. As
Luisa did so, the fork she held dripped scalding grease
onto a square of the worn linoleum beneath her. Luisa
would have to drag out the mop again to clean it so no
one would slip and fall. She would have to be careful
not to step on the spot before then, not to track grease
throughout the apartment.

'Why couldn't Papa bring us to a nicer place?' Luisa
thought, pushing the purple-rimmed medallions around
the frying pan, mindful not to crowd them as Mama
instructed. It wasn't that Brooklyn was so bad, but their
second-floor walkup was. The Leedys and Joneses and

all the rest weren't as clean as the Tozzis were. *'Il sapone costa poco,'* Luisa's mother reminded her one day as they scrubbed the floor side by side on their hands and knees.

'Soap is cheap,' Luisa translated, hoping her mother would catch on and repeat the phrase in English. But she never did. Assunta never even *tried* to learn English.

There were mice, sometimes even rats, but not because the Tozzis weren't immaculate. It was the other families. *Sciattoni.* Slobs. Especially the Irish, Luisa's mother would say. *Soprattutto gli Irlandesi. Bastardi!* The vermin was the only reason the family was permitted to have a cat. Gatto, a scrawny tabby who meowed relentlessly in the alley below until the Tozzis finally took him in. To name the stray "Gatto" was her mother's idea. Gatto meant "cat" in Italian. How unimaginative! How silly!

Luisa herself would have named the cat "Caruso" after the opera singer. Once the girl had heard Caruso singing "*Là Ci Darem La Mano*" through an open window when a neighbor across the way played the record on their Victrola. It was so lovely it gave Luisa the shivers. Luisa decided that she would offer the Great Caruso her hand (as he pleaded in the song) and more. Errico, now, Enrico, was a Neapolitan, not Calabrese like Luisa. But she would forgive him that one transgression.

As if Gatto knew she was thinking of him, Luisa felt the soft brush of his body against her legs. Checking first to see that Mama wasn't lurking, Luisa fished a circle of eggplant from the oil, first draining it and cooling it on the newspaper-coated plate. She took a bite then offered the rest to Gatto. He swallowed it hungrily, careful not to gore Luisa with his needle teeth. She patted his belly, feeling his ribs beneath his loose skin.

"Luisa!"

She cringed at the way her mother barked her name. *"Si, Mama."*

"L'acqua..."

"L'acqua non bolle ancora," the girl lied. The water wasn't boiling yet because Luisa had forgotten to light the burner. Quickly, Luisa flicked on the gas beneath the pot and struck a match. The burner hissed then exploded into a blue ring of flame.

A moment later, Luisa's mother lumbered in, rubbing her swollen belly. Assunta's threadbare cotton housedress strained in the middle, threatening to rip. Then the door burst open, and the boys charged in, Dom blaming his brother for the noisy trespass and vice versa. *"Basta,"* their mother cried. *"Serafino…"*

"It's Sam," the boy corrected, insisting on Americanizing his name. Assunta herself balked at being called "Suzy," the whitewashed version of her beautiful given name. The majestic name "Assunta" was in honor of Our Lady, of the Assumption, of Mary defying death and rising to heaven on a puffy cloud as a queen. Assunta reminded her children of this as often as she could, though she knew deep inside that she was a lowly excuse for royalty.

"Sam?" their mother repeated, the texture of the sound unfamiliar on her foreign tongue.

Then Dom slipped on the linoleum grease—Luisa had forgotten all about wiping it up—and Sam tripped on top of him. They began punching and wrestling in the middle of the kitchen floor, knocking Luisa from her wooden cooking stool. And who do you think got smacked for it? Luisa. Always Luisa.

After supper, Luisa squeezed onto the narrow bed beside her brothers, struggling to stay off the wet spot that neither boy would admit to. "You *both* wet the bed," she grumbled, then took the blanket to sleep on the fire escape. To escape her brothers. To escape her parents' creaking bed beyond the thin tenement walls. 'Why can't Papa stay off her?' Luisa asked herself. 'Why? Why? Why?'

There were no answers.

CHAPTER THREE

Henrietta

'Each day he gets further and further away. How is that possible when Antonio is right here?' Henrietta asked herself. 'Somehow, he is more distant than when he was in Udine, sewing instead of fighting. I know it irked him, that he felt less of a man than those in combat. Only, this mother's heart was grateful. Relieved. Only, when he returned, it was not to San Vincenzo. He was still in a faraway land.'

Henrietta gazed out the window at the craggy hills, a sight which usually gave her pleasure. But not this day. She worried, not about her youngest, Francisco, who was naïve enough to find joy in everything. Franco, her change of life baby, her embarrassment at forty-five, as if men and women didn't seek pleasure in each other's bodies at that age.

But Antonio, Antonio had always been a worry. Colicky at birth, he would pull from her breast and cry relentlessly, staring into her face as he sobbed and she sobbed helplessly in return. Refusing Henrietta's full, overflowing breasts in favor of the chamomile tea and other soothing herbs the midwife brewed. Henrietta felt rejected, shunned, but still, she adored her firstborn son. Perhaps even more than her second.

Antonio, so sullen, even as a boy. With his heavy-browed, deep-set eyes that contemplated life so intensely, even the blue of the sky. 'That one will always be trouble,' her husband Giovanni told her. But Henrietta refuted this even though she feared it was true. Antonio would never be content, she worried, at least not on their dry, dusty farm.

Giovanni wanted a son whose hands were willing to harden with farm work, one who could easily wield a hammer, wring the neck of a chicken or pull a gasping calf from the sticky haunches of its mother. Early on, Antonio showed a preference for the needle rather than the shovel. He would rather help Henrietta with the sewing than sow a field with tomatoes. And he was skilled at darning, soon a better seamster than Henrietta was.

Antonio had delicate, fine-boned hands, topped with long, graceful fingers. In sharp contrast to Franco's short, stout digits, which were more suitable for fieldwork. This pleased Giovanni—at least one of his offspring would follow in his muddy footsteps.

If they could've afforded a piano, Henrietta suspected that Antonio would be proficient at playing. He had an ear for music and could repeat the notes of a concerto he'd heard only once, humming as he sewed. Antonio also had an affinity for opera. The first time he'd seen *Tosca* when a troupe breezed through one summer was an epiphany for him. To watch her son's face as he listened to *"Vissi d'arte"* brought tears to Henrietta's eyes. Any neighbor with a phonograph was subsequently pestered by Antonio to play whatever classical records they might have.

Henrietta guessed that Puccini and Verdi were more real to Antonio than the people in their village. 'That one…' Giovanni would begin, then shake his head.

'…that one will be worth the trouble,' Henrietta would insist, placing her hand over her husband's soil-encrusted fist which would slowly relax and unfurl with her urging. Now, all she had to do was convince herself.

Blessings on Gennaro Pucci for hiring Antonio back again as a tailor since his return from the war. Especially when the young man seemed so unmoored, wandering off to walk the hills until twilight to "clear his head." Perhaps Gennaro's kindness was because he had lost his own son in the Fifth Battle of Isonzo. Or maybe it was because Gennaro knew how unhinged wartime could make a fellow, he himself a veteran of the Boer Wars.

Since Antonio had secured gainful employment, he seemed less unhappy. Or perhaps he was simply less vocal about his discontent.

But at times Henrietta's son still roamed the scrubby hills when he couldn't sleep. Which was often. Henrietta would rise, stare out the window and follow the light of the lantern her son bore across the slopes. She would follow the beacon as it moved, swinging through the brush, until she could see it no more.

Sometimes, as her husband and second son snored, Henrietta softly cried, cried for her eldest's restless soul and wounded heart. Because there was nothing she could do to calm either.

CHAPTER FOUR

Assunta

Something about her daughter annoyed Assunta to a degree that her other children did not. And her two boys were hellions. Assunta secretly hoped the baby she was carrying was a girl. Not only to replace the daughter she had lost but because girls were easier. Quieter. More obedient. Less trouble. At thirty years of age, having pushed out four children and mourning one (whose name she refused to speak, or even think), Assunta was tired. Exhausted, even.

Perhaps she would attempt to cook a meal today. As much as Assunta hated to admit it, she missed feeding her family. She missed putting a frugal but filling dish on the table. Like *minestra de pane,* a thick soup made with wilted vegetables and stale bread that was sheer deliciousness. The peeling, chopping and grating required was slightly above a ten-year-old's skills set. Even one as bright as her Luisa.

But the stench of garlic simmering in olive oil turned Assunta's stomach and brought on a wave of nausea so strong, she had to run for the slop bucket. Or relegate herself to the battered armchair by the window. These days, she was suited to do nothing more than crochet, the steel hook an extension of her fingers. The basket of

tiny baby hats and sweaters beside the armchair was
steadily growing.

Now, Assunta worked on a blanket of pale rose with
yarn Mrs. Leedy had given her. 'It was in the clearance
bin at Kreske's,' the woman trilled, almost apologizing.
'I figured with pink, you'd surely have a girl.' Then
the Irishwoman lowered her voice as well as her gaze,
'Boys are so troublesome, aren't they?' To which Luisa,
Assunta's faithful translator, gave a small laugh. Assunta
did as well after the girl told her what their neighbor
had said.

'Grazie,' Assunta said, dipping her head and smiling.
She looked lovely when she smiled, her hard, weary
features momentarily melting.

'You're welcome, dear,' Mrs. Leedy told Assunta.
Then, to Luisa, she queried, 'Lu, how do you say it
in Eye-talian?'

The child thought for a moment. *'Prego, caro.'*

'Prego, caro,' Mrs. Leedy repeated, without rolling
the 'r.' 'Gee, who would have guessed I could speak
Eye-talian,' she said proudly. 'Make something pretty,
now, Suzy,' Mrs. Leedy told Assunta before she left.

She didn't bother to remind her neighbor that her
name was Assunta, not Suzy. Assunta tried to correct
Mrs. Leedy regarding her name many times but the Irish
lass never listened.

'Fare qualcosa di carina, ora,' Luisa told her mother,
translating Mrs. Leedy's parting words.

To which Assunta huffed, *'Faccio sempre qualcosa
di carino.'* Because everything she crocheted was
pretty, Assunta didn't appreciate being told to make
something nice.

As her fingers tucked through the pink yarn, Assunta
watched her daughter at the kitchen table. Luisa wasn't
preparing the meal but doing her homework. A stubby,
flea-bitten pencil was clutched in her fist. A warped
marble composition book was set in front of her. Public

School 104 had opened only the year before, just two blocks away, on Gelston Avenue, a stone's throw from Gatling Place. Otherwise, the child would not have gone to school at all. It was too much trouble and there was so much to be done at home. Besides, what purpose did knowing how to read serve a girl?

As it was, Luisa started attending school late, but she caught up with her lessons quickly. Unlike her brothers, Luisa cared about learning and was conscientious about her studies. She didn't grumble about squeezing in housework and homework but bore the burden of both without complaint.

Yes, her Luisa was a good girl. But then why was Assunta so harsh with her? Luisa was smacked and pinched more often than her horrid brothers were. The way she glowered at Assunta, defiant, refusing to cry. Those large, luminous eyes brimming but never spilling. They reminded her of... No, Assunta would not speak her dead child's name. She would not permit herself to even *think* it.

But carved into Assunta's memory was the girl's ashen, fallen face a decade earlier, her inky black eyes stricken as she bellowed, 'Mama! Mama!' Giuseppe guided Assunta by the shoulders and into the wagon that awaited them, stuffed with several suitcases that carried their meagre possessions. Baby Luisa clung to Assunta's chest and began bawling when she heard her sister's plaintive cries.

Assunta tried not to look back but what mother could resist doing so? Her last memory of her daughter Beatrice was of the three-year-old breaking free of her grandmother's grasp and chasing the wagon, barefoot, hair streaming wildly as she ran. Though Assunta shouted and wailed, *'Fermare! Fermare!'* her husband didn't stop; he whipped the horse harder so it would go faster. Little Beatrice stumbled and fell into the dirt, grabbing handfuls of soil and throwing it at the departing wagon, still screaming for her mama.

Assunta watched until the child was just a speck on the horizon as the wagon took the three of them from Longobucco to the port of Naples and her destiny. Giuseppe sold the horse and wagon at the dock for cash to help them in their new home. A ship called *Madonna* carried them to America. Assunta considered this name a good omen—they would be taken in the arms of the Blessed Mother to a distant shore. Clearly, she would protect them.

What choice did the Tozzis have but to leave Calabria? The farm was in ruins, thanks to Giuseppe's idiot of a brother, who was supposed to be tending to the livestock while Giuseppe was off fighting in the Boer War. The animals began dying one by one, first the smaller beasts like the chickens, then the sheep, goats, and finally, their modest herd of cows.

The Tozzis held on for as long as they could, Beatrice coming along less than a year after Giuseppe's return, a blue-eyed, dusky man who no one recognized upon his homecoming, his flesh so toasted from the South African sun. *'Melanzana! Melanzana!'* a village boy called when he spied a Black man coming over the hill and into Longobucco. This eggplant-skinned man turned out to be Giuseppe.

Upon finding his livestock dead, Giuseppe sold the farm for a pittance. They moved in with Assunta's mother, a hard woman who harbored a resentment for the man who could not support her daughter. Giuseppe learned the simplest trade he could, stonemasonry, but there wasn't much work in town for the people had little money. At times Giuseppe took jobs as distant as Cosenza, but that was almost seventy kilometers away, and he could only visit his wife and newborn child on his one day off, if at all. Then came another *bambina,* Luisa, and making ends meet was more difficult with another mouth to feed.

But America…in America it was rumored that there was plenty of work. In America, tall buildings were rising from the sea. In New York, it was said that a sixty-story tower would soon grow from the foot of Manhattan Island and more just like it would spring up beside it, like weeds. Giuseppe's friend Luigi had written to him of the job opportunities, the lodgings with running water and indoor plumbing. Luigi lived in a place called Brooklyn which was *paradiso,* he said.

Paradise turned out to be a cold-water flat with a shared toilet in the hall. Soon after the Tozzi Family arrived in Bay Ridge, Assunta's milk dried up and Luisa cried inconsolably just as Beatrice had when her mother abandoned her. Those eyes, those big, wet, baby eyes staring at Assunta reminded her of Beatrice. That was the first time Assunta had pinched Luisa…to silence her. It worked.

Why was she thinking of this? Why was Assunta thinking of Beatrice as she crocheted? As she watched Luisa diligently doing multiplication problems at the kitchen table? Why was she permitting herself to remember her lost girl when she swore that she wouldn't?

Luisa looked up from the table at her mother. They had the same eyes. The same mournful sable eyes. Luisa and Beatrice. Beatrice and Luisa. Sometimes it angered Assunta, how much Luisa resembled her sister. Sometimes it made Assunta want to strike Luisa. This is how much she pined for her lost daughter.

With difficulty, Assunta rose from the armchair by the window, first putting down the crochet needle and the square of pink blanket. Slowly, Assunta worked her way across the apartment to the kitchen, to her daughter sitting there, writing so intently. Instead of striking Luisa merely for living, Assunta bent slightly and pressed her lips to the girl's forehead in a kiss.

Luisa put down the pencil and cupped her fingers around her mother's, savoring the sweetness of the moment, for sweetness was so rare in this home.

Today, Assunta decided she would teach the girl how to make *minestra,* complicated as it might be for a child Luisa's age. They would work side by side, just as Assunta used to do with her own mother, and it would be a blessing.

CHAPTER FIVE

Antonio

He kept the steamship schedule close to his heart, in his breast pocket, for weeks before he dared to even look at it. The tri-folded brochure was there as he worked in Gennaro's shop, his foot furiously pushing the pedal of the sewing machine, up and down, down and up. Antonio patted the brochure occasionally to confirm that it still resided there, nervous it might somehow jump out and spill his secret. He was leaving. He was leaving. He didn't know when yet but someday, someday soon, Antonio was leaving San Vincenzo.

He slipped the schedule from his pocket to beneath his pillow each night, careful his brother Franco didn't see from his slender bed, inches from Antonio's. At ten, Franco was curious about everything and couldn't keep a secret even if you gave him a few *liras*.

Antonio sat on the edge of the bed in his underdrawers and smoothed the wrinkled paper against his knee. Franco mumbled, *"Vanessa, per piacere... Vanessa..."* Antonio smiled at his brother's dream. He could only imagine what Franco was begging the milkman's daughter to do. When Antonio was certain his brother was fast asleep, with his back turned, Antonio lit the lantern and read.

The *Giuseppe Verdi* made its passage from Naples to New York City several times a year. It typically took three weeks to cross the Atlantic, give or take. *Sette d'Octobre* leapt off the crinkled page at Antonio. The date waltzed before his eyes, tugged at his ear, poked his ribs and nudged his shoulder like an insistent suitor. Seven had always been Antonio's lucky number. And October was his favorite month, not too cold, not too warm. It seemed fortuitous to start his new life on October seventh.

Besides, Antonio's friend Vittorio, who had made the voyage two years prior, claimed that autumn in New York was like nothing else. The tree boughs shimmered with leaves of brilliant gold and crystalline ruby. The air was especially sharp and crisp and fragrant in one's lungs in the fall.

Leaving in October would give Antonio months to save from his wages plus he could take on private clients, making a dress here, a jacket there. Pucci didn't mind and permitted Antonio to use the shop's equipment after hours, free of charge, if the young seamster had side work. Sometimes his boss even gave Antonio lengths of remnant cloth that weren't enough for the large orders Pucci Tailoring produced.

Antonio had no shortage of private clientele, mostly single girls seeking a husband, eager to get the shy, dark-eyed artisan alone so they could brandish their charms like a soft sword. Though Antonio tried to be professional, his hands trembled and he perspired when he held the measuring tape to a slender waist. His normally strong voice faltered when he described the merits of linen over wool. Antonio worried that these women would guess his secret—that the suave, elegantly dressed sartor was practically a virgin who had never even kissed a woman. Save for those scant moments with the nameless prostitute on his eighteenth birthday in Udine, Antonio had scarcely bedded a woman. And besides, she didn't count. To him, only true love counted.

Passage to *L'America* was almost 160,000 *lire* and then there were food and living expenses to contend with once he arrived in New York. Vito assured Antonio that he could get him a job at the midtown shop where Vito worked. He also said Antonio could secure cheap lodgings in the Harlem rooming house where Vito stayed.

For Antonio, traveling steerage, crammed into a dormitory with a hundred or more strangers, was out of the question. Perhaps he could afford third class if he were frugal with his earnings from now on. His finger trailed across the brochure's page, following the columns of prices and amenities. Antonio knew he could deal with four or six to a cabin that featured washbasins and running water, though the notion of a shared toilet concerned him. However, it would only be for less than a month, so Antonio supposed he could bear it. He would spend most of his time on the splendid promenade decks and take his meals in the special third-class dining room.

His heart racing, Antonio convinced himself that he could do it. Save. Leave. Make a new life in a new world. *"Io posso...Io posso...Lo farò"* he began in a whisper that grew louder.

"Puoi cosa?" muttered Franco, wondering what it was that his brother could—and would—do. Could Franco be trusted to hold Antonio's secret? Was he old enough to keep Antonio's revelation to himself?

Despite his better judgement, Antonio told his younger brother his plan to escape to America. It was a relief to get his secret out into the stagnant air under the cover of night.

CHAPTER SIX

Luisa

'Having a baby is a messy business,' Luisa told herself. 'So much blood, slime and screaming...' In the basement washbasin, she scrubbed the stain on the white bedsheet. She doubted the angry red mark would ever come out, no matter how hard she scoured. Luisa added more bleach.

'Is it possible to wear your fingers to the bone?' she wondered as she rubbed even more vigorously. The old bed garment was beginning to wear thin, as was all the Tozzis' clothing. Even the new baby, a sister named Barbara, had garments that were worn to a shine, passed from neighbors who shared infant togs just as old hobos shared a bottle of rotgut around a fire. Except for the clothes Assunta had crocheted with gifted yarn, all the newborn's wares were hand-me-downs.

Luisa remembered how her mother's hardened face eased when Mrs. Rosenthal told Assunta that Jews honored the dead by naming babies after them. They used the first initial of the departed's first name so that they could be remembered, live on, in a sense. Of course, Luisa translated this for her mother, but clumsily, because it was a difficult concept to convey. But once she did, Assunta smiled and nodded; she understood. So, the nameless child became Barbara. In memory of Beatrice, the girl who was buried far across the ocean beneath foreign soil.

When the loud, ugly birth process had begun, Sam and Dom were whisked off to Zia Claudia's house. Galina, the midwife, commandeered Luisa to help, against her will. The girl would have preferred to read a book, to have pastina with butter topped with little snowlike piles of grated pecorino as her brothers were enjoying at Zia Claudia's. Luisa was sure they could hear Assunta's anguished cries even two blocks away on Dahlgren Place where *zia* lived.

'*Ragazza, prendere l'acaua…Ragazza, piu stracci…*' and once it was, '*Rapidamente, sei una ragazza lenta e stupida.*' But Luisa didn't want to fetch more water or more rags. She may not have been the brightest girl in the fourth grade, but she wasn't stupid. Or slow. She was faster than most of the boys, in fact, whenever they ran relay races in the schoolyard.

And Luisa did not want to see her mother's *fessa* stretched like a gaping wound beneath the bedsheet. Oh, to have a bowl of warm pastina, the miniscule stars sliding down Luisa's throat, no need to chew. But here she was, heating water on the burner and rummaging for old, clean towels while her father smoked his cigar on the front stoop, probably cringing with each of his wife's cries, sighing with guilt every time his name was uttered with a flurry of curses behind it.

This was the second day Luisa was forced to miss school this year—and today Mrs. Fitzpatrick was reading the class a chapter from *The Wonderful Wizard of Oz* as she did on Friday afternoons. Now Luisa would be a chapter behind. Maybe two if Assunta forced her to neglect her studies and help care for the baby. The girl longed to be doing anything else but this, to be anywhere else instead of here. To be on the concrete playing Jacks or even Johnny on the Pony. Instead, she was Galina's slave, hauling water, being called stupid and slow.

But when the baby came out, slick as a seal in the Central Park Zoo, Luisa's heart unfurled. The newborn was covered with a caul, which Galina expertly parted with her hands. At first, the tiny creature was purple and lifeless. Luisa and the midwife held their breath, each silently praying the child wouldn't be stillborn like Mrs. Rosenthal's son. But then Assunta's baby gave a swimmer's gasp and bawled even louder than its mother.

Galina made the sign of the cross. *'Un'altra ragazza,'* she shrugged, peeking at the swollen mound between its legs. Assunta nodded, eagerly taking her baby girl into her arms as Galina busied herself with the afterbirth. Luisa couldn't tell if the women were pleased or disappointed, but she, for one, was glad the child was female.

After the midwife and the girl cleaned the room, changed the sheets, washed the baby in a basin of warm water and opened the windows to release the stench of birth, Galina shouted out the window for Giuseppe to come meet his new daughter. He and Assunta exchanged private words that no one else could hear, their foreheads pressed together.

Soon after, Zia Claudia arrived with Sam and Dom in tow. Cradled in her hands, *zia* carried a bowl of pastina, covered with a thick dishcloth to keep in the heat. "How is my favorite goddaughter?" she asked, kissing the side of Luisa's head and her thick, black hair.

Luisa shrugged, shellshocked from what she'd witnessed on her mother's birthing bed.

"Sit," Zia Claudia told her. "*Mangiare.* Everything else will wait."

Luisa sat at the scarred kitchen table. It had been there when the Tozzis moved in, passed from immigrant family to immigrant family. Luisa ate quickly, like a starving street dog, spooning the star-shaped pasta into her mouth with a velocity that shocked her.

The pastina was still warm.

CHAPTER SEVEN

Henrietta

A ntonio worked so much that Henrietta rarely saw
him. He went to Gennaro's tailor shop before
the sun came up and arrived home long after it
had set. On the stove, his mother kept a plate of whatever
they'd had for supper waiting for him. Hearty, peasant
fare: cornmeal with fresh tomato sauce, spaghetti with
sardines, boar stew. Whatever it happened to be, Antonio
accepted it gratefully and ate it with the same gusto.
'Grazie, Mama,' he always said before tucking in.

Henrietta was often already in bed when her son sat at
the table, alone. *'Prego, figlio mio,'* she would say sleepily
from the adjoining room.

But this particular night, Henrietta forced herself
to stay awake, sitting in the uncomfortable, stiff-backed
kitchen chair that her husband had crafted with his
own hands. Light blue rosary beads between her fingers,
Henrietta mumbled a string of Our Fathers and Hail
Marys, worrying the notches in the crystal strands.

It was past nine when Henrietta saw the swing of the
lantern light as her eldest son approached the farmhouse.
She counted the seconds it took for his relaxed stride to
bring him to the threshold. Eleven.

Antonio's shoulders stooped deeper than a
twenty-year-old's had a right to. Dark circles were

etched beneath his eyes. Weary as he was, Antonio still smiled when he saw his mother. "You're up late," he said.

"There's stuffed eggplant," she responded, "with raisins and breadcrumbs, just how you like it."

Henrietta began to rise from the table, preparing to heave her thick, farm wife's body from the rustic chair. "That's all right," Antonio told her. "I can get it myself. Sit."

But Henrietta couldn't sit. In the village she was from, women served men. Even if the man was your son. Men sat; women stood. "But you serve yourself every night," she said. "I'm here. Give me the honor."

Antonio sighed and listened to his mama. He sat. She pressed her palms to the tabletop and stood. Henrietta uncovered the plate of dark purple vegetables warming on the stovetop and placed it before him. She slipped a fork, knife and a cloth napkin beside the chipped plate. Antonio bowed his head in thanks and prayer as his mother severed one, then two slices of bread with the sharp-toothed knife. This knife was meant for bread only; it never cut anything else.

"It's good," Antonio told her, with a full mouth. He hadn't eaten since breakfast and had sewed right through lunch. Henrietta nodded in response. She knew she was a fine cook, but it was nice to hear it sometimes.

From the gallon jug, Henrietta poured a tumbler of dark wine, then another. Antonio raised his eyebrows as he chewed, the raisins' sugariness a perfect complement to the tang of the garlic. "You never drink wine," Antonio remarked in surprise.

"Maybe it will help me sleep," Henrietta conceded. The nearby sounds of her husband and youngest son snoring gently were barely audible but still, she heard them. They emitted slightly different tones, like woodwinds warming up in an orchestra, mocking her wakefulness. "Lately, I've been having trouble sleeping," she tagged on.

Antonio dabbed his lips with the cloth. "Worried?"

"A mother always worries," Henrietta said.

"Franco will find his path," he assured her. "We all do."

She shrugged.

"Papa?" Antonio asked.

"Not Papa," she said.

Their eyes met above his plate, which was almost empty. "Me?"

Henrietta took a swallow of *chianti*. Giovanni made it in the autumn with his friend Stefano, who had a small vineyard. "You work day and night," she began. "You're hardly ever home. When you're not here, you don't eat and I..." The words poured from her in a torrent, like a river that had overrun its banks.

Her face was grooved with such concern that Antonio had no choice but to tell his mother of his plans. "When?" she crowed.

"Soon," he told her.

"I won't ask why," Henrietta sighed. "Because I already know. I've known for a long time that I couldn't... that this place couldn't hold you."

Silence, then more wine. "I'm happy for you," she said. "Truly I am. What mother wouldn't be? But I'm sad for myself." What mother wouldn't be?

Henrietta rose from the table, not even clearing it. She didn't want her son to see her cry, otherwise, he might not go. But he had to go; it was best for him.

Before Henrietta could flee, Antonio caught her by the waist. He wrapped his arms around her and held his mother close, this tiny dynamo who only reached his shoulder. Antonio kissed her wiry curls so unruly they escaped her ropelike braid. They smelled of hay and kitchen and regret and tenderness, but mostly of hope. "I'll never see you again," she feared aloud.

"You will," he said. "I promise."

37

Henrietta broke from his embrace—any type of physical affection, even from one of her sons, made her uncomfortable. "I will hold you to it," she told Antonio.

"You will come visit me. I'll send for you."

She shook her head sadly. "My place is in this place," she said with finality. "I was born here and I will die here."

Then Henrietta went into her room, changed into her nightgown and slipped into bed beside her husband. Half asleep, Giovanni drew her close. His hands, rough from the plow, were a comfort. "Antonio is leaving," she wept.

"It's time," Giovanni said. "*Tutti gli uccelli devono volare.*" All birds must fly.

CHAPTER EIGHT

Assunta

S he didn't need a calendar to tell her that the end of summer was nearing because late August, without fail, Luisa always begged and pleaded with Assunta to be permitted to attend school in September. While the boys begged and pleaded not to go to PS 104, Luisa was just the opposite. Such a strange girl. What child liked school?

On the free calendar that Uccello, the butcher, gave away, Luisa had even scribbled *"Scuola"* and underscored it three times in the square that announced the first day of school. Fifth grade, this year. Ten years old this past March. My, how quickly time passes. Already, Barbara, the baby, was ready to spout teeth. Assunta could feel the hard nubs beneath her gums when the child nursed. Thank God Barbara was an easy baby, despite her urgent, untidy entry into the world.

But Luisa…what good could school possibly do a girl? It could only cause trouble. It could only make her desire things she couldn't have. It could only make her desire more. More than this squalid, second-story walkup apartment filled with the odors and filth of others that was impossible to wash away. More than a husband who worked until his back ached, hauling bricks in a wheelbarrow, mixing cement to build grand, tall buildings he would never enter once completed.

Most children Luisa's age begged to go outside and play. But the girl had long given up on this request. There was so much work at home. Three children to care for besides herself and six mouths to feed. And Assunta was always so tired.

Luisa was a help, a blessing, but in other ways, she was a curse. Always asking why. *Perché? Perché?* Always staring at Assunta with those deep, dark eyes. Accusing her. But of what? Of everything, but of nothing in particular.

In the spare moments she managed to steal away, the girl could be found writing in a little book with a red cover that tied closed with a ribbon. *"Che cos'é?"* Assunta wondered, snatching it from her.

"É un diario…Il mio diario." Luisa snatched it back, risking a slap. "It's mine. It's private. *Privata. Personale."*

Even if Assunta could read the squiggles that filled the pages, she would not have understood. She couldn't read much Italian, let alone *L'American.* But perhaps she would have understood the sentiment, the longing in the lines. Perhaps not.

The cloth-covered book was a gift from that blasted teacher for winning some sort of contest. Luisa had tried to explain it to Assunta in an excited mix of Calabrian slang and English, but Assunta was lost. She pretended to grasp what the girl was saying: "Spelling bee…best in class…*migliore delle classe…*'parallelogram' was my word…Mama! *Per favore, ascoltare!"*

But Assunta couldn't listen. There was so much to do all the time. Like take the laundry from the line, fold it and put it away. It was surely dry by now. Then the baby cried.

"Un momento," the girl pleaded, sitting at the table with a hard-backed book. *Una Piccola Principessa,* Luisa had said it was called. Was this another gift from that infernal Mrs. Fitz-something? The cover was pink with

gold lettering and there were drawings inside. Magical drawings. Luisa showed them to her mother occasionally, trying to explain about Sara Crewe and Becky and that mean *strega* Miss Minchin. Sometimes Assunta caught Luisa reading passages aloud to the baby in a whisper as though a four-month-old could understand.

Chopping an onion at the counter, Assunta glanced over to see her daughter lift Barbara from her basket on the floor. Luisa read intently, bouncing Barbara on her knee as Luisa held *A Little Princess* in one hand and with her free hand, wedged a knuckle into the teething child's mouth. Barbara seemed happy, Luisa, even happier.

Assunta slipped the chopped onions into a sizzling pan of olive oil then reached for the head of garlic. She broke off one clove, then another. With her fist, she brought the side of the paring knife's blade onto the cloves one by one, then slipped them from their papery jackets. The girls started at the sound. *"Un momento, Mama,"* Luisa said again. "I'm almost done with this chapter."

Yes, Assunta would give the girl a chance to finish reading. But she couldn't spare a second more.

CHAPTER NINE

Antonio

Antonio was ill for the first three days of his journey across the Atlantic, as were two of his companions in the six-person cabin. Luckily, Antonio had secured a space on a lower bunk; it was closer to the slop buckets. Those who were not sick had compassion for their fellow berth mates, bringing them warm mugs of strong tea, bowls of crackers and emptying the buckets into the toilet in the restroom down the corridor when the stench became overpowering.

Whenever Antonio thought of his mother and their tearful departure at the bus station, he felt even worse, the stab deep in his heart rather than in the pit of his gut. He'd told Henrietta there was no need to see him off in Naples—it was almost 500 kilometers from San Vincenzo to the Neapolitan docks—and she relented. But Henrietta insisted on accompanying Antonio to their town's bus depot. It was harvesting time and his father was busy in the fields. As it was, it took some convincing for Giovanni to excuse Franco from his work to see his brother off.

'I'll never lay eyes on you again,' Henrietta sobbed, as she had countless times in the weeks prior.

'You will, Mama. I promise.' Antonio hoped he could live up to that promise.

As he boarded the bus, he glanced back only once, and that was to see Henrietta collapsing into Franco's arms. The ten-year-old struggled to hold his mother's weight. '*Andare*,' Franco mouthed to his brother when he saw Antonio pause. '*Andare.*' And Antonio went. He did not look back again.

On the ride to Naples, Antonio forced himself not to think of his mother, the family or the farm. He was glad he decided to take the bus rather than the ferry to the port. Although the trip took longer, he reasoned that he would be spending enough time on the water during his Atlantic voyage. Three weeks, at least. And besides, he wanted to say goodbye to the dry, rocky, desolate land that his father tried so hard to farm. He wanted to say goodbye to the antiquated villages. Goodbye for now, possibly forever.

As the *Giuseppe Verdi* pushed through the waves, Antonio recalled his difficult sendoff at San Vincenzo's bus station. It was all he ruminated upon from his sickbed.

Like a phoenix from the ashes, like Jesus from the dead, on the third day, Antonio rose from his berth. He shakily made his way to the wash basin and splashed water onto his face. The notion of running water—and flush toilets in the corridor, via a box above the bowl with a pull chain!—was a source of wonder to him. Since no one was in the room at the time, Antonio took the opportunity to run a damp rag under his arms and over his privates.

His legs were still rubber as he navigated the narrow passageway to the dining hall. It was the first time he felt well enough to sit in one of the turned brass and mahogany swivel chairs. The long tables were covered with linen and the drinking glasses were finer than any Antonio had used in San Vincenzo. So too were the plates, pure white, not marred like the farmhouse crockery. Plus, all the utensils matched.

The dining saloon was expansive; more than three-hundred passengers could be seated comfortably there at one time. Though the *Giuseppe Verdi* set sail from Naples, most on board hailed from different parts of Italy and from neighboring countries, so they spoke many tongues. Although the travelers were civil, passing the butter and salt cellars with the hint of a gesture, few could have deep conversations because of the varied Italian dialects and assorted languages they spoke.

Most days, Antonio spent his time walking through the smoking rooms, lounges and on the covered deck reserved for people of his class. There were accommodations for 100 in first class, 260 in second class and 1,825 in third class, but the ship didn't seem overly crowded. Antonio always managed to find a deck chair to laze upon, though he preferred to stroll, to study the steel-gray waters, dimpled with waves, to be moving as the ship moved forward.

He kept to himself, occasionally seeking out a tufted leather chair and table in the men's lounge to write a letter to his mother, scrawled on thin onionskin paper. Unlike most women in San Vincenzo, Henrietta could read and was often called upon to recite letters their neighbors received from relatives. Antonio would mail his correspondence to his mother in order, little by little, after the ship made landfall.

Antonio walked in rain, in sunshine, when it was blustery and when the air was static. Sometimes, he imagined he saw land, but it was just his eyes playing tricks on him. It was just the monotony of the sea. Antonio was anxious to begin another life, excited to see *La Signora.* The Lady. She who resided in New York Harbor, bedecked in robes of blue copper, right arm raised. She who wore a seven-spiked crown yet was not a queen.

"Give me your tired, your poor, your huddled masses yearning to breathe free…"

On the deck of the *Verdi* was the only place Antonio felt he could truly breathe. Would his friend Vito be waiting for him when Antonio was released from immigration on Ellis Island? Would Antonio pass through processing as hale and healthy or would the doctors discover a reticent disease and send him back? Would he miss his family with the same ache he felt now? Did he break his mother's heart?

There were no answers to these questions. Not yet. So, Antonio walked. He walked the wooden outdoor decks. He walked the litosilo decking below. He walked and walked.

"Send these, the homeless, tempest-tossed to me, I lift my lamp beside the golden door!"

1923

CHAPTER TEN

Luisa

The day after she graduated from the eighth grade at Public School 104, Luisa found herself at a sewing machine at what could only be called a sweatshop. There was no corsage, no special meal, no gifts upon her graduation. A present or flowers would have been frivolous. There were so many mouths to feed at the Tozzi home and Luisa was told that she needed to help. So, she had no choice but to help. Going to high school was not an option, especially for a girl.

The job they gave to a young woman with no experience as a seamstress was a buttonholer. Luisa hated it. She couldn't seem to get the rhythm right. The needle kept hitting the button, snapping in two. She kept hiding the broken needles, the scarred buttons, afraid she'd get in trouble, frightened they would dock her pay. Her skirt pocket was tinkling with them.

When she'd destroyed her last button, Luisa had to ask the floor manager for more. He smiled at her sheepishness and said she was doing well, then sent her back to her machine with a pat on the bottom and a sack full of unblemished buttons. Luisa blushed crimson and slunk back to her Singer. Her knee shook as she worked the pedal.

Luisa didn't want to be there. Where she really wanted to be was the library, hidden between stacks of books. What she really wanted to be was a librarian, but she would need more schooling to do this. And more schooling was not possible, not for a girl. *"Tu sei pazzo?"* Assunta laughed when Luisa suggested it. *"Con che soldi?"*

No, Luisa wasn't crazy and she would find the money, somehow. She and her mother continued scrubbing the tub of undershorts in the basement. There was a profusion of *muthandis*. Long underwear, and socks too. Socks so filthy they could practically stand and walk off on their own. Luisa was stewing as she scrubbed. 'Why do men smell so bad?' she wondered. Assunta didn't seem to notice the odor or her daughter's anger. 'Why does she keep having children?' Luisa asked herself.

Giuseppe's back was acting up again. The physician from the bricklayers union had written a scrip for him to get pills that Luisa's father couldn't afford to fill. Not with six hungry mouths to feed. It was either quell his pain or feed his family. The rotgut wine his friend Belloni fermented in his musty cellar took the edge off the ache and it cost only pennies.

The doctor also prescribed that Giuseppe refrain from work until his back mended. But the foreman on the job only laughed at this notion and pushed the paper back into Giuseppe's face. "I got plenty to take your place," the pink-faced boss scoffed. "It don't take no genius to push a wheelbarrow filled with bricks, Joey."

So, Luisa worked. Especially after her father told them his foreman's reaction to Giuseppe's injured back. Already Sam and Dom were doing their part, taking on odd jobs after school. When they graduated, they would learn a trade like their father. There was protection in unions.

Luisa's only solace was her books. Her nose was buried in them on trolleys. Books occupied her time not only on restroom breaks at work but as she munched on the hard Italian bread slathered with butter and sugar that comprised her lunch. Luisa didn't care that her coworkers snickered behind her back, calling her names. At times they did so to her face. *Kniha dievĉa. Chica del Libro. Książkowa Dziewczyna. Ragazza Libro.*

But Luisa didn't care. There were worse names to be called than "Book Girl" in a myriad of languages: Slovak, Spanish, Polish, even Italian. Luisa didn't care because she had found refuge from the constant whir of machines, the constant prick of fingertips on needles, the constant chatter.

As she worked, hunched over the black Singer sewing machine, Luisa was someplace else. She rose far above the warped floorboards littered with scraps of thread and fabric—the garments they made were the only bright spots in the huge warehouse. As she sewed, Luisa escaped to Emily Brontë's West Yorkshire Moors, to Louisa May Alcott's Massachusetts, to Jane Austen's Highbury. These were all women who had written books when women weren't meant to do such things.

Though she was tired from her day in the factory, Luisa took the trolley several stops further to the Fort Hamilton branch of the Brooklyn Public Library. Before mounting the steps, she gave a silent benediction, thanking Mrs. Gelston of toney Shore Road for donating a collection of books that later became the Fort Hamilton Free Library. She thanked Andrew Carnegie, an immigrant like Luisa, but from Scotland, who believed it was it important to build libraries for the poor, like her. Luisa even thanked the architects Lord and Hewlitt, who designed Carnegie's branch of the Brooklyn Public Library, a uncomplicated brick building with limestone trim, overhanging eaves and high windows that let in the sunlight.

Luisa scurried to the fiction aisle, which she knew so well, she could find it in the dark. She dashed to "F" then to "T," pulling out thick volumes, then hurrying to the front desk. She was meant to cook supper that night and couldn't be late. Luisa returned *Wuthering Heights* and *Little Women,* exchanging them for *Madame Bovary* and *Anna Karenina.*

"Ah, you're broadening your horizons," Mr. Szczesny, the librarian, remarked.

At first, Luisa didn't get the joke; she worried that she was breaking an unwritten rule by borrowing too many books. Then she saw Mr. Szczesny's smile.

"Taking a trip to Europe, I see," he said, tapping Bovary's hard, red woven cloth cover. "Do you have your passport?"

Luisa handed Mr. Szczesny her library card, crinkled from use. "This is better than a passport," she told him.

There was no time for small talk. Luisa nodded, took back her card, shoved the books into her satchel then scuttled down the steps. She still needed to stop at Silvio's shop for zucchini and two knobs of garlic. Hopefully, her brother Sam had remembered to get the half-price, day-old loaves of bread from Lobue, the baker, as he was instructed. But Sam often forgot.

Luisa glanced at St. Patrick's Church cattycornered from the library. If Assunta asked why she was late, Luisa would say that she ducked into St. Pat's to light a candle. For Beatrice, naming her unspoken sister. That would satisfy her mother, though it would be a black mark on the girl's soul for lying. And lying about praying in favor of reading. But Luisa didn't care. Books were worth lying for.

She quickened her pace and turned the corner at Ninety-Second Street, hustling toward Gatling, and home. The fourteen-year-old had so few pleasures. Work. Home. Cook. Then maybe if she wasn't too exhausted, she would read aloud to Barbara at bedtime, careful not to burn the pages of *Anna Karenina* on the candle stub.

CHAPTER ELEVEN

Henrietta

A ntonio's letters never arrived frequently enough for Henrietta's liking. Even one each day would not be adequate. Still, she savored his every word and tried to picture what her son described in his graceful, loping handwriting. The streets of Harlem. The tall, brick rooming house where he slept. The large, green park that bordered his neighborhood. The stone canyons of buildings he wandered through.

No wonder Antonio had been drawn there, Henrietta admitted to herself. Manhattan lacked the repetitiveness of farm life. Of planting. Of weeding. Of sowing. Of watering. Then doing it all over again from season to season. Manhattan was different, exciting.

What could Henrietta write back to her son? That she missed him? That she pined for him with the empty desolation that only a mother could? This, he already knew. Before he departed, Henrietta assured Antonio that she understood why he was leaving but still...still... it didn't make his leaving any easier to bear.

At suppertime, Henrietta would read Antonio's letters aloud to Giovanni, who never bothered to learn to read, and Franco, who had. She sat at the rough-hewn farm table, her voice rising with emotion, then laughing like a wind chime when Antonio wrote of the streetwalker he'd mistaken for a maiden in distress.

As Henrietta turned the translucent paper and continued reading, her husband chewed and nodded. Franco listened, rapt, fork and knife suspended in midair. Henrietta feared that her youngest son would leave too when he was old enough. Following in the footsteps of his brother. Footsteps across the sea.

Sometimes Antonio tucked in a private note for his brother, not marked with his full Christian name, "Francisco," but with his affectionate nickname, *"Faccia Buffa."* Funny Face. Though tempted, Henrietta never read the letters intended for Franco. Some things were personal, even in a cramped farmhouse.

Henrietta knew that Franco kept his brother's letters, as she did, in a not-so-secret place, tied with string. (Her collection was thicker, though.) She also knew that her son treasured Antonio's words as much as she did. But not Giovanni.

In one such letter, sent soon after he'd arrived on Manhattan Island, Antonio had slipped a black and white photograph he'd bought from an industrious photographer who sold snapshots to new immigrants. It measured no more than two inches by three inches and depicted the 1919 New York City skyline. A full moon was suspended above a double-spanned stone bridge and the pointed tops of several tall structures pierced the clouds.

Henrietta had never seen so many buildings crowded into one place, but her son's letter explained that the whole city was like this. Antonio's dark blue script clarified that the photo had been taken from a place called Brooklyn, which was across a river called East. The bridge itself was named the Brooklyn Bridge and linked Manhattan to its namesake.

Henrietta displayed this photograph in a willow frame that Giovanni had crafted specifically to hold it.

Only Henrietta was permitted to touch it. She cleaned the wood and glass lovingly, and often.

Beside the photo was another, also in a handcrafted frame. It showed her son, slightly stouter, four years older, hands in pockets, fedora set at a jaunty angle, slight smile on his full lips, bow tie a bit crooked, posing on a street called Duffield. It had been taken by a professional photographer outside his studio, Antonio had written. Henrietta studied it so often that she remembered every detail with her eyes closed, down to his camel topcoat and polished, pointed shoes.

Inside the envelope that had held Antonio's letter and photograph, her son had tucked in American dollars with the instructions for Henrietta to use the money to have a picture taken of the three who remained in San Vincenzo. Antonio said he missed them terribly and was saving up to come visit. He wanted to see for himself how Franco had grown and how his parents had grown older, seasoned like a good wine. Truth be told, though Antonio was saving a fair portion of his earnings, he wasn't sure if he could ever visit his homeland again. But he pretended he would, as much for his mother's benefit as for his own.

Henrietta did as she was asked. She marched her husband and youngest son to Enzus's Fotoshop on *Spozano Piccolo* so Enzus could take their portrait. Henrietta, Giovanni and Franco were scrubbed and starched, wearing their Sunday best. Giovanni's mustache was sharply waxed; Henrietta's matronly shift and black lace collar accented her dark hair, recently threaded in gray. Franco seemed startled, ready to run. Standing stiffly against the painted backdrop of a city that was not theirs, the trio wore fake smiles and forced their eyes to stay open wide, just as Enzus commanded.

The result, seen weeks later, were remote renderings of the three, shadows of the rural, hardworking people they truly were, encapsulated in varying shades of tobacco. As little as the photograph resembled his family, when Antonio received it in his Harlem room a month after it was mailed, his mother knew that her son would be pleased, if not slightly wistful.

But the question remained: would Henrietta ever see Antonio again?

CHAPTER TWELVE

Assunta

Assunta couldn't help but notice the way boys looked at her Luisa, and even, (for shame!), some men. When the girl ran for the trolley. When the girl sat reading on the grass, not far from her family at a picnic on the hills of Shore Road. When the girl pushed the buggy with her most recent sibling, another brother. 'Do they wonder if the child is Luisa's?' Assunta asked herself.

She watched these randy males watching Luisa from afar as Assunta nursed little Paolo, he of the endless appetite. 'This is the last child, truly,' she promised herself, her body weary from carrying, then expelling, then suckling her babies. But somehow, Assunta knew he would not be the last.

Married off not much older than Luisa was now, Assunta feared that her daughter was too headstrong to become a wife. Luisa did things her own way, no matter how many times she was warned, smacked or reprimanded. *'Aiutami, Signora,'* Assunta would plead to the heavens. But even Mother Mary couldn't, or wouldn't, help with this one.

Young Luisa clearly had no gift as a seamstress. Her mother was forever finding crushed pearl buttons and snapped needles shoved into the girl's pockets. Perhaps

Luisa would fare better as a cutter or a presser. But Luisa's heart—or mind—wasn't in her work; instead, both were dug deeply into her books.

It was no secret that the girl read late into the evening—maybe this was why she faltered at her work. Because Luisa was exhausted from reading about hearts that beat beneath floorboards, tired from being chased by the Creature through the hills in *Frankenstein*. Luisa tried to share these stories with her mother as they shelled chestnuts or skinned sardines at the kitchen table. But Assunta didn't understand the allure of books. The macabre stories only ended up frightening Barbara.

Assunta knew of Luisa's late-night reading marathons because the candlelight shone from beneath the bedroom door. It irked her—they couldn't afford all those foolhardy candles Luisa was burning. But Assunta tried not to complain. The girl worked hard both at home and at the factory. 'She should marry a candlemaker,' Assunta sighed. 'If he would have her.'

Out of her five children, Luisa was the one Assunta worried about most. And not solely because of her obsession with books. Barely fourteen, the girl was shut into a sweatshop twelve hours a day, six days a week. Assunta knew her daughter wasn't happy. But then again, who was happy?

Then there was the matter of safety. Luisa was a clumsy child, always running into a doorjamb or a piece of furniture because her head was in the clouds—or in a paperback. Her fingertips were littered with red pinpoints from needle pricks. And just yesterday, a needle had pierced her palm, requiring pliers to remove it and a shot of whiskey to calm the girl. The floor manager patched her up and immediately sent Luisa back to work. She didn't tell her mother about his customary pat on the rump, however. It would have thrown the woman into a tizzy.

Although it had occurred a dozen years earlier, the Triangle Shirtwaist Factory fire had taken the lives of one hundred and forty-six workers, mostly young Italian women like Luisa, and Jewish immigrants.

Not much had changed since then but at least foremen no longer locked the doors to exits and stairwells. To use the powder room, workers had to jump through hoops. At least there was a fledgling union, of which Luisa was a member. Slowly growing, the International Ladies' Garment Workers' Union would hopefully protect its laborers from future disasters.

But Assunta would never forget the March day in 1911, when she forced her neighbor, Mrs. Rosenthal, to read the news article reprinted in the *Brooklyn Daily Eagle* from the *Milwaukee Journal* a couple of days after the disaster. It was a firsthand account from one William G. Shepard, a reporter who was a helpless eyewitness to the tragedy. At first, Mrs. Rosenthal refused, proclaiming it too sad. But Assunta pressed her kindly neighbor, and afterwards regretted it.

Trudy Rosenthal cleared her throat and reluctantly began. She read it very slowly so Assunta could understand. Trudy's voice quivered toward the end when she came to this part:

"...*A young man helped a girl to the window sill. Then he held her out, deliberately away from the building and let her drop. He held out a second girl the same way and let her drop. Then he held out a third girl who did not resist. They were as unresisting as if he were helping them onto a streetcar instead of into eternity. Undoubtedly, he saw that a terrible death awaited them in the flames, and his was only a terrible chivalry.*

"*Then came love amid the flames. He brought another girl to the window. She put her arms about him and kissed him. Then he held her out into space and dropped her. But quick as a flash he was on the window sill himself. His coat fluttered upward—the air filled his trouser legs. I could see that he wore tan shoes and hose. His hat remained on his head..."*

There was more but Trudy stopped abruptly. Assunta's neighbor's tears hit the newsprint in splats, she recalled. Then she let the *Eagle* slide from her fingers and threw herself into Assunta's arms. They cried together until Luisa, then only two, woke from her cradle, wailing too.

And now, at fourteen, Luisa was working in a sweatshop like those Triangle Shirtwaist girls.

At home, Assunta had her daughter's eyes to contend with; they were so dark and sad and accusatory. What could Assunta do? Of course, she wanted her daughter to be content, not to be so exhausted and bleary-headed at the end of the day. Besides, this type of work would prepare Luisa for life itself. For a life of discontent and dullness, which was most often a woman's lot. Not misery exactly, yet not quite joy.

1926

CHAPTER THIRTEEN

Antonio

Several years passed, each like the one before it. Antonio could hardly believe he had been in the United States going on seven years. Although he sent letters to San Vincenzo regularly, he hadn't been back home once. He knew this broke his mama's heart, but he had no choice. He was building a life here, a future in America. There wasn't a future for him in that insignificant Calabrian town as a farmer's son, and to visit was so expensive.

Antonio still resided at the Harlem boarding house. It was clean, well-appointed and Mrs. Rizzo provided two balanced meals a day—a simple breakfast and supper. Hearty peasant fare like his mother used to make—greens and beans in rich broths with not much, if any, meat. Just as his mother did, Mrs. Rizzo kept the evening meal warm on the gas stove's pilot light if Antonio had to work late. If he arrived in time to share dinner with the other boarders, hearing the Calabrese dialect traded across the tabletop was a balm to his spirit. It was just like home. Well, almost.

Because of his frugal lifestyle, Antonio was able put aside quite a bit each week, more than half his salary. He usually slipped a few bills into the envelope along with the letters to his family. He hoped his mother would spend it and not save it. He hoped she didn't ache too deeply for him and could think of him fondly.

Though the Metropolitan Opera was only a handful of miles from his uptown home, Antonio dared not squander his pay on a ticket. Not even when *Tosca,* his favorite piece, was performed. Sometimes on a Sunday afternoon, he would take a brisk stroll downtown to the opera house just the same, if only to watch the fancy people arrive at the crossroads of Broadway and Thirty-Ninth Street, then disappear inside the opulent building, the doors whooshing closed, clearly marking the distinction between the haves and have-nots.

Antonio would stand near the entrance as though waiting for someone, and if he were lucky, he might catch the rousing first strains of *Rigoletto* or *Carmen,* thrilling as a circus calliope. Well dressed in a fine suit and coat sewn of his own hand, a smart hat topping his head (he'd befriended a milliner who worked in the building, and Abbruzzese often gave Antonio his samples), the young man cut an impressive figure.

Once Antonio had the good fortune of being gifted a ticket to *Aida.* He stood there speechless when a comely lady slipped him a scrap of paper, explaining that she would rather go shopping at Macy's than sit next to "some schmo" for three hours and watch "a fat broad" sing. Then she gave Antonio a hurried peck on the cheek and dashed off giggling with her girlfriend, remarking that Antonio was "a dead ringer for Valentino."

As he was shown to his seat in the parterre beside the ticket-giving lady's pouting would-be suitor, the tearful opening violins tugged at Antonio's heartstrings. Then the kettle drums stirred his soul. The young Italian ignored the daggers cast at him by the ditched boyfriend and allowed himself to be transported to ancient Egypt, swallowed up by the tale of a captured Ethiopian princess, ardor, backstabbing and ultimately, death. Always death. And the music...oh, the music... Verdi at his best.

Only after the lights rose hours later, did Antonio realize that his face was drenched with tears. Hoping no one would notice, he mopped his face with a linen handkerchief his mother had sent, embroidered with his initials, *AD*. Antonio DeMarco. A regal name, he thought.

By day, he worked in the Garment District, in a tall building a stone's throw from the Metropolitan and from the theatres of Broadway. Other venues Antonio could not afford to visit. Although his specialty was men's apparel, Antonio could make—or mend— just about anything. His talented hand was equally suited for thick cloth as well as the gossamer of ladies' lingerie.

Staying late one evening, Antonio heard a commotion. The manager from Costuming on the floor below was frantically searching for a tailor to do a quick repair to a chorus girl's costume. It had caught on a dressing room nail an hour before curtain time. *"Lo faró,"* Antonio said, then, in hesitant English repeated, "I will do it."

The floor manager disappeared and the chorine threw off her trench coat, revealing a perfectly pear-shaped, exposed left breast and a pink sequined bodice torn to the navel. Antonio blushed from top to tail, feeling his manhood stir immediately. He motioned for the woman to step behind the curtain to disrobe. She did so swiftly and handed Antiono her skimpy costume. It smelled of Chanel and sex.

Threading his needle with flamingo-shaded cotton, Antonio avoided Beverly's gaze and set to work. "Please, be snappy," she entreated, clasping the trench coat around her voluptuous body. "Curtain's at seven." Beverly played one of the Revue Girls in *Americana,* "It's way the hell up on Forty-Eighth Street at the Belmont."

The chorine spoke so rapidly that Antonio understood nearly every other word, but he worked as rapidly as he could. When the dancer cackled something about Rudolph Valentino, the tailor shrugged, *"Non capisco."*

"I'd like to *capisco* you, hot stuff," she muttered, "if I had more time."

When Antonio returned Beverly's sheer garment, she claimed that she needed help getting back into it. Without waiting for a response, she pulled Antonio behind the curtain, dropped the trench coat and shimmied into the bodysuit. "It's a job for two," she grunted, guiding his hands along her thighs to aid in stretching the tight fabric up over her generous bottom.

It was impossible not to see the protrusion in the handsome mender's slacks. Boldly, Beverly gripped it with her fist and squeezed. He groaned and immediately released, spilling inside his trousers like a schoolboy. "If I didn't have a cab waiting for me downstairs..." Beverly lamented. She kissed him on the mouth, grabbed her coat, then left. Antonio was breathless—and confused.

Sunday, Antonio's day off, was the most difficult day of the week, for Sundays were long and lonely. Sometimes he wandered the streets, journeying to the southernmost tip of Manhattan at South Ferry then back uptown to 125th Street. Antonio would linger at Battery Park, gazing out at the Lady, in her bright green splendor. Or he would look toward Ellis Island, the place where his fate changed when he passed through its immigration point without a second glance. After all, Antonio was young, healthy and clear of mind, not even twenty-one at the time.

On his Sunday sojourns, on his way back uptown, Antonio would saunter past Trinity Church, the Woolworth Building, City Hall Park and the towering Municipal Building, detouring into Chinatown and Little Italy, perhaps to have an egg roll or a cannoli from a street vendor. Antonio would then whisk up Broadway, past Union Square, and other unremarkable squares named "Worth" and "Herald."

Rushing through the Theater District, Antonio vacillated between hoping he saw and hoping he didn't see Beverly, that randy chorus line dancer. He never did. Then he headed home for Mrs. Rizzo's Sunday *ragú.*

Antonio's friend Vito had been badgering him to accompany Vito into the wilds of Brooklyn. Bay Ridge, to be precise. Vito was keeping company with a Brooklyn girl named Anita who was from an old-fashioned Genoese family. Whenever they met at the Capozzi home, there had to be chaperone. "Wouldn't it be nice to double date with us?" Vito asked. "She's got a friend…"

Antonio rolled his eyes. "There is always a friend," he told Vito.

"Lu's quite a dish," Vito insisted. "Plus, she's a nice girl."

"I have no interest in nice girls," Antonio said. *"Only cattive ragazze."*

"Ah, Lu is not a bad girl, but I think you'll like her just the same."

Despite his grumbling, Antonio agreed to meet this mysterious Lu. And on this brisk autumn Sunday, his life suddenly changed.

CHAPTER FOURTEEN

Luisa

L uisa had no desire to accompany her friend Anita and Anita's beau Vito on a clandestine double date that Sunday. She would rather sit and read on an out-of-the-way bench in Owl's Head Park. Luisa was certain that Daisy, Jay, Nick and Jordan would be infinitely more interesting than the fellow Anita wanted to set her up with.

"Oh, come on…" Anita begged. "Vito says Tony's very nice. A real gentleman. And handsome. Says he looks like Rudolph Valentino."

Luisa groaned and rolled her eyes. "More like Lon Chaney as Quasimodo, I bet," she said.

Anita clapped her hands together. "The Hunchback of Notre Dame! Hey, you never know. Maybe Tony likes those darned books as much as you do. Maybe he's even read that one."

Luisa permitted her friend to rouge her cheeks. Then with her pinkie, Anita applied a blush of red lipstick to Luisa's mouth. "There!" Anita chortled approvingly. "You look just like Clara Bow."

They arranged to meet Vito and Antonio at a park near 101st Street. Neither Luisa nor Anita had told their mothers that they were meeting gentlemen there, although Anita had been seeing Vito, with a chaperone (usually her younger sister Anna-Marie), for a handful of months. Anita wanted to see Vito privately, she explained, to "pitch woo," whatever that was.

The wind was strong that day. It barreled along the Narrows, which separated Brooklyn from Staten Island. Fort Wadsworth was visible across the water. A ferry chugged between both boroughs.

Cannonball Park was Luisa's second favorite spot to read. She often did so on one of the benches facing the Rodman gun, a massive black cannon which gave John Paul Jones Park its descriptive nickname. A string of cannon balls lined up before it like a metal caterpillar. There were also two rows of cannonball tripods to tempt young children into leapfrog. Luisa's brothers liked to climb them. Although it was frowned upon, the hellions still did it. Now this sacred place would be forever ruined for Luisa because she was meeting a man she didn't wish to meet here at Cannonball Park.

Even though Vito and Antonio needed to take three subway trains and a trolley (a pilgrimage of more than two hours), to reach this remote corner of Brooklyn, they were already waiting when the girls arrived. Anita flew to Vito's side, hugging him and being so bold as to plant a kiss on his cheek. "This is my Vittorio, Lu," Anita introduced. "And fellows, this is my friend Luisa."

"Vito," he corrected, then added, "Ladies, this is my friend Tony."

"Antonio," he said.

"Antonio," Luisa repeated, her small, pink tongue softening the "t" as a native Italian speaker would. Vito hadn't lied; Luisa was pleasing to the eye. She had a round, full face, expressive brown eyes and a curvaceous frame. Her salmon-shaded dress was well-made. Its classic lines featured fine stitching and was cut from good cloth. On her head, Luisa wore a cloche. What Antonio could see of her hair was jet black, wavy and abundant.

He didn't notice much about the other woman. Alicia? Annette? No, Anita. But she seemed pleasant enough.

Vito and Anita hadn't seen each other for several weeks and their hunger was evident. Excusing themselves, they immediately secreted off to a bench around a bend beside some bushes. Conversely, Antonio and Luisa chose to walk. She wore sensible yet well-crafted shoes with low heels. He liked a woman who liked to walk and had the shoes to prove it.

Luisa soon discovered that this young gentleman's obsession was not books but opera. He spoke with passion regarding the music he loved in the language of their childhoods. Of the time he saw *Aida* at the Metropolitan Opera House. Of his veneration of Verdi and how he came to this country on the steamship *Giuseppe Verdi.*

She smiled at Antonio as he talked, amused by his delight. Luisa's teeth were white and strong and straight. Her lips, plump. *"Destino,"* Luisa said, tickled by the fact that the ship which brought Antonio to these shores was named for his favorite composer. Destiny. Fate. Luisa countered that she came here on the *Madonna* with her parents when she was a babe in arms.

Just for a moment, Luisa could picture a baby in *her* arms. Perhaps Antonio's. She shook the foolish notion from her head then spoke of her favorite books, something no one in her family could appreciate. Not even Anita. They wouldn't understand. But she thought Antonio might. And he'd asked her favorites; the others never asked.

Luisa responded to his question. *"A Passage to India, Heart of Darkness,* and anything by Poe. Or women…" She had to stop herself, rein herself in. Luisa was becoming breathless. Breathless with books. And breathless with this man who listened to her so intently, who smiled slightly as she spoke, as though charmed by her words.

Once or twice, Luisa was brave enough to look directly into Antonio's eyes. They were a warm shade of chestnut where hers were deep brown. Yes, she and Antonio would have dun-eyed children, Luisa decided, then felt her olive skin coloring. His brows were thick, his nose, patrician, where hers had a slight curve at the bridge, a souvenir of when she'd fallen from the front stoop as a toddler.

Luisa and Antonio stopped at the large granite boulder which contained a bronze tablet. When Luisa offered to read the inscription, Antonio nodded his consent. (She didn't yet know that Antonio read flawlessly and devoured the news two times each day, once in English and once in Italian, as though he didn't trust either *The Daily News* or *Il Progresso*.)

The bronze tablet said:

To commemorate the first resistance made to British arms in New York State, August 1776. Erected by the Long Island Society Daughters of the American Revolution, A.D. 1918

Antonio took the opportunity to mention that he himself had been in a war, the Great War, and had come home to San Vincenzo the very same year the monument had been erected. Luisa sensed that he didn't wish to speak of the war, for if he did, he would have. They walked on.

When they stopped to rest on a pebble and wood bench in view of the Rodman gun, Luisa fiddled with the tassel on her purse, alternately afraid Antonio might kiss her, then afraid he might not. Studying his profile, Luisa decided that Antonio did indeed resemble Rudolph Valentino, who had died that August in Manhattan. But Antonio was more handsome, she thought.

"Che cosa?" he asked when he caught her studious gaze upon him.

"Niente," she said, blushing deeply. But it wasn't nothing.

As if reading her mind, Antonio raised his brows in a dramatic gesture. "Valentino," he sighed, tracing his profile with his fingertip.

She shook her head. *"Più bella."* Had she just told Antonio that he was more handsome than Valentino? Aloud?

Instead of embarrassing her, Antonio took Luisa's compliment in stride, amusing her with his experiences following Valentino's unfortunate, premature death two months earlier at age thirty-one from sepsis. More than 100,000 had lined the streets surrounding the Frank Campbell Funeral Chapel on Madison Avenue. Windows were smashed as his grieving admirers tried to enter the funeral home.

"Mi ricordo," Luisa said. She also remembered that suicides of despondent devotees were reported.

On the day of Valentino's funeral mass at Saint Malachy's, an unsuspecting Antonio was chased down Broadway by crazed fans who believed their screen idol's demise had been a hoax and that Antonio might indeed be the true Valentino. Antonio was terrified, tried to flee, and was ultimately rescued by police officers who finally disbursed the out-of-control mob.

Luisa laughed at Antonio's story. He liked the sound of her laughter; to him it was reminiscent of the opening strains of an opera.

That was when Antonio took Luisa's hand. She wished she'd worn gloves as proper young ladies did. But Antonio made no mention of the scars of her trade—the pinpricks, the scissor slices, the place where the sewing machine needle had entered her palm. The touch of the smooth tailor's hand on hers quietly elated her.

On their pebble bench in Cannonball Park, Luisa and Antonio somehow gained the courage to stare into each other's eyes. When he squeezed her hand, she squeezed back and smiled. 'This is the man I'm meant to marry,' she told herself.

CHAPTER FIFTEEN

Henrietta

"Your brother has a beau!" Henrietta shouted through the open kitchen window. Though it was almost November, the weather was mild and warm. Franco was in the yard just beyond the house, tending to the chickens as they scrabbled for grubs and other insects in the dirt.

"How's her eyesight?" Franco asked.

Henrietta didn't understand his joke. *"Che cosa?"*

"Is she blind?" Franco said in explanation. His mother sighed in frustration and threw a mealy onion out the window at him. Henrietta would never understand the grudging love between the brothers; they would do anything for each other but tortured each other mercilessly.

"Her name is Luisa," Henrietta continued, undaunted. *"Americana?"*

Henrietta shook her head. "She and her people are from Longobucco. You know, it's on the road out to the sea."

Giovanni came out of the barn. "Ah, that's unfortunate," he said. "Nothing but thieves and witches in Longobucco. And big mouths." He rolled the rotting onion toward the cluster of chickens and watched them peck it to bits. "Perhaps this Luisa bewitched him."

"Buffone!" Henrietta scolded her husband then slammed shut the window.

Later, at the supper table, Henrietta still couldn't let go of the notion that her eldest son might soon be a husband and that she may one day have grandchildren. Grandchildren she would never see, never hold in her arms. "Antonio says he's coming to visit," Henrietta told Giovanni as she sawed off pieces of semolina bread.

"Quando?" her husband wondered, grabbing the bread's heel and dipping it into the rich, red sauce.

She turned the letter's pages, searching the words for this detail. "When? He doesn't say. But soon, *io credo."*

Giovanni chewed thoughtfully and nodded. *"Credi? Io credi Susanna volaró!"* He gestured out the window at the sow rutting through the dusty yard for any scraps the chickens may have left behind. A spot of red dirtied the table as Giovanni waved the hunk of bread in the air while he ranted.

Though Franco found the image of Susanna, their pig, soaring above the rocky hills of San Vincenzo very funny, he stifled his laughter because he could see that his mother was near tears. Seven years after his brother had left home, Franco could still hear Henrietta crying for her lost son in the night as his father unwittingly snored beside her. Or did Giovanni know Henrietta still ached for their prodigal son, but just didn't care?

Henrietta silently folded the letter and slipped it into the onionskin envelope. Later, after she finished the supper dishes, she would put it with Antonio's other letters.

CHAPTER SIXTEEN

Assunta

He was certainly handsome, Assunta would give him that. But who did this Antonio fellow think he was in that fancy suit, with those fancy manners, dabbing his lips with a cloth napkin between bites like some lesser duke. Antonio complimented Assunta's lowly home as though it were the Doge's Palace instead of a tired tenement apartment. He had even brought her flowers. Flowers! In December! What a waste of a coin. But the daisies were lovely.

Antonio looked slightly uncomfortable, squashed between brother and sister and *madrina* and all the rest around Assunta's crowded Christmas Eve table, which was set up in the parlor. It wasn't even a table—just a pair of sawhorses and a four-by-eight Giuseppe had "borrowed" from the construction site. (He would return them after the holiday and none would be the wiser.) Still, it did look splendid, the discarded piece of muslin Luisa had rescued from the factory embroidered with curlicues courtesy of Barbara's hand. The scraps of evergreen the older boys had filched from the Christmas tree vendor and fashioned into a garland gave the place a festive countenance. You could smell the minty pine above the heady aroma of garlic and fish.

Giuseppe had worked overtime for weeks so they could afford the traditional Feast of the Seven Fishes. Just to prove what an excellent provider he was, there were eight types of seafood at the Tozzi table, including the oysters that had "fallen off the truck." But who was counting? For days, the women worked, preparing the fish, soaking the *baccala* for twenty-four hours, changing the dried cod's salty water often. They kept the vegetables fresh on the cold fire escape; it was better than the already-crowded icebox.

Assunta was glad she'd listened to Luisa and donned the dress her daughter had made for her, a jade green print the girl said brought out her light hazel eyes. Assunta insisted on protecting her new frock with an apron as she, Barbara, Luisa and Zia Claudia, ferried dish after dish to the table. Although Assunta insisted that Claudia was a guest and should sit and be served, Claudia scoffed at this notion and reminded her that a *madrina* was part of the family.

Studying Antonio across the table, Assunta supposed, 'He must be at least ten years older than Luisa…and she is far too young to have a *bello.*' But then Assunta reminded herself that by the tender age of seventeen, she was married, with a baby on the way, and that Guiseppi was almost nine years *her* senior.

When they had barely cleared the supper plates, Guiseppi brought out the cigars, procured from Luis, a Cuban woodworker at the construction site who brought them to New York regularly. 'My husband is pulling out all the stops,' Assunta thought. 'Falling all over himself to impress Luisa's good-looking suitor. He even changed his undershorts for the occasion.'

The women piled the plates in the sink, first scraping remnants of cod and calamari, clam and mussel shells into the trash before they started the coffee pot and took out the desserts.

That morning, Assunta had baked a coffee cake in a Medaglia d'Oro can. Barbara was busy whipping the fresh cream that would top it. Zia Claudia uncovered the *pizzelle* while Luisa unwrapped the platter Antonio had transported all the way from Harlem. Arranged upon it were a sea of seven-layer cookies, a sugary rainbow of red, white and green sponge cake held together with sweet preserves then bracketed by dark chocolate. Scattered here and there were *pignoli* cookies. *"Molto costico,"* Claudia noted. Pine nuts and almond paste were indeed expensive.

Claudia and Assunta raised their brows at such a posh dessert. Those rainbow confections originated in Venice; the ladies were peasants from the south, like the earthier *pignolis*. *"Da una panetteria,"* Assunta scoffed.

"They're not from a bakery," Antonio, who was escaping to the restroom, clarified. "My landlady Mrs. Rizzo baked them. She wishes you a *Buon Natale.*"

Assunta nodded her gratitude. *"Grazie. E a lei."*

"I'll be sure to tell her," Antonio said.

Claudia and Assunta sighed at almost getting caught gossiping. "Serves him right for wandering too close to the woman's world," Assunta elbowed Claudia.

"A man shouldn't be anywhere near the kitchen," Claudia agreed.

"Voi due siete incorreggibilli!" Luisa scolded. It was true—together the two were incorrigible, a force to be reckoned with.

Besides the cakes, there was also a fresh fruit salad, made from ingredients that were almost past their prime and therefore sharply discounted at Silvio's. Assunta marinated the fruit in a bit of Guiseppi's chianti from Belloni's secret cellar. Wine was contraband during Prohibition, but no one was the wiser. However, the colorful, spiked fruit was barely touched with so many confections on the table.

Of course, Serafino and Dominic grabbed for the rainbow cookies, their hands and faces still stained with spaghetti sauce. After much complaining, they gave a cursory wash at the kitchen sink then darted back to the desserts, as though they feared the cookies might be gone in the moment it took to clean one's hands. *"Animali,"* Assunta said with affection. She gave Little Paolo, safely ensconced on her lap, a rainbow cookie too. At three, he was a healthy eater and pleasantly chubby.

Luisa entered the makeshift dining room with the coffee pot and milk, Barbara followed close behind with the bowl of whipped cream she worked so hard to beat into swirls. After coffee was served and the desserts tucked into, Antonio cleared his throat and rose to his feet. 'Is he leaving so soon?' Assunta wondered. 'How rude!'

But instead of leaving, Antonio fell to one knee before Assunta's eldest daughter. He fumbled in his jacket pocket then came out with a square red velvet box. He held the box in his palm and opened it so all could see. Inside was a ring, a gold band topped with a small blue stone. Aquamarine, Luisa's birth gem.

In a quivering voice, Antonio asked Luisa for the honor of being his wife. In both English and Italian, so everyone in the room could understand. Two languages made it doubly important. He ended with, *"Posso avere la tua mano nel matrimonio?"* May I have your hand in marriage?

Luisa covered her face, clearly shocked. Zia Claudia burst into tears. Assunta, who was never at a loss for words, was speechless. Breaking the silence, Serafino piped, "Just her hand? How about the rest of her?"

Assunta whacked her son across the bottom. *"Basta."* She glanced at her husband, who was beaming, tears gleaming in his dark eyes. Antonio had clearly gotten Giuseppe's permission first, yet her husband hadn't uttered a word. That man was full of surprises. Still.

When she took her hands from her face, Luisa's cheeks were wet and flushed pink. "Yes," she breathed. *"Si, si, si...* I will marry you."

Antonio slipped the ring onto Luisa's finger.

1927

CHAPTER SEVENTEEN

Antonio

W hen he left nearly eight years earlier, Antonio truly believed he might never see his mother again. But there he was, walking the unpaved road toward the farm, his rocking, slightly bow-legged gait carrying him closer to his past with every step.

Henrietta must have been waiting by the front gate for hours. To Antonio, it looked as though she were holding herself back from running to meet him, gripping the coarse fencepost to keep her racing heart in check.

Steps away, Antonio broke into a slow canter, first dropping his secondhand, travel-worn leather satchel in the dust. He would clean it off later and polish his shoes as well, he thought to himself, unused to the grit of his former life.

Antonio's mother felt frail and angular in his arms. They held each other and cried happy tears, she murmuring his childhood nickname over and over again, "Tonio…Tonio…" then, "Are you hungry? You can have some bread and cheese and olives before supper if you are."

"No, I'm not hungry," Antonio smiled. Some things never changed. Mama still put him before herself. She put everyone else's needs before hers.

Antonio's father, of course, was in the fields, unable to tear himself from the weeds and seeds, even for a few moments, even to greet his son. And Franco had no choice but to toil at his father's side. There was always work to be done, Poppa said.

A wild boar *ragú* was simmering on the stove, the scent of which permeated the rooms of the small stone farmhouse. Antonio was grateful there was time for a private cup of coffee with his mother before the place was "invaded by barbarians," as she so delicately phrased it. *"Barbari,"* she smiled and repeated, for Giovanni and Franco were her very own barbarians.

"So, tell me about this woman, this Luisa," Henrietta said when they'd had several sips of coffee and several bites of almond *biscotti,* which she'd baked herself that very morning.

"Il mio fidanzata," Antonio politely corrected.

His mother acquiesced. *"La tua fidanzata."* Fiancée. It was so recent a notion for Henrietta that her eldest was getting married, that he would soon be a husband. 'Antonio has a betrothed,' she reminded herself. "What is she like?" Henrietta wondered aloud.

Antonio beamed and rattled off a laundry list of his intended's attributes, careful not to gush. "Luisa is smart, pretty, hard-working, devoted, kind...and like you, she loves to read." His mother nodded pensively.

How would his father describe Henrietta, Antonio reflected. 'Henrietta is a good cook and has a strong back,' his son decided Giovanni would say. This is how the man would likely describe his wife of three decades. A dedicated housekeeper and maid, nothing more.

"Can she cook?" Henrietta posed.

"Very well," Antonio said. "The family has me over for supper once a week, on Sundays, and Luisa does most of the cooking."

Henrietta dipped the crisp cookie crescent into her cooling coffee, took a bite. A coughing fit suddenly overtook her. "Are you sick?" Antonio asked.

"I'm not sick," his mother assured him. "A crumb just caught in my throat." But in truth, Henrietta had a cough she couldn't shake since the turn of the new year. "It's not a concern," she swore.

Supper was delicious. The sauce had simmered on a low flame all day and had a rich, smoky quality. The strips of hand-cut fettuccini had been dried on a clean, white sheet spread across Antonio's old bed. The pasta cooked up succulent, perfectly chewy and bouncy. There was also freshly-baked bread to sop the extra sauce.

Arm slung across the chair back, Giovanni ran his tongue over a toothpick he'd carved from a piece of birch. His father offered Antonio one, but he declined; Antonio had always found cleaning one's teeth at the table a despicable habit. Time hadn't improved the tense relationship between father and son. If anything, the years had made it even more uncomfortable.

"So, you were fired, were you?" Giovanni blurted out. Henrietta's spine stiffened as she prepared the evening coffee. Although these bouts of verbal sparring were common between the two, they still filled Henrietta with uneasiness.

"Not fired," Antonio told him with a good-natured smile. "Laid off."

"Ah, so there's a difference," his father said. "Explain."

Antonio took a breath. "There isn't much call for men's suits in the heat of summer," he replied calmly. "So, the factory laid off all but two workers in Haberdashery."

Giovanni clamped the toothpick with his molars, steadying it to speak. "How can you be so sure you'll have a job when you get back?"

"In this life, nothing is certain except death and taxes," Antonio responded, quoting Benjamin Franklin. Antonio was fairly confident his unlearned father wouldn't have an inkling who Ben Franklin was. "But it's happened before, this seasonal layoff," Antonio qualified, "and I've always had a job when summertime was over."

The perennial peacemaker, Henrietta burst in. "We're just so pleased you were able to visit," she said, pouring the coffee then placing her hand on her husband's shoulder to quell any further outbursts. Franco observed this exchange as intently as he would watch a soccer match in the town green.

"I scrimped and saved so that I could finally come," Antonio told them. "And Mrs. Rizzo, my landlady, gave me permission to sublet my room for a few months, so that's a help. I'm getting a dollar more than my rent."

Giovanni scoffed even at this. He removed the toothpick from his mouth, the better to banter. "Even so, it seems foolhardy to squander money on a pleasure cruise. *Follia.*"

Henrietta fixed her hands on her narrow hips. Her cheeks colored and her breath came in short bursts. "Folly! Are you crazy?"

"No, I'm not crazy," Giovanni insisted, amused at his wife's passion. It was her passion that drew him to her in the first place. This and her once-full bosom. Now she was skinny as a broom. "I'm just joking," Giovanni said. "Pulling your leg." He drew Henrietta close and kissed her shoulder. Not entirely satisfied that he was kidding, she huffed and pulled away.

"But on the other hand, you'll have a wife to support," Giovanni persisted with Antonio, gearing up for the second round in this sparring session.

Henrietta groaned and took the plate of sponge cake from stovetop to table. She must have been baking all morning, Antonio decided. "None for you," Henrietta told her husband, moving the dish from his grasp. For a moment, her son wondered, when nighttime came, if his father reached for Henrietta in the dark, would she move her body from his grasp as well?

Antonio pushed his parents' nocturnal activities from his mind and once again, confronted his father. "We will support each other," he said. "Luisa and I."

Giovanni grabbed a hunk of cake when Henrietta's back was turned. "Ha! A wife shouldn't work," he barked at his son, yellow cake crumbling from his full mouth.

"Ha!" Henrietta parried, indicating the full sink of dishes and the remnants of the meal surrounding them. "So, I don't work?"

"I didn't mean…" With just a glance from his wife, Giovanni was quiet and popped the toothpick back into his mouth.

In bed later that evening, Antonio and Franco spoke in low voices, just as they used to. It was as though no time had passed. Except somehow, Franco was now a man who shaved, drank wine and who knows what else. "Papa would never let me go," Franco told his brother. "He says I'm needed here."

"The wedding would be after the fall harvest. In November," Antonio said, staring at the wooden planks that comprised the ceiling. "I have savings…"

"So do I," Franco swore. "When farm work is done, I do odd jobs for Pucci, delivering suits and dresses, cleaning up."

Antonio was proud of his brother's entrepreneurial spirit and said so. "But you need to get out from under Papa's thumb," he added.

"And what about Mama? She would be all alone with that ogre, no one to protect her."

"Mama can take care of herself," Antonio assured his brother. Then a beat later he added, "Mama could come too."

Franco shook his head, the shadow of his movement streaking across the moonlight-bathed wall. "She would never leave him. Even for a short time."

There was nothing else to say, for Antonio knew this was true. The sound of Henrietta's muffled coughing sifted in from the next room. Then there was silence.

Though exhausted from his long voyage and from the dusty ride to San Vincenzo, Antonio couldn't sleep. There were times during the day—and there would be many times in the days to come—when he couldn't breathe. Antonio felt smothered by the stagnant air of this place that never changed, at the dust that never seemed to settle. He had to remind himself to take deep, measured breaths. That his destiny was not to stay in the place of his birth. That he now lived in the United States. That this was just a visit. That he had Luisa, his future bride, patiently waiting for him in Brooklyn. But just how long would she wait? And how long could he force himself to stay in this godforsaken, unbending hill of rock?

In San Vincenzo La Costa, time seemed to stand immobile. Nothing seemed to change. But in reality, everything did. Time raced forward, waiting for no one, not even Antonio. It was the insufferable sameness of his hometown that was smothering him. But Antonio needed to stay put, at least for a few months. After all, the voyage took three weeks and was costly besides. He had to get his money's worth. But how could he weather this visit without Luisa by his side? He was so lonely before she came along. He didn't want to risk losing her. Would she grow weary of waiting for his return?

Checking that Franco was asleep, Antonio reached into his satchel for the photograph he carried of his fiancée. It had been taken just a month earlier, Luisa in her bathing costume, knee deep in the crowded Coney Island surf. The tank top barely hid her bulging breasts, the short skirt caressing her thighs. Antonio had never seen so much female flesh in real life, save for Beverly, the chorine. But this was different.

Lying on his back in bed, Antonio's manhood stiffened and he knew it would be impossible to sleep until he stroked himself to satisfaction. While gazing at Luisa's picture in his left hand, he pleasured himself with his right. He tried not to make a sound when he climaxed but, in his mind, murmured, 'Luisa…Luisa *mio*…'

He cleaned himself up, stowed the photo and blew out the candle stub. Antonio decided right then and there that he would marry Luisa as soon as he could upon his return to *L'America*. At twenty-eight, he had no time to waste. Then and only then, after this decision, was Antonio able to sleep, and sleep soundly until dawn.

CHAPTER EIGHTEEN

Luisa

"Na-na-na-poo-poo," Luisa's brothers Sam and Dom sang in unison. "He's not coming back." Everyone in the family teased Luisa that Antonio would never return from Italy. Everyone, from the kids to her Papa and cousins. Even Zia Claudia, who rarely said an unkind word to anyone, couldn't resist. And don't forget Mama. "You are..." her mother began in English, *"come si dice...abbandonato...Ah, jilted."*

Luisa usually met this foolish talk with a polite smile, much like another Italian girl, the Mona Lisa. But unlike Luisa, the Mona Lisa was an affluent lady from Florence, a lofty city in the north, instead of a Southern country bumpkin whose father raised livestock before turning to stonemasonry and cement work. Luisa didn't think herself beautiful, not like that classic ideal of feminine loveliness. But nevertheless, men looked, and sometimes even said things, as she passed on the sidewalk. And Antonio told Luisa that she was pretty quite often. She tried to believe him.

Despite the taunting, deep inside, Luisa knew her suitor would come back. Why would he not? The pleasantries Antonio whispered to her, the dreams they shared, the thrilling clutch of his arms around her, his firm, inquisitive kisses upon her mouth that left her wanting more... She and Antonio had similar histories: both were children of farmers, both were full of longing. They were both in the rag trade, though Antonio enjoyed his work much more than she did.

Yet in the dark of night, sisters pressed against her in the bed they shared, sometimes Luisa's heart beat furiously and fearfully in her chest with the thought that maybe, just maybe, Antonio might *not* come back. Not to her, anyhow.

"It's been two months," Luisa's father reminded her. "But who's counting?" Luisa's response was a shrug and her *La Gioconda* smile.

But Luisa indeed was counting: it had been two months, five days and four hours. Antonio left just before summer and promised to return before the end of that season. He wrote often, short, affectionate letters in his sweeping hand. Antonio said that he missed her. That he was helping Gennaro Pucci, the local tailor, who was buckling under arthritis and a glut of work. That his mother had a nagging cough which only grew worse as time passed.

Luisa worried that maybe Antonio would decide to stay. Maybe he had found a beau there. Maybe, maybe, maybe...

"There is no flame but the one I hold for you," Antonio assured Luisa when she voiced her trepidation in writing.

If she dared to ask when Antonio would return to her side, all he wrote was, "*Presto, amore mio, presto.*" Soon, my love, soon...

Luisa worked hard, often putting in extra hours at the factory. She gave her father her earnings. Well, almost all her salary. Luisa neglected to tell Giuseppe that she'd been granted a raise or about the time she'd won a contest for the most shirtwaists sewn in an hour. This distinction earned her a dollar. She squirreled it away in her "mad money" box.

When it wasn't too hot, Luisa walked across the Brooklyn Bridge to work, saving her trolley fare. She hid her stash beneath a loose floorboard that no one, not even her sisters Barbara and Filomena (Mina'd come along two years earlier with little hubbub) knew about. 'A woman needs to keep some secrets,' Luisa reasoned, trying not to feel guilty for her dishonesty when she withheld her bonus earnings from papa.

In the evening, Luisa, her mother and Barbara hand-sewed the sheets, pillowcases, dishtowels and undergarments that would become Luisa's trousseau. Zia Claudia, who worked in a trim and fabric shop, had gotten a good price on the delicate, Venetian lace that would be transformed into Luisa's veil and ankle-length gown. It was her godmother's gift to the girl, and she sewed the garments evenings as well.

"You will look like an angel at your wedding," Zia Claudia beamed at Luisa's last fitting. *"Una angela."*

"If there will be a wedding," Luisa sniffled, clutching the ivory-shaded lace to her chemise.

"Of course, there will be a wedding," Zia Claudia snapped, giving her goddaughter a playful smack on the *culo* to ward off such foolish notions.

"But *zia*, what if Antonio doesn't come back?" Luisa choked on a sob. "You said it yourself."

"I was only joking! Why wouldn't he come back? Your *fidanzato* is no fool. And you are such a prize." Luisa tried to believe her *madrina's* words.

Then, one Sunday in late August (the twenty-first, to be precise), when Giuseppe and boys were bathing at Coney Island, there came a knock on the Tozzis' door. Several knocks. Assunta, Luisa and Barbara were in their slips, sewing on the fire escape, trying to evade the thick, oppressive heat. Mina was napping beside them. This is why they didn't hear the persistent knocking at first. When Luisa finally opened the door, there stood Antonio, suntanned, smiling and bearing presents.

The moment he laid the heavy satchels on the linoleum, Luisa flew into his arms. He embraced her tightly, just a thin cloth separating him from her perfect, olive skin. *"Bella, bella..."* he whispered into her coils of ebony hair. At that moment, Luisa did indeed feel beautiful.

Being a gentleman, Antonio waited in the parlor for the other females to don their summer shifts, sipping on a sweating glass of fresh lemonade. Soon the room was full of babbling women. They spoke over each other. "We figured you weren't..." and "Where were you..." and "You were gone so long we..."

But Luisa said nothing. She just sat in an armchair across from her betrothed, gazing at him. He looked back at her, ignoring the questions of sister and mother, then reached into one of the haversacks.

Antonio's gifts were thoughtful and numerous. There was something for everyone and these "somethings" were exactly what the recipient liked. For Giuseppe, there was fragrant tobacco. For Assunta, a set of rose-pink rosary beads from Santa Maria Della Neve. For Luisa's two sisters, a bracelet and a necklace. The boys had trinkets like knives and wooden toys to fight over. However, there was no present for Luisa. 'Antonio is gift enough,' she told herself.

In the second satchel was a bounty of dried sausage, jars of preserved tomatoes, an array of marinated olives, aged cheeses, candied lemon peel and a variety of sweets. There would be no cooking that night, just an easy feast of delicacies from the Old Country. Assunta sent Barbara to fetch three loaves of bread from Lobue's on the corner. The others would return from the beach soon, ravenous.

Meanwhile, Assunta sliced and chopped, preparing the bounty on a board they usually reserved for rolling out pasta. *"Vai, vai!"* Assunta gestured to Antonio and Luisa, encouraging them onto the fire escape, a place where she could both watch them and they could have some privacy.

The couple spoke in hushed whispers, quickly describing the happenings in their time apart. They talked of their loneliness, trying to verbalize their ardor in a matter of moments. "I want to marry you," Antonio said, kissing Luisa's rough hands. Her engagement ring still sparkled, pale blue and full of promise.

"Yes, we will marry," she laughed. "November, you said, after the harvest so that maybe..."

"No, November is too long to wait. Sooner. Next month."

"But my dress..."

"Next month," he said with urgency. "The last Sunday of the month. That will be enough time, no?"

Luisa paused. "All right," she told him. "Yes."

Although she ached to ask about his rush to wed, Luisa couldn't find the words. Why the hurry? Could he wait no longer to have her in his marriage bed? What had happened in Italy? Why was he so anxious? Perhaps the answer would surface in the coming days, perhaps not. But Luisa was glad Antonio had returned, glad he still wanted her and that he hadn't rekindled an old flame while back in San Vincenzo.

They sat on the fire escape's black wrought iron steps that had been painted so many times, they were sticky in the heat. Antonio above, Luisa slightly below, between his parted knees, silently staring at the sky that was beginning to color and darken. Assunta peered out the window to ensure that nothing tawdry would transpire.

"Oh, I almost forgot," Antonio said. He fished a small, plastic box from his breast pocket. Swirls of coral and white decorated its cover and "Cosenza" was stamped in blue upon it.

"Take it," he said. "It's for you."

Luisa slid the box's top from its bottom. Upon a square of cotton lay a pair of earrings, eighteen-karat gold, teardrop-shaped. "These are the last tears I hope to give you," Antonio said.

She wished this were true but knew it was impossible. Love brought tears and so much more.

CHAPTER NINETEEN

Henrietta

It all happened so quickly. Antonio was back on a steamship in the beginning of August and the next thing the DeMarcos knew, a wedding invitation arrived in the post. It was pale bone, on heavy stock, printed in a no-nonsense black script.

Even if Franco had been permitted to make the transatlantic voyage, even if there had been *lire* to spare, there wouldn't have been enough time to attend. At first, Henrietta was hurt but then she recalled the finality of Antonio's last conversation with his father. Though her son remained polite, her husband did not.

The relationship between Antonio and Giovanni was never what Henrietta would call close. There was always a distance between the two. Jealousy? Perhaps. It was as though her husband resented the attention the child took from him. By the time Franco arrived almost ten years after their firstborn, Giovanni was resigned to his change of status with his wife. He was glad to have another farmhand and not one who hated to soil himself with field work. Giovanni didn't have much use for one who favored the arias of Puccini over the lowbrow antics of Punchinello. Where did this Antonio character come from?

Henrietta coughed into her elbow. The dry hackle had grown worse since Antonio had left. Sometimes she found it difficult to catch her breath or to breathe without wheezing. Although she tried to hide its severity from Antonio, Henrietta suspected he knew that it was more than *niente*. Hardly a day passed when he didn't suggest she visit Dr. Gilardi.

What Antonio didn't know is that his mother had already been to the *medico*. And to a lung specialist in Rende. By then, her condition was too far gone for treatment. Nothing could be done except soothe the coughing with herbal teas spiked with lemon and honey. This would give her a brief respite before the hacking began again.

Henrietta traced the raised lettering of her son's wedding invitation with her worn fingertip. Black embossed pearl paper. Classic and refined, just like her son.

Mr. and Mrs. Joseph Tozzi
request the honor of your
presence at the marriage of their daughter
Louise

to

Mr. Anthony DeMarco
on Sunday afternoon, September 25, 1927
at five o'clock
at St. Patrick's Church
4th Avenue & 95th Street, Brooklyn, N.Y.

BRIDE'S RESIDENCE
142 GATLING PL.
BROOKLYN, N.Y.

BRIDE'S FUTURE RESIDENCE
7407 5TH AVENUE
BROOKLYN, N.Y.

Henrietta couldn't speak for the girl's stylishness—or lack thereof. She didn't know Luisa and never would. The young woman was the same age as her son Franco. Just eighteen years old. Only a child, really. But this Luisa or Louise, as the invitation referred to her, must be special to have won Antonio's heart. He was very picky, ever since he'd been a child. Choosy about what he ate, how he dressed and who he kept company with. For a time, Henrietta feared he would die a bachelor. As it was, Antonio was marrying at twenty-eight, practically elderly for San Vincenzo.

'But Antonio isn't in San Vincenzo any longer,' Henrietta reminded herself. 'He is far, far away and I will never see him again. Not in this life.'

Although it pained Henrietta that her son lived across the ocean, at least he was happy. At least he'd found the lid to his pot.

Henrietta examined the wedding card more closely. Everyone's given names were Americanized. Why? Had they forgotten who they were? Where they came from? And this "Tozzi"…was it shortened, courtesy of an Ellis Island agent, from something like "Tozzolino." Did people now call Henrietta's son "Tony"? Did he call his betrothed "Lu"? And what was this Lu's mother's name? Had she been a humble farm wife like Henrietta? Or a rich merchant's wife? How many children did this Mrs. Joseph Tozzi have? Did any of them die at birth as Henrietta's daughter Maria had?

In another world, in another country, Henrietta and her mystery in-law would have shared cups of strong coffee and homemade cake together. They would have traded stories about what their children were like as children. They would have crocheted sweaters and soft blankets for the *nipoti* they were sure to have. But now, in two different lands, separated by more than seven thousand kilometers, there was no connection at all.

Henrietta sipped her tea, sweetened by honey procured from the bees which roamed the wildflowers in their field, spiked by the juice of lemons larger than her fist which hailed from her friend Alessandra's trees in Sorrento. The tea soothed Henrietta's burning throat but not her aching heart. And this soothing, this relief, was only temporary. Soon she would begin coughing uncontrollably again, struggling for air.

Memories of Antonio coming down the road months earlier brought a smile to Henrietta's dry lips. She recognized his distinct, rocking gate even before she could decipher his face. He broke into a trot, then a run, dropping his satchel and scooping Henrietta into his arms.

Antonio had looked well, slightly heavier, his darkly handsome face rounder. As usual, he was impeccably dressed, even for travel, even when visiting a farm. His childhood home. This place called America clearly agreed with her son. Henrietta knew the moment she laid eyes on him that he wouldn't stay long. That he couldn't wait to leave. That he had only returned for her sake, and Franco's. Antonio had no use for Giovanni, and vice versa.

During his time back home, Antonio spent many solitary hours walking the hills surrounding their village. For this purpose, he dug out his old hiking boots from beneath his bed. Other times, he dipped into town itself, visiting old friends or buying little trinkets for his intended's family from the local shops. Antonio would tell Henrietta who he saw and where he went, showing her the treasures he'd purchased. Once she spied him disappearing into Phillipi's jewelry stall. He never showed her what was in the pink and cream-colored box, however.

Gennaro Pucci told Henrietta that he'd offered Antonio his old job back on a long-term basis. And that her son had thanked him profusely, but informed Pucci that he had work back in New York and a sweetheart waiting for him.

Lucia, who had always fancied Antonio, told Henrietta that he refused to go on a stroll with her. That his heart belonged to another. *"Ma é un solo passeggiata!"* Lucia had told him.

To which Antonio responded, *"Non e mai solo uno passeggiata,"* explaining as kindly as he could that it was never just a walk.

Though Antonio stayed more than two months, Henrietta sensed that her son was anxious to return to his life. She felt it in his silence as he helped her snap string beans. She heard the longing in his voice when he spoke of his Luisa, saw the spark in her son's eyes when he described his beau's virtues, a spark which she knew Giovanni never held for her.

Should Henrietta send the couple a wedding gift? Certainly, she should, but what? Antonio had brought sacks full of local treasures back to America with him. What more could Henrietta give Luisa except her firstborn son? Perhaps she would begin embroidering a coverlet for their marriage bed then a blanket for their baby.

But deep inside, Henrietta knew that there would not be ample time for either. A tickle began deep in her throat. The tickle soon became a burning which erupted into a deep cough that rattled through Henrietta's chest like a wet, violent storm. She collapsed onto the tabletop, gasping for breath, helpless tears streaming from her eyes. If only there were time, more time…

CHAPTER TWENTY

Assunta

Luisa and Antonio's wedding was undeniably beautiful. Spills of white roses decorated the altar of St. Patrick's. (The new church had been dedicated only the December before.) Assunta's oldest daughter resembled a princess with her lacy cap and veil that trailed the ground behind her. Her tasteful V-necked lace sheath had scalloped edges that fell just below her knees. Luisa carried a huge bouquet, also of roses and ribbons, which was twice the size of her head. Dark spit curls snuck from beneath her cap and a thin strand of borrowed pearls clasped her neck.

The wedding party itself was small. Paolo (age four) and Filomena (who was just two) served as ringbearer and flower girl, respectively. Mina (Filomena's preferred name) carried a basket of rose petals. Her dress echoed her oldest sister's with its pointed hem. The girl groused that the headpiece, with a carnation at each ear, itched and made her resemble a mouse. Paolo carried a heart-shaped pillow with streamers. He hardly complained about his short pants and knee socks but tried to pull off his lace collar when his older brothers teased that he looked like a sissy.

Vito stood up as Antonio's best man and Anita was a fetching *damigella d'onore.* She wore a picture hat that perfectly matched her cocktail dress of beaded lilac and cradled an armful of pink roses. Antonio, Vito and the father of the bride looked dapper in their rented tuxedos, bow ties, vests and boutonnieres.

The remaining Tozzi children's clothing—and even Assunta's pale seafoam frock—was borrowed from neighbors. Although this saved on expenses, Assunta still agonized over where all the money was coming from. The invitations on fine, eighty-pound stock, the calling cards, the roses...all those roses in a rainbow of shades. Giuseppe told his wife not to be concerned, that he'd been saving his *tombola* and pinochle winnings for years. "Winnings?" Assunta yelled. "You said you always lost."

To which her husband winked, "We all have our secrets, no?"

"Lies, you mean!" Assunta was cross with him for hiding money.

"Ah, how could I not put aside a little something? You've given me so many daughters," he sighed.

Assunta recalled this conversation as she sat in the church pew beside a handful of her children, who were remarkably well behaved. Watching Giuseppe walk Luisa down the aisle to the strains of Pachelbel's "Canon in D" on the pipe organ, how could Assunta not cry? How could she not wish a good life for her Luisa, an easier life that she herself had. Yes, Assunta loved her children, but her body ached from carrying them. The girl they'd lost, her dear Beatrice, was never far from her mind. Assunta prayed that Luisa would never know the pain of losing a child.

Thanks to the skill and quick hand of Zia Claudia, Luisa's dress was flawless. To save a bit of coin, maybe it could be passed along to the other girls for their own weddings. Money, Assunta was always fretting about money.

She couldn't understand Antonio's rush to get married. After all, Luisa wasn't going anywhere; it was he who'd fled to his homeland for two whole months. And Assunta knew her daughter wasn't with child for she'd watched her wash out the rags from her flow only the week before. Besides, Luisa was a good Catholic girl. But Assunta wasn't too confident about her son-in-law's integrity, what with his flashy looks, pointed sideburns and slicked-back hair like some lesser B-movie matinee idol. Time would tell.

Assunta had the foresight to position Barbara on the bench beside her so the girl could translate Father Kent's words. (Why couldn't an Italian priest have been secured for the ceremony?) Barbara's warm breath pulsed in Assunta's ear, saying that love was patient and kind and never failed. *"E ora restano questi tre: fede, speranza e amore. Ma il più grande di questi è l'amore,"* Barbara said. "And now these three remain: faith, hope and love. But the greatest of these is love." She said it in two languages because the words were so important.

The large rebuilt church was half full. In its previous iteration, Luisa and her siblings had received their holy sacraments, and all but Luisa had been baptized there. It was said this structure cost two-hundred-and-fifty-thousand dollars to erect. The marble altar, mural of the crucifixion and elaborate stained-glass windows seemed almost too sumptuous for this unassuming parish of immigrants from many different lands but it suited Assunta's daughter well.

Giuseppe assured his wife that he (well, he and Zia Claudia) would handle all the details of the reception that followed the wedding. *"Non dovrai muovere un dito,"* he smiled, wiggling his pinkie finger. And indeed, Assunta didn't have to do anything involving her little finger or any other body part. After the procession down St. Patrick's long, marble aisle, after the receiving line, they all wandered over to the adjoining church hall.

When Assunta entered, she almost wept. The table was covered with foods brought by the family's friends and neighbors. Their signature dishes sang from the distant shores of their native lands. Pierogi from Poland sat comfortably beside a tray of baked ziti. Swedish meatballs bathed in a rich, brown gravy were complimented by a tub of German-style potato salad, glistening bacon and onion. A platter of *spanakopita* beckoned, feta cheese and spinach oozing out from between the perfectly-browned phyllo dough. And of course, to bring the newly-wed couple good luck, a vat of traditional Italian wedding soup bubbled away on a hotplate.

Another table held the desserts: Mexican wedding cookies, anisette toast, *vaniljkakor* with their bellybuttons of raspberry jam peeking through. Lobue's Bakery provided the wedding cake, complimentary. When Assunta ordered it, Calogero, the baker, told her it would be his honor to give Luisa's cake as a gift. At first, Assunta balked, thinking it charity, but when he reminded her of how many loaves of bread the family of eight had eaten over the years, she bowed her head and thanked him for his generosity. *"Non é niente,"* he said. It's nothing.

In attendance was Calogero and his wife Bella, who also brought a tray of Sicilian "S" Cookies—Bella knew they were the bride's favorite. Assunta also knew that Bella would slip Luisa one *sulla casa* when Calogero wasn't looking. Bella thought that Luisa was such a sweet girl and besides, she was friends with their daughters Lisa and Jessica. So, that warranted a free cookie now and again, no? When Luisa came home with golden crumbs dusting her lips, Assunta would smile at Bella's kindness. Fine people, the Lobues.

Then there was Mrs. Leedy and her brood, Mrs. Rosenthal and even Mrs. Fitzpatrick, one of Luisa's grade school teachers at PS 104. Mrs. Rizzo, Antonio's landlady, had made the trek down from Harlem with Vito. Mrs. Rizzo was sorry to lose such a faithful tenant, but was glad Antonio had found his mate.

Look at Luisa, radiant with joy, eyes glistening with glad tears for all who had come out to celebrate her wedding. They must have read the announcement in the church bulletin's "Bans of Marriage," for Assunta hadn't invited this many. And Antonio, he looked happy, if not a bit overwhelmed, his tranquil life invaded by this loud, brash Brooklyn family and their friends. Antonio's only guests were his *il testimone della sposo* Vito and their landlady.

The satin *a busta* satchel Assunta had sewn for Luisa was bursting with envelopes, some thick with dollars and others jingling with coin. Assunta smiled, recalling the afternoon she tried to explain to Mrs. Leedy exactly what *a busta* was as she stitched: a sack to discreetly stash cash gifts. Assunta's broken English and comical pantomime hand gestures baffled the immigrant from Londonderry even more. The language gap between them widened until Barbara said, "In Italian, *a busta* means 'envelope.'"

"For Pete's sake, that's brilliant," Mrs. Leedy exclaimed.

A third table was covered with presents: a coffee pot, a toaster, dish towels and such. Luisa and Antonio would want for nothing.

After rushed farewells, the couple dashed off to catch the overnight train from Pennsylvania Station to Niagara Falls. ("My, that's an Irish goodbye, if I ever saw one," Mrs. Leedy remarked.) The guests ate and drank and danced even after the guests of honor had gone.

Would Assunta's daughter lose her virginity in a Pullman compartment on the Buffalo Star speeding north? Assunta worried about whether she'd told Luisa enough about what to expect on her wedding night. 'Grit your teeth and pretend...'

Giuseppe sidled up to his wife and planted a kiss on her cheek. *"Non é bello l'amore?"* he said with a sigh.

Assunta smiled. Yes, love was indeed beautiful. 'Sometimes there is no need to pretend,' she decided.

CHAPTER TWENTY-ONE

Antonio

L uisa was extremely quiet during the taxicab ride to Pennsylvania Station, Antonio noted. Pensive. All the way across the Brooklyn Bridge and to the center of Manhattan, she said barely a word. 'Perhaps, like me, she has never been in a taxi before,' he ventured. At first, Luisa fretted that it was an extravagance, but they couldn't have taken the trolley, could they? With all their valises? And they knew no one with an automobile who could give them a lift.

She grasped Antonio's hand tightly in the vehicle's expansive back seat. He studied the lines of Luisa's face, the snub-nosed, strong-jawed profile he had grown so fond of, so familiar with. Antonio could have drawn it with a charcoal pencil in the dark. The setting sun provided a blazing background beyond the smudged windows.

Could he make this woman happy for the rest of her life? Could he provide for her? Would be an adequate husband? Father? Barely eighteen, so many people adored Luisa. So many turned out to wish her well in her married life. With him! Why had Luisa chosen Antonio? What made him so special, so worthy of her affection?

These were questions one didn't ask another person, even one's wife. At least a bashful soul like Antonio didn't. Couldn't.

Four days was all either of them could afford to take off from work. Another extravagance! But Antonio felt it was important to take Luisa away, to celebrate their union as husband and wife someplace scenic, foreign, exotic.

The next few days were a jigsaw jumble, even more so than their wedding ceremony and the potluck afterwards. Snapshots flashed through Antonio's mind: Luisa in her wedding gown, her comely face draped in lace, Luisa laughing with her friends from the factory as they told bawdy jokes, Luisa in awe of the city as night fell, Luisa's wonder at Pennsylvania Station, her first time seeing its majestic columns, the sweeping, vaulted ceilings of its main waiting room, the enormous clock (Timed by Benrus) in the main concourse. Then, Luisa's enchantment with their Pullman car, the polished wood interior, the tiny sink, the bunk beds. "Sam and Dom would love this," she laughed.

"They would," Antonio agreed. "Do you?"

Luisa wheeled around. "Yes!" she told him. "And I love you as well."

Antonio smiled so Luisa knew that his feelings were mutual, but for some reason, he couldn't say that he loved her. Not yet. There was so much he couldn't put into words. Not yet. But he hoped Luisa knew that he loved her. Of course, she knew, didn't she?

Until their wedding night, Antonio had never seen Luisa with her hair down. Though he had spied more than her ankle in her bathing costume when they'd gone to that crowded beach at Coney Island, she'd kept her dark, wavy hair fastened in a low bun with a sea of u-shaped hairpins. Now, her tresses cascaded over her shoulders as she sat on the berth's lowest bunk, wearing an ethereal white peignoir set (a gift from the factory girls), knees demurely tucked together as she removed pin after pin from her thick forest of hair. So many pins!

To facilitate the unfastening, Luisa invited Antonio to join her on the low bunk. It creaked under their combined weight. As he searched her scalp with tentative fingers, Antonio's breath quickened. Her hair was so soft, so lush and there was so much of it. The faint scent of violets rose from Luisa's skin as he dropped pin after pin into the collection pooled in her lap. When there were no more pins to be found, she gathered them into a round tin and feathered her mane. It reached the small of her back.

Had Luisa not beckoned Antonio to the space beside her, he may not have been so brave as to consummate their marriage. Surely not on a moving train bounding toward Buffalo! What happened next was a tangle of tresses, hot skin, wet mouths, parted thighs, searching fingertips and then, monumental relief.

Afterwards, Luisa brought Antonio a warm washcloth, dampened from the miniscule sink in their compartment, then cleansed herself. The washrag was pink with blood afterwards; she rinsed it clean.

As Antonio began his climb to the top berth, Luisa stopped him. "No, stay down here with me," she said, "but only if you'd like." They slept, bodies curved around each other, two demitasse spoons nestled in a drawer, rocked in the arms of the Buffalo Star.

He'd splurged on their trip and booked a room at the Harmony Inn on Wadsworth Street. Luisa gasped when she saw the sprawling, many-gabled, orange brick Queen Anne mansion. "This is the right place," he assured her, taking Luisa's arm to climb the steps to the parlor. It was filled with red damask sofas, oak paneling, tiled fireplaces, stained-glass windows and terra cotta ornamentation.

Theirs was the Sparrow Suite. Painted in the colors of this common, humble bird, it featured a plush double bed, a mirrored wardrobe, a slate fireplace and fine oak furniture. It was the nicest place Antonio had ever stayed, and he surmised this was true for his wife as well. He hoped it wasn't the last vacation they would take together for soon enough, it would be back to the grind: work, bills, then God willing, babies.

The following two days, Luisa and Antonio explored Buffalo by foot, gazing at the Falls from different angles, walking across Peace Bridge into Canada. Dedicated only two months earlier to great fanfare, Peace Bridge featured five spans and an impressive steel arch. At night, when the Falls were lit in a rainbow of changing colors, Antonio was gratified by seeing the delight on Luisa's face as she watched the spectacle.

Since they were honeymooners, they also felt obligated to visit Honeymoon Bridge. It was a magnificent metal structure, completed in 1898, and at the time, was the biggest steel arch bridge in the world. "It looks too flimsy," Louisa said, halfway across its span, her worried countenance dampened with the spray from the American Falls. She swore she could feel Honeymoon Bridge trembling. At Luisa's beckoning, they returned to the surety of solid land.

Back in the Sparrow Suite, the couple properly explored each other's bodies in the gentle lantern light. Antonio marveled at the soft down that covered his wife's skin. He thumbed the dimple of the smallpox vaccine scar near her left shoulder, kneaded the thighs that eventually clung to his waist. Luisa, in turn, wrapped her fist around Antonio, in wonderment of how his manhood grew, then fell.

All too soon, it was back to Brooklyn, to their apartment above Heffernan's Confections, the rooms strung together like railroad cars, one after the other. Perched on Fifth Avenue, near the corner of Seventy-Fourth Street, the scent of sugar and the tang of cocoa wafted up through the floorboards. Antonio was convinced this was a portend of the sweet days to come.

CHAPTER TWENTY-TWO

Luisa

S he had never been on a train like this before. The
Buffalo Star was much more grand than the
Sea Beach or even the wood-paneled trolley. To
Luisa, Buffalo seemed a kinder, gentler New York City.
And the inn! It was more sumptuous than anything
she had ever seen in Brooklyn. Like a page out of
Sense and Sensibility.

Luisa kept whispering to her new husband that these
frills, these extravagances were too rich, too dear for the
likes of them, two factory workers. *"Troppo caro,"* she
blurted out when the shopkeeper told the couple the cost
of the keepsake photo he wanted to take of them in his
studio in front of a watercolor backdrop of Niagara Falls.

Antonio just smiled. "It's not too expensive," he said
to Luisa. "Not for my bride. Besides, it will be something
nice to show our children."

Luisa knew that after the Buffalo Star carried them
nearly four hundred miles south to their home, she and
Antonio would put their noses to the grindstone. They
would work hard and save for a house of their own one
day. A splurge such as this picture was permissible, she
persuaded herself.

The photographer had Luisa perch on Antonio's knee
and clasp his left shoulder. His arm slung across her back,

no one could see that he brazenly squeezed her buttocks the moment the flash exploded; this was the reason for Luisa's cryptic Mona Lisa smile.

Weeks later, Luisa contemplated the Niagara Falls photograph, now in a gilded frame on the coffee table of their modest apartment. She gazed at the picture as she mopped the kitchen floor. True, it was hard work, laboring outside the home then returning to cook a quick, economical supper then laboring inside the home. But such was the lot of women in 1927.

Antonio was grateful for all Luisa did. He insisted on washing the dishes each night after Luisa cooked. She liked how meticulously he worked, scraping the remnants from the plates into the wastebasket with a balled-up sheet of *Il Progresso* in his fist. He filled one side of the double sink with hot, soapy water and rolled his shirtsleeves to the elbows, humming happily as he scrubbed. "*Là Ci Darem La Mano*," usually.

Almost nightly, Antonio sought Luisa in the dark, sometimes even as she dried plates beside him at the kitchen sink. This both pleased and concerned her. It was too soon to have a baby and Luisa was confused by the advice her friend Nieves had given her. Was Nieves's information on fertility and the Rhythm System reliable? Or did something get lost in translation? And remembering to write down the start of Luisa's last flow, counting days on the calendar...who had time for such nonsense?

Luisa enjoyed making a home for herself and Antonio in the small railroad apartment above Heffernan's. Did it always smell like sugar or was this just her imagination? Just her bliss shining through.

She dumped the bucket of dirty water into one side of the deep kitchen sink then tiptoed across the damp floor into the parlor. Antonio would be working late so she still had a few stolen moments to herself while the linoleum dried.

Luisa picked up *The Sun Also Rises* from the end table, a wedding gift from her fourth-grade teacher Mrs. Fitzpatrick. "May the sun always rise on bright days for you, my dear Luisa," Mrs. Fitzpatrick had inscribed on the title page. This present alone was a thoughtful gesture but the fact that the woman had tucked a ten-dollar bill between the pages was incredibly moving.

In fact, the generosity of all the wedding guests touched the newlyweds deeply. The presents sent from Italy—most notably, a lovely, embroidered nightie from Henrietta, who was ailing. In a kind note, she apologized for not being able to attend their wedding. "But I will meet you someday," Luisa's mother-in-law had written in shaky letters. "You make my son very happy, and for that I am grateful."

From other family members overseas, there were crocheted doilies, carved wooden boxes and satchels filled with fragrant dried lavender. From across Gatling Place there were waffle irons, stock pots and even a patchwork quilt. The couple had everything they needed.

Turning another page in Hemingway's book, Luisa couldn't decide if Brett Ashley, with her bobbed hair and carefree attitude, was a charming bohemian or a shameless hussy. Luisa did, however, take a liking to Jake Barnes, an expatriate American journalist with a war wound that rendered him unable to copulate.

Luisa was almost at the end of the story. Though she looked forward to seeing her husband's tired but handsome face after the late shift, she hoped Antonio didn't return until after she finished the novel. She read feverishly, trying not to skim, breathless with anticipation of where the couple who loved each other, but could not consummate their love, would end up.

On the last page, Brett says that she and Jake could have such a terrific time together. However, Jake, soured by life, tells her that it's a pretty thought but not...

A heavy knock on the door made Luisa jump. She put down the book. Suddenly, she was not in Spain in the cab with Brett and Jake any longer but back in the Bay Ridge flat. Had Antonio forgotten his key? Again?

Luisa tread lightly across the now-dry linoleum and unlatched the door to see a Western Union delivery boy standing there. "Telegram for Mr. Antonio DeMarco," he said and thrust an envelope at Luisa. "All the way from Italy," he added. Luisa fumbled in her apron pocket for change and emptied coins into the Western Union boy's cupped hand. He doffed his cap at her in thanks.

'Telegrams are rarely good news,' Luisa sighed as she put the buff-colored envelope on the kitchen table then lit the flame under a pot of water to begin preparing supper. Her husband's name, handwritten, showed through the cellophane window.

Somehow, Luisa knew what the message would say. The loss of Antonio's mother would break his heart.

CHAPTER TWENTY-THREE

Assunta

'What a nice home my daughter has made,' Assunta reflected, surveying the railroad apartment's rooms. She sat in the parlor, where the sparse furnishings were pushed to the side to accommodate a large folding table which had been borrowed from a neighbor. From this vantage point, Assunta could see the kitchen, steamy with bubbling pots, and beyond it, the bedroom and the spare room, little more than a closet. 'Spare rooms rarely stay empty for long,' she noted.

Though Assunta offered to help Luisa prepare Sunday supper, the girl refused assistance. Several times. *"Sei sicuro che non posso aiutarti?"* Assunta called out.

"No, Ma," Luisa said in English. "I already told you I didn't need help. *Siediti. Rilassati."* But Assunta couldn't sit and relax. She glanced into the kitchen again. Tendrils of Luisa's hair framed her face, curling in the humidity. Her apron was stained with red sauce. Though it was November, her skin was damp with perspiration. The girl was pale and looked sickly. Once already, she excused herself and ran for the washroom. Assunta could hear her daughter retching beyond the closed door.

The table was set with china Luisa had "inherited" from old Mrs. Tuttle, their neighbor on Gatling Place, who'd passed the week before the wedding. Mrs. Tuttle's daughter was cleaning out the apartment and had china of her own, so she offered her mother's to the Tozzi girl. ("You were so good to my mom," Lynn Tuttle had explained. "She'd want you to have it.") The tablecloth was neatly ironed and the silverware (also from Mrs. Tuttle) was polished to a high gloss. The drinking glasses were simple but sparkled too.

This was the first Sunday supper Luisa and Antonio were hosting. Assunta knew Luisa wanted this meal to be perfect and that she'd worked hard all week: planning the menu, washing and pressing the table linens, cleaning, shopping, then purchasing all the ingredients after scrimping and saving for several weeks. The only dish Luisa permitted her mother to bring was dessert: a ricotta cheesecake crafted from their neighbor Mrs. Ricci's not-so-secret family recipe.

Luisa did, however, allow her sister Barbara to help. They worked silently and deftly, innately knowing what needed to be done and doing it. Young as Mina was, she was able to carry bowls of olives, lupini beans and caponata to the table.

The males of the family were on the roof, Antonio tasked with showing them Mr. Grant's pigeon coop, then retrieving a gallon jug of Belloni's homemade wine from its cool hiding place. Prohibition still raged so one could never be too careful.

Assunta's three sons flew down the roof ladder's rungs, abuzz with talk of homing pigeons, how fast they could fly (up to sixty miles an hour!) and how they helped during the Great War. In fact, one of Mr. Grant's birds, Cher Ami, was named in honor of the "war hero" who received France's *Croix de Guerre* for having delivered a dozen important messages despite being badly injured.

Serafino tried to coax Assunta up the ladder to have a look for herself. *"Per favore, mama,"* Dominic begged as well. But their mama wouldn't relent.

Antonio's hand briefly cupped the swell of Luisa's belly as he placed the gallon of wine on the sink's edge.

"Per piacere," Paolo echoed, flinging himself into his mother's lap.

"Sono troppo vecchio e grasso," Assunta told him, swatting the boy from her as one would brush away a fly.

"You are neither old nor fat," Luisa said to her mother as she slid the ravioli into the teeming pot one by one with a slotted spoon. *"Cinque minuti,"* she informed them. "Only five minutes. In the meantime, pick on this stuff," she added, gesturing to the *cicchetti* Barbara had set out on the table. "But don't snack too much. You don't want to spoil your appetites."

Assunta batted the boys' hands from the serving bowls. *"Lavati le mani,"* she reproached, imagining dirty pigeon feathers, fleas and other nastiness coating their skin. The trio stomped off to the washroom.

At the head of the table, Antonio said, first in Italian, then in English, "It is through God's grace that we are together today in good health, with good food, and I pray that we can all be together again soon." His normally strong voice faltered as Luisa clasped, then squeezed his hand.

Assunta lowered her eyes. She knew her son-in-law was thinking of his recently-departed mother. The woman, Henrietta, wasn't much older than Assunta herself. She thanked the Lord that she was blessed to sit at this table, surrounded by those who loved her. *'Per gracia di dio,'* she silently prayed. Yes, Antonio was right; it was all through the grace of God.

The Tozzi men descended upon the feast like a pack of jackals. Antonio paused and waited until all had taken their food, even the women, before he served himself. There was ravioli, gravy meat and escarole enough for twice the amount of people present. Plates of grated cheese, lemon wedges and hunks of bread were passed from one to the other.

Luisa took very little, then barely ate what was in her plate, Assunta noticed. Her coloring had gone from stark white to grayish green but at least she didn't have to dash to the restroom during supper.

When the subject of work arose, Antonio said that the shop had been very busy lately. Luisa said the same about her place of employment, making it a point to speak in English. (She tried to get her parents to practice the language of their adopted country whenever possible, but they usually reverted to Italian, especially with the family.) Full of Mr. Belloni's red wine, Giuseppe piped up, "No wife of mine ever had to work."

Assunta set aside her fork. "You made sure to keep me pregnant, so how could I work?" she said, then smacked his arm. "And cooking, cleaning, raising your children..." Assunta continued. "You don't call that work?"

For once, Giuseppe was dumbfounded. His wife's fiery demeanor had attracted him to Assunta in the first place. Spitfire out of bed, spitfire in bed, as the old saying went. In Assunta's case, it was true.

Taking pause, Luisa brewed a pot of espresso but didn't indulge herself. Even the children had a drop of coffee in their cups of hot, sweetened milk. Luisa didn't even take a wedge of Mrs. Ricci's cheesecake, her favorite, making the excuse that she was full. But Assunta knew the truth: her daughter's belly was full of baby.

1928

CHAPTER TWENTY-FOUR

Antonio

Could it be possible that Luisa grew even more beautiful as her pregnancy progressed? Antonio didn't think so, yet, like a lingering rose in the dead of winter, the young woman blossomed. Thankfully, she was no longer as ill as she'd been during the first months. Luisa's already full breasts burst from the top of her brassiere, the moons of her dark areolas visible. Antonio desired Luisa more than he had before but took her more gently now, devising innovative and unusual methods to bring them both pleasure.

The father-to-be worked harder than ever and managed to stash savings in the Colibri cigar box he kept under their bed. As was the custom, Luisa stopped working in the factory as soon as she began to "show." But she immediately started taking in piecework and doing alterations for neighbors, turning the kitchen table into a sewing emporium. She enjoyed this more than the rushed, frenetic pace of the sweatshop.

Luisa not only mended, hemmed, let out and took in garments but she created unique, one-of-a-kind fashions. Gowns, frocks, skirts and even bespoke slacks. You name it, Luisa could sew it. Plus, faster, more reasonably and more expertly than any seamstress in the neighborhood.

Though he was weary, Antonio often helped Luisa when he came home after his own dance with the needles.

Often, when supper was over, Antonio and Luisa sat in the parlor, darning this and that while listening to "The Voice of Firestone" on the radio. Antonio's favorite program, it played a mélange of classical music. While Luisa tapped her slippered toe in time to the melodies, Antonio became totally swept away by the music. Lost. "Our child is going to come out humming the overture to *Don Giovanni*," Luisa joked.

At this, Antonio bristled. Not because he lacked an appreciation for Mozart (although he did prefer the works of his countrymen to those of the Austrians) but because it sparked memories of his father, Giovanni, who bore the same name as the opera's title character. Since the death of Antonio's beloved mother Henrietta the previous October, his father's health had taken a turn for the worse. Though Giovanni seemed to treat his wife carelessly when she was alive, he fell apart after her loss.

Franco wrote to Antonio that the fields had gone fallow and the animals often went unfed and unwatered. Franco did what he could, but he kept long hours as a carpenter's apprentice. The farm no longer supported itself and they relied on Franco's income to stay afloat. The young man frequently found his father passed out at the kitchen table he had built from trees felled by his own hand, on his own land, a spilled-over jug of wine leaving a blood-red puddle at Giovanni's feet.

On one such evening, Franco came home to discover that he could not rouse his father from his drunken dreams. Giovanni was cold as stone to the touch, probably hours dead. A telegram enlightened Antonio of his father's unceremonious passing. Antonio responded immediately, telling Franco what he should do. The nineteen-year-old made burial arrangements for their father and sold the family farm, which was underwater in debt anyhow.

When all was said and done, there was only a million *lire* (the equivalent of roughly six hundred dollars) in profit—from selling the beasts, the few sticks of furniture and the land. This inheritance, Franco would divide evenly with his brother. It was how they did everything, fair and square and split down the middle. After all, Antonio was expecting his first child that summer.

As Franco was emptying his mother's bureau, he discovered a parcel of letters tied with crude twine in her unmentionables drawer. Antonio's letters. Franco sat on the edge of the bare mattress to read. Tucked between the notes was another envelope, this one stuffed with American dollars. All the money Antonio had sent Henrietta over the years. Franco permitted himself to weep, but just for a moment. He would return the envelope to his brother, which Antonio would later divide with Franco. Henrietta's posthumous legacy of sorts.

It was without question that Franco would join his older brother in America. And that he would move in with Antonio and Luisa. The young man arranged passage on the next ship leaving from Naples. He would gladly occupy the DeMarcos's spare room, which would soon be transformed into a nursery.

Francisco DeMarco made passage on the brand-new *Conte Grande* eight years after his brother had boarded the *Giuseppe Verdi*. All Franco brought from home were a handful of belongings like his clothing and his shaving kit. In Franco's breast pocket was the moonlit photograph of the New York City skyline Antonio had sent to their mother. It had been her most prized possession.

Antonio was stunned by the lanky manchild who bounded toward him after disembarking the Ellis Island ferry. Franco scooped his older brother into his arms. The young man had grown like summer wheat in less than a year. His collar was frayed but clean and his dress suit was worn but neatly pressed. His slacks wandered above his shoe tops. Antonio would soon remedy this.

Due to her delicate condition, Franco hugged his sister-in-law with less vigor than he had his brother, but not with less emotion. *"Mi dispiace per le tue perdita,"* Luisa offered, then corrected herself, *"Perdite."* Giving condolences for his losses, not loss. Giovanni and Henrietta DeMarco had died within months of one another.

When Franco lagged behind, Luisa took the opportunity to whisper to her husband, "He's so skinny! But I'll soon fix that."

"Andiamo," Antonio called to Franco. "Let's go!"

On the trolley across the Brooklyn Bridge, observing the instant rapport between his wife and his brother, Antonio puzzled if the two might be more suited for each other than he and Luisa were. After all, they were closer in age, born only weeks apart in the spring of 1909, while Antonio himself was rapidly approaching thirty. But he pushed this foolishness from his mind, fortified when Luisa glanced at him and smiled. She was truly his *solo amore*. His only love. There was no doubt.

With pleasure, Antonio sat back and watched his wife excitedly pointing out the spire of the Woolworth Building, which her father had helped build, the blue metal expanse of the Williamsburg Bridge before them, and the Williamsburg Savings Bank's tower, in Brooklyn, which was still under construction. *"Mio padre é un costruttore,"* she noted proudly. The expression of surprise on Franco's face made Antonio chuckle; he was certain his brother believed that Luisa's father had built all of New York City singlehandedly, brick by brick.

Everything in Franco's newly-adopted land was a source of marvel for the country boy—the buildings stuck so close together, the people so smartly dressed, and the paved streets themselves. Franco even admired the fold-away bed they'd borrowed from Mrs. Brincko down the hall. Luisa hung a picture resembling the rugged San Vincenzo countryside to make Franco feel more at home. But Antonio was sure his brother wanted nothing of home save for his memories.

Franco promised that he wouldn't be in the couple's hair for long and that he would be settled in his own place in a month, two at the very most. Before Antonio could protest that Franco wouldn't be a bother, Luisa piped up, *"Non sei un fastido!"*

After they dropped off Franco's satchels at the DeMarco's apartment, they walked to Luisa's parents' place on Gatling. The newcomer thoroughly enjoyed the milelong stroll on Fifth Avenue. It took twice the time because Franco kept stopping at shop windows, admiring the wares or complimenting the superiority of the produce in America over that of Italy. "Everything is better in *L'America!*" he exclaimed in thickly-accented English.

Antonio and Luisa stole smiles at each other as they walked. He squeezed her hand. She squeezed back. It was good to have Franco here; he managed to find wonder in everything, even apples. The local bakery was also a source of rapture. They let Franco pick out the dessert they would bring to her family—a gooey cheese Danish.

As they rounded the corner of Gelston Avenue, Franco told them he'd been studying the green and red chapbook Antonio had sent several Christmases ago, the one with "Learn to Speak English" embossed in gold on the cover. "It shows," his big brother complimented Franco. Again, the young man beamed.

Before they climbed the row house's cement stoop, Luisa warned Franco, *"Sono molto rumorosi e ce ne soni molti."*

Antonio took the cake from Luisa so she could hold onto the railing. Her ankles had begun to swell in the latest stage of her pregnancy. "In English," Antonio sweetly reminded her. "Franco needs the practice."

Luisa nodded, then repeated in English, "My family is very loud and there are a lot of them."

However, nothing could quite prepare the fellow for the swarm of Tozzis that descended upon him. Sam showed Franco the pocketknife Antonio had brought back from San Vincenzo. (Meanwhile, Franco had been at his brother's side when he picked out the gift last year.) Mina, who was only three, showed him the handkerchief Barbara was embroidering with his initials, much to the protest of her older sister. "You spoiled the surprise!" Barbara chided then clomped out of the room.

'Could it be that the girl has a crush on the stranger from across the sea?' Antonio pondered.

Paolo staked claim to Franco's lap, squirming as the man tried to drink his espresso. This was so different than the somber meals of his youth in the ramshackle farmhouse. However, Franco seemed to be coping well, relishing it, Antonio noted.

Throughout supper, Luisa reminded her family, "In English! In English!" as they spoke excitedly to the newcomer. It warmed Antonio's heart to see how even his in-laws struggled to comply with Luisa's request so that his brother would learn the tongue of his adopted home more rapidly.

Antonio's mother-in-law pulled out all the stops in her *"Benvenuto in America"* meal. Besides the colorful antipasto—a dark rainbow of olives, glistening roasted peppers, earthy marinated mushrooms and an array of cheeses—there was a deep red sauce covering mounds of rigatoni and bowls of gravy meat (regular and hot sausage, plump meatballs, beef braciole, curls of pork skin and a chicken quarter to sweeten the pot), a garlicky string bean salad, loaves of crusty bread and more. Then there was dessert! *"Non mangiamo così tutti i giorni,"* Assunta explained.

Luisa heaved herself up from the table to get more cream. "Of course, we don't eat like this every day," she laughed. "Or we'd all weigh five-hundred pounds. *Cinquecento libbre.*"

Giuseppe stroked one edge of his handlebar mustache, satisfied with the abundance of food his backbreaking work had brought. Then he told Franco that he knew a fellow in the Carpenters Union, but they only hire the best. Giuseppe asked his son-in-law, "Is he any good?" gesturing to Franco with his chin.

"He's very good," Antonio assured him.

Giuseppe sucked his teeth and took a gulp of Medaglia d'Oro. "Tomorrow, I will speak to Roberto about getting Franco a job."

Antonio looked around the table. He was surrounded by faces he hadn't known two years prior but now knew as well as his own. Each beauty mark, each furrow, each whisker. And then there was his Luisa, heavy with his child, ever so lovely. It felt like family. 'It *is* family,' Antonio reminded himself. 'Your family.'

The sky was beginning to color as Luisa took his arm and the three of them strolled back toward Seventy-Fourth Street. She was already in bed when Franco handed his brother a small parcel: a stack of envelopes wrapped in a rough twine. "Mama kept every letter you ever wrote to her," Franco began. "Every photo. Even the money you sent."

Antonio blinked and nodded, taking the parcel from Franco. They still smelled of his mother, of the farmhouse: of hay and onions and slight discontent. Antonio waited until he knew Luisa and Franco were asleep. Then he sat alone at the kitchen table and silently wept.

CHAPTER TWENTY-FIVE

Luisa

With every passing day, Luisa had more difficulty with routine activities—climbing the stairs, standing at the stove, the sink. Antonio and Franco took on more responsibilities at home, despite Luisa's protests. She felt slightly guilty with her feet up on the ottoman as Antonio washed and Franco dried the supper dishes. As often as he could, her brother-in-law cooked a simple supper, explaining, "I had to learn fast after Mama died."

In the Dyker Theater, Luisa sat between the two brothers, watching *Sadie Thompson,* the latest Gloria Swanson picture. It was no secret that Miss Swanson was her husband's favorite movie actress and that he carried a flame for the sultry Chicago native with the alluring mole near her chin. Enroute to the Dyker, Antonio had regaled them with talk of how Gloria Swanson not only produced and starred in the film they were about to see but was also nominated for Best Actress for this performance at the first annual Academy Awards.

Luisa perched her sore feet on the base of the seat in front of her, gazing at the expanse of fluffy clouds painted upon the Dyker's high ceilings. It was her favorite movie theater in Bay Ridge. As the newsreel played, Franco mouthed the words he was unfamiliar with, and in hushed whispers, Antonio and Luisa took turns explaining their meanings to him.

Luisa's brother-in-law smelled fresh and clean, just as her husband did, with a hint of bay rum. He was closer to her age, born just ten days before her. Franco was less guarded, more outwardly happy than Antonio was. The DeMarco men spoke very little of their parents, of their home, which led Luisa to wonder if their father had ruled the broken-down farmhouse with a violent hand that even a mother's adoration couldn't temper. Franco could make Luisa laugh like a child in a way that no one else could. Yes, Luisa did love Franco, but like a brother, not in the same deep, serious way she loved Antonio. Of this, she was certain.

Though the Sadie Thompson story was gripping and a bit decadent—Sadie was a woman of ill repute eager to start an honest life in Pago Pago—Luisa soon fell asleep, her head lolling onto Franco's shoulder. He did not nudge her away. These days, the very act of breathing seemed to tire Luisa. She stole sleep whenever she could.

One day, Franco came home from his job at the Brooklyn Navy Yard carrying a bulky object shrouded in a potato sack. "Did you take the trolley home with that?" Luisa wondered.

"Ray gave me a lift with his truck," Franco answered. Luisa marveled at how his English had improved in the short months he'd been there. He mastered even American slang.

Franco insisted they wait until Antonio came home before he unveiled his mystery gift in the Long Island Big Boy potato sack, jokingly swatting Luisa's curious hand when she tried to touch it. *"Pazienza,"* he scolded her.

Though supper was ready (just leftover rigatoni and broccoli fried crisp in a pan), Luisa demanded they open the present first. *"Come un bambino la mattina di Natale,"* Antonio grinned.

"Yes, she's just like a child on Christmas morning," Franco agreed.

Antonio covered his wife's eyes with his hands as Franco carefully slipped the object out of the burlap bag. Before them lay a cradle, crafted from oak and hand polished to a high sheen. Luisa immediately burst into tears. Practically everything made her emotional these days, but her brother-in-law's heartfelt gesture touched her to the core. "It must have taken months," Luisa said through her tears.

Franco admitted it had. "I collected the scraps when I was building the desk for the officer's cabin on the *Pensacola*," he explained. "I picked only the best pieces."

"I can see that," Luisa said, touching the smooth wood. "It's soft as butter," she remarked.

"Your mother made the little mattress," Franco told them. It was covered with a sunny yellow and white gingham check. (Mina had a dress of the same material.) Most everyone was positive Luisa was having a boy because she was carrying so low, but Luisa was sure it was a girl. In any case, yellow was a cheerful color, no matter the child's gender.

On July 5, 1928, Gloria Maria DeMarco made her way into the world amid some commotion and a great deal of blood. Briefly stuck behind her mother's pubic arch, the doctors at Bensonhurst Maternity agreed that they might have lost both mother and child if the father hadn't insisted his wife give birth in the hospital rather than at home.

Although it was traditional to name the firstborn girl after the husband's mother, Antonio suggested they name the child for his favorite actress, Gloria Swanson. Her middle name, Maria, was Henrietta's middle name. It also gave a nod to the Blessed Mother.

Luisa was secretly relieved when Antonio suggested they name her "Gloria." It would have been cruel to saddle a wee one with such a long, unwieldy name. Even though the modest farm wife sounded like a wonderful person indeed, "Henrietta" did not trip lightly on the tongue. Luisa was content to honor her mother-in-law with the child's middle name.

Gloria was a beautiful baby, weighing in at a whopping nine pounds and thirteen ounces, her perfectly round head topped with a mound of black ringlets. Upon seeing all that hair, Luisa thought, 'No wonder I had *agita!*' (Italian folklore taught that carrying a baby with a full head of hair gave the mother heartburn during her pregnancy.)

Adorable as she was, the child was colicky and could cry herself into a gasping, red-faced tizzy, sobbing for hours if she wasn't held tightly and marched throughout the apartment. At her most fussy, only Franco could calm her, singing "Huggable You" to her in a hushed voice, the words peppered with his thick accent. Luisa's eyes watered when his voice wavered on these lines,

"When I gaze at you
My soul skips a beat
I lose my words
And trip on my feet…"

When the girl calmed, Antonio would take over, wrap his arms around her and coo,

"Don't be a bad girl
Come to Daddy, come to Daddy,
please do…"

Luisa would watch from the stove or from the kitchen table, her heart full and think, 'How lucky am I?'

CHAPTER TWENTY-SIX

Assunta

If you asked Assunta, her daughter and Antonio's brother Franco were a bit too close for comfort. But no one asked Assunta. Perhaps this bond was because they were nearer in age, born just days apart, while Antonio was ten years older than Luisa. This was an even larger age gap than Assunta and Giuseppe had.

But her daughter seemed happy with Antonio, noticeably happier after Franco's arrival. Luisa giggled like a schoolgirl at his jokes, and they were always sharing secrets when they sat side by side. Antonio seemed to appreciate the closeness of their relationship, but their amiable chatter raised Assunta's hackles. How dare her daughter be so cheerful?

Assunta was convinced Luisa's bright mood would wane when the baby came, even after such a difficult birth. But no, Luisa was as glad as ever after Gloria Maria was born, troublesome as she was.

And who did Antonio think he was, insisting that Luisa have the child in a hospital? 'He's always been so high and mighty,' Assunta huffed to herself as she scoured the kitchen sink. Home birth was good enough for Assunta (seven times!) and all the generations of Tozzis and Nigros before her. What made Luisa so special that she had to give birth in a cushy maternity center?

Did her son-in-law think women who had babies in their marriage beds were savages? No, it had been done from the beginning of time. Even sweet Lord Jesus Himself was born in a manger. And what was good enough for the Virgin Mary was good enough for Assunta. Why not Luisa?

True, her daughter did have a tough time, even with her wide hips. Luisa lost a great deal of blood and might have lost the baby as well as her own life if she hadn't been in a hospital. At least that's what Antonio said. Who could believe him, though?

But when Assunta was permitted to see her daughter at Bensonhurst Maternity, Luisa looked as pale as the bed sheets. Assunta's angry heart melted when she saw her eldest look so weak and wan. And the first time she held that dark-haired, dark-eyed cherub in her arms, Assunta was a puddle.

But for the love of *Gesù*, the child's name! Who ever heard of naming a baby for a motion picture star? A *puttana* with painted-on eyebrows, all that makeup and the mark of the devil on her chin. Was Gloria Swanson's mole even real? Or was that fake too? And sure enough *Piccola Gloria* had been born with a tiny mole on her upper lip.

In Assunta's mind, the couple had disgraced Antonio's recently-departed mother when they gave the child a movie-star name instead of honoring the girl's maternal grandmother with a namesake. When pressed, Assunta would admit that Henrietta was a hideous thing to call a baby—even an adult—but customs were customs. If people didn't cleave to tradition, they were no better than *animali*.

And what was wrong with the name "Assunta?" It was a perfectly-fine name, a strong name. Plus, it honored the miracle of the Blessed Mother being scooped up into heaven, without even experiencing death. But the couple claimed that they wanted a name that sounded

more modern, more American than either Assunta or
Henrietta. Ha! A baby named for a stranger!

Still, the girl had a good birth date. Lucky numbers.
Assunta herself had been robbed of her birthday. When
they came through Ellis Island, Assunta Nigro Tozzi's
birth date was changed from June 18 to June 13. Perhaps
a clerk's poor penmanship was to blame or maybe it was a
twisted sort of revenge because the lowly worker resented
all these dirty Guineas invading his country. For decades,
Assunta had been angered by her birth-date change;
thirteen was such an unlucky number.

Ah, and *Piccola Gloria* was so spoiled! She demanded
to be held so much that Luisa fashioned a cloth sling
that she wrapped around her body so the child could
be swaddled close to her mother as she did her chores.
"Chinese mothers do this working in rice paddies,"
Luisa pointed out sweetly when Assunta confronted her
about it. "African mothers too. I saw it in a newsreel,"
she added.

'Imagine, a child so fussy that her uncle can calm her
better than her own parents can,' Assunta muttered to
herself as she swiped gook out of the enamel drainboard.
Well, perhaps it wasn't fussiness, just colic. But Antonio
and Luisa wouldn't even permit Assunta to feed the
baby spoonfuls of chamomile tea. "Dr. Cortes said only
breastmilk for the first few months," Luisa reminded her.
Hmmm! *Té alla camomilla* was a remedy that had worked
for centuries yet it wasn't suitable for *la Principessa*.

'And a baby sharing a room with a grown man!'
Assunta groused to herself as she moved on to scrub
the remnants of dinner from the range top. *Pazzo!* Luisa
insisted that Franco was a help, calming Gloria when she
woke in the middle of the night, ravenous, appeasing her
until Luisa could reach her. This way, the girl wouldn't
wake the whole tenement with her hungry cries.

Assunta stopped for a moment. Why was she so
full of rage, she asked herself. Franco was a decent sort.

Gloria was an angel of a child. Luisa was a capable, loving mother and Antonio, a caring father who only wanted the best for his family. But sometimes, out of nowhere, Assunta was flooded with red-hot anger, then the next moment, was weeping for sheer gladness.

She knew the source of her pendulum-swing emotions but couldn't admit the reason to herself. It began with those uncontrollable flashes of warmth that soaked her bed sheets in the middle of the night and caused her to fling open windows in the middle of winter. These odd feelings, these rages began when Assunta's flow became irregular. She wasn't yet forty, it was too early for her to go through the Change. Maybe having all these babies put her body out of whack.

Already, Assunta was thickening in the middle and her stubborn chin sprouted an unruly hair or two. Even more troubling than her unpredictable rage was when her "friend's" visits became few and far between. At first, Assunta worried that she was pregnant, but this didn't feel the same as being with child. This didn't feel like something was beginning but instead, like something was ending.

For Assunta, there would be no more babies. No more giving life. Would Giuseppe still want her? Would she still want him?

There, in her drab kitchen, Assunta scrubbed and cleaned and tried to make her worn home shine. She was certain that her own time to shine was over. But maybe, just maybe, her children, and their children, would be beacons of some sort.

1931

CHAPTER TWENTY-SEVEN

Antonio

A ntonio didn't know how they would survive the
Great Crash but somehow, through the grace
of God, they did. All his life, Antonio had no
difficulty finding work but when the factory closed, he
felt untethered, for there was no shop work to be found
anywhere. He worried about how he would care for his
wife and his toddler. As Little Gloria learned to master
the art of walking and talking, Antonio worried about
how he was going to feed her.

"There are some who have no food, let alone delicious
food like this," he reminded Luisa, who apologized for
serving pasta for supper yet again. Whatever Luisa served
was delicious, whether she managed to procure a bruised
eggplant for a penny, a rogue jar of anchovies or simply
served spaghetti with browned garlic and olive oil. "There
are some who have no homes. We are lucky," Antonio
tagged on. "We have both food and shelter, and we have
each other."

Luisa, his Brooklyn Mona Lisa, would smile vaguely
at him, as she fed Gloria pastina drowned in butter from
a demitasse spoon that bore the child's teeth marks. "We
are," she agreed. "We are very fortunate."

Antonio was glad he hadn't trusted Banca Stabile
on Mulberry Street with all his savings. He had several

Colibri boxes of cash stashed in various hiding spots throughout the apartment. Unbeknownst to Antonio, Luisa had been ferreting away any surplus from her weekly household allowance. Since they'd gotten married, she had amassed quite a healthy stash. Drawing from their clandestine savings, they managed to eke by.

Although most factories and sweatshops folded after the unfortunate events of October 29, 1929, people still needed clothes. They didn't have the means to buy new apparel, but instead, sought to mend what they had. After all, seams always tore and hems needed to be taken up or down on castoffs. Dresses and slacks needed to be let in.

Luisa was already known as a quality seamstress throughout Bay Ridge, so her business only amplified after the Crash. Charging as little as possible, Antonio and Luisa created a handy cottage industry of fixing and sewing their neighbors' clothing. It wasn't much, but combined with their secreted savings, it was just enough to get by. This sustained them until Antonio got word that Frazzetta Limited was reopening after two years. They asked Antonio to return to his former position as master tailor—but for less money. Antonio had no choice but to accept their offer. Luisa continued mending at home, Little Gloria at her feet.

His brother Franco also managed to survive, even though the Brooklyn Navy Yard had reduced its workforce of four thousand by one-quarter. Italians and other immigrant ethnic groups were the first to be let go, Franco among them.

But just like garments, structures like staircases and flooring collapsed and needed fixing, even during the Great Depression. Franco became Bar Ridge's go-to handyman and remained busy throughout the years following the Crash. Though he charged a pittance for his services, he was able to contribute to the household. Antonio was proud of his brother's resourcefulness. In fact, he was proud of how his entire Brooklyn family muddled through such difficult times.

When construction resumed with the cruiser, the *USS New Orleans* in early 1931, Franco eagerly returned to the Brooklyn Navy Yard. Soon after, he secured a studio apartment on Clermont Avenue, a stone's throw from the Yard. The adjoining Wallabout neighborhood is where Franco met Rosa, the daughter of Italian immigrants from Salerno. Soon, Franco and Rosa began keeping company in her parents' parlor, her younger brother and sister on the sofa beside them to ensure that no hanky-panky transpired.

When Franco brought Rosa to Sunday supper at his elder sibling's apartment, Antonio took an immediate liking to her. As did Luisa and Little Gloria, who insisted upon calling her *"Zia,"* despite being gently corrected. "I suppose you remind her of Luisa's sisters," Antonio explained to Rosa.

"I'm honored," she blushed from the kitchen. Gloria clung to Rosa's leg as their guest grabbed a dishcloth. Rosa insisted on helping, despite Luisa's protests. As Luisa washed and Rosa dried, they gossiped about picture-show stars, half in English, half in Italian, young hens, cluckling with decadent delight.

"Non lasciarla andare," Antonio told Franco under his breath.

Franco assured his brother that he wouldn't let Rosa go. *"Questa è un custode. Se lei mi avrà."*

"Oh, she will have you," Antonio said in a low voice. Rosa smiled at them both from the kitchen as the men cleared the remaining dishes from the linen-covered card table in the parlor. They saved room for the *tiramisu* Rosa had made that morning. Not only did it survive the trolley ride, but the rum-and-espresso-bathed ladyfingers soon put three-year-old Gloria to sleep.

Toward the end of 1931, the DeMarcos were just starting to get back on their feet and put aside meagre savings. Antonio had just been promoted to floor manager at Frazzetta's. Luisa had more work than she could handle and sometimes took on her sister Barbara to help fulfill her orders. The couple was saving to buy a home. Nothing large or ritzy, just a place of their own.

Then came Luisa's news.

CHAPTER TWENTY-EIGHT

Luisa

uisa could never get used to the hollow, haunted eyes of the people she saw on bread lines. They seemed deeply embarrassed by their lot in life, though it was through no fault of their own. The young mother felt compelled to hug them, as though this might make a difference. But it would probably make things worse because Luisa knew she couldn't hug them without crying.

However, it was the children, the hardened eyes of the hungry children, that made Luisa really want to weep. She would shove spare pennies into their dirty hands then scuttle off, crablike. Pushing her clean little girl's carriage before her (a hand-me-down from neighbor to neighbor), Luisa fisted away her own tears. 'There but for the grace of God,' she thought and crossed herself. 'This could be us.'

She and Antonio had enough, barely enough at times, but they never went to bed hungry. True, often their stomachs were filled with only a bowlful of polenta, the hearty cornmeal mush slathered with a dollop of leftover marinara sauce and a scant sprinkling of parmesan, but still, they were full.

Gloria managed to grow plump from Luisa fattening her with milk from her own body and eggs from Mrs. Murphy's chickens, when the resourceful housewife managed to secure them. (Luisa would trade her neighbor mending for eggs.) At a year and a half, Gloria's short, sturdy legs were topped with rolls of fat, even though the girl was an enthusiastic walker.

And now, at age three, Gloria liked to run, her coal-black ringlets bouncing with each step. She slipped comfortably back and forth between two languages, often in the same sentence. Gloria was smart as can be and healthy, thank God. Luisa had seen far too many skinny babies wasting away during the difficult times. *Tempi difficili,* as they were called in the DeMarco home. Hard times.

Luisa's parlor transitioned into a tailoring shop as she took on mending, then later, as the economy improved, clothing orders. When Old Mrs. Brincko passed, her daughter Justina asked Luisa if she might want her mother's ancient Franklin sewing machine. Luisa quickly said yes to this generous gift, Justina politely refusing the money Luisa offered. The woman closed Luisa's fist around the cash, covering Luisa's hand with hers. "You were so good to Mama," Justina choked, her eyes shining with wetness. "Looking in on her, bringing her supper, inviting her over for tea. And how she went on about your wee one! I don't think Mama would have lasted this long if it weren't for your kindness."

Luisa didn't know what to say, so she pulled the woman into a tearful embrace. At times, when she worked late into the night, Luisa swore she could feel Mrs. Brincko's benevolent gaze upon her, satisfied that her trusty sewing machine had outlived her, that it was helping Luisa contribute to her own family's support.

When he was let go from Frazzetta Limited during the early days of the Depression, Antonio gladly helped Luisa with her work. For her, it was quiet bliss, sewing side by side with her husband, Glorina (yet another nickname!) nearby, chattering happily to a handmade ragdoll. Luisa was tinged with guilt for feeling so gratified, so blessed, when others had so little.

"Sono molto contento," she would grin at Antonio when she caught him staring at her as they stitched.

He would take in the simple room, the frayed curtains, his wife's worn housedress and admit, *"Anch'io sono molto felice."* That they could be happy with next to nothing surprised them both.

Then Luisa's flow abruptly stopped and she began to feel tender and seasick, especially in the mornings. Her heart chilled at the notion she could be pregnant. 'I've been so careful,' Luisa told herself. But had she truly? Four years after her marriage, the Rhythm Method still confused her.

It bothered Luisa how she desired her husband, even in her condition. Did respectable, Catholic wives do this—crave their spouse's touch, lie in bed hoping he would reach out for her, wedge himself against her body. How Luisa would sometimes reach for him. 'Should I confess this to Father Kent on Saturday?' Luisa worried. She couldn't bear the shame, the embarrassment.

As Luisa darned Signora Borghese's voluminous bloomers, Luisa paused to cup her growing, softly-curved belly. Had Antonio noticed the fullness of her breasts, the swell of her stomach? Should she go to Dr. Lewy to confirm her condition? There was no need because Luisa already knew. She knew her body even better than her husband did, though he sometimes dared to taste it, and she to taste him.

Again, should Luisa declare these transgressions to Father Kent? Hearing a young woman's voice in the confessional box, he grilled Luisa through the screen, asking if she used birth control. This was bad enough. She couldn't imagine telling Father Kent about lusting after her own husband. And now her impure desires had gotten her into trouble. She was pregnant again.

Antonio took the news agreeably, in stride, as he did most things, a smile slowly tinging his lips. "It's the wrong time," Luisa fussed, bursting into tears.

"Is there ever a right time?" Antonio posed. This gave Luisa no comfort. She covered her eyes with her palms. Antonio tried again. "Perhaps it will be a boy this time," he ventured. "But another girl would be nice too." He took Luisa's hands in his and pressed his lips to them.

Antonio proposed they leave Gloria with Assunta for a few hours so he and Luisa could go visit Dr. Lewy together. Afterwards, he insisted on taking her to lunch at Woolworth's, an extravagance, true, but chow mein sandwiches were in order. They shared a banana split, though Luisa claimed she was stuffed. Walking back to Gatling Place to retrieve Gloria, they held hands. On the way to their apartment, Antonio pushed the pram as Luisa tried to imagine what life with two wee ones would be like.

Just as Luisa had expected, the rabbit died two days later.

Luisa's emotions vacillated between profound pleasure and raw dread. 'How can I bring a baby into a world where so many are suffering?' she worried. 'Is it foolish? Selfish? Neither? Or both.'

A newsreel at the Loew's Alpine just the other day showed the devastating droughts in the Great Plains, soil eroding into dust, farmers and their children skeleton thin. This begged the question, would there be enough food to feed the hungry mouths in faraway Brooklyn with farms in the Midwest crumbling?

Luisa looked at her chunky, cheery toddler with the bright, brown eyes and worried. *"Bella! Basta!"* Antonio would scold her as lovingly as possible when Luisa agonized in the dark in the middle of the night. "Enough," he told her. "Haven't I always taken care of you? Of Gloria?"

"We take care of each other," Luisa politely corrected him, remembering how she often sewed into the night and how she kept a neat home.

"Si," Antonio agreed. "We'll get by."

He would stroke the side of her cheek in rhythmic circles to calm her, his hand drifting to the pillow as he fell asleep. But just before dropping off herself, Luisa would remember Japan's invasion of China or the devastating earthquake in New Zealand and begin to worry all over again. Luisa would force herself to think of Little Gloria's pure glee when she watched Charlie Chaplin in the boxing ring in *City Lights* and reminded herself that there was still joy in this world.

Then there was Franco, newly moved into his own small but clean and bright studio apartment, newly enamored with a wonderful woman named Rosa. Luisa immediately liked her; they fell into a lively conversation, as familiar as sisters. She was so pleased to watch the ardor rising between Rosa and Franco like a flower stretching toward the sun. Yes, love bred hope too.

As Luisa's belly grew, her fears grew less, though she was concerned about her mother's health. Assunta had become very tired as of late and had barely enough energy to walk the dozen blocks to visit her only grandchild. Her chores often went undone, the children picking up the slack. Assunta was in her early forties yet appeared older. She walked as though the weight of the world bore down on her shoulders. The stubborn woman refused even a visit to Dr. Lewy. *"Troppo caro,"* she barked.

"It's not too expensive," Luisa chided her mother. "It's your health. Besides, I can make it up in trade. I can do mending for Mrs. Lewy and the doctor's visit won't cost a thing."

With rest, Assunta regained her strength—she told them that Dr. Lewy said her body was just exhausted from having so many babies and she needed to relax. Her health improved slightly, slowly.

Life was good.

Then one day, without warning, while Luisa was hemming a gown at the Franklin, she felt a sharp stab in her abdomen and stood abruptly. Then there came a gush of blood and another stab.

CHAPTER TWENTY-NINE

Assunta

Though Assunta had birthed seven children, she had never seen so much blood. She and Mina were on the Fifth Avenue bus to visit Luisa when the young woman's pain began. There was no time to even call a neighbor for help, for when Luisa stood, she said there was a flood of thick, reddish-brown fluid then another searing pain. That was all Luisa recalled before her mother and littlest sister found Luisa on the floor in a pool of blood, poor, Little Gloria standing beside her, sobbing, "Mama! Mama!" over and over.

While Mina calmed her niece with a cold cup of milk and a cookie, Assunta tended to her daughter. The girl was gray and lifeless, and for a moment, Assunta thought she was dead. But then Luisa stirred, whimpering. Assunta dashed for the telephone mounted to the kitchen wall, grateful her son-in-law had splurged on what she had first tut-tutted as frivolity. *"Per la emergenzie,"* Antonio had told her. And this was most certainly an emergency.

Amazingly, Assunta was able to remain calm and managed to speak English. Dr. Lewy happened to be in his office and left immediately, though he had a waiting room full of patients. He drove the three miles from Borough Park to Bay Ridge in record time, flying up the staircase.

Luisa was conscious when he arrived, softly sniffling because she knew she'd lost the baby. Dr. Lewy fell to one knee, opened his black bag and took out a syringe. "This should slow the bleeding," Dr. Lewy told Assunta. "Though she will probably bleed for several weeks." Assunta didn't need Mina to translate; somehow, she understood. The doctor gave Assunta a vial of pills. "This should help with the cramps," he said. "I'll come by tomorrow to see how she's doing."

Before he left, Dr. Lewy helped Assunta get Luisa into the bedroom, taking care to put out an old towel on the bed before letting her lay down. Luisa was so weak and had lost so much blood, she could barely walk. "And how have you been feeling?" Dr. Lewy asked Assunta. When she looked at him searchingly, he gestured to her belly. "The pains," he explained.

"Very good," she lied. "*Tutto finito.* No more."

As Mina sang Gloria to sleep in the next room, Assunta sponged Luisa's body clean then wrestled her into a fresh nightgown. Only then did she deal with the disaster in the parlor. 'Life is so messy,' Assunta thought to herself. 'Being born, losing a life and everything in between.'

She wiped up the fluid and clumps of matter. Would this have been her grandson? Or another granddaughter? Assunta crossed herself and continued, placing the remnants in a mop bucket with a quiet reverence, then dumped the contents into the toilet. She pulled the cord on the box above the bowl to flush.

On her hands and knees, Assunta scrubbed the parlor rug with a mixture of bleach and water. This is when Antonio walked in from work. It had all happened too quickly to phone him, and when Assunta remembered to ring Antonio, he had already left the factory. But that had been hours ago. Where had he been?

Instead of supper waiting for Antonio when he entered the apartment, there was his mother-in-law's scowl. Assunta blamed him for her daughter's suffering, for her miscarriage. Luisa worked too hard yet never complained. Antonio couldn't support the family, so her daughter had no choice but to take in sewing. Never mind that Luisa swore she liked the work, having a shop in her own home, chatting with her customers. There was a sense of fulfillment in creating christening gowns and wedding gowns, she claimed. But Assunta didn't believe her.

She blamed Antonio's inferior seed and his age for her daughter's miscarriage. Assunta blamed him for everything she could, but in the end, she knew it wasn't Antonio's fault. It was no one's fault. It was *il volere di Dio*. The will of God.

Antonio gave Assunta his hand and helped her off the ground. "What happened?" he asked. "Where's Lu?"

All Assunta could say was, *"Il bambino…"* and they collapsed into each other's arms. She had never been this close to another man besides Giuseppe. It was odd, not entirely unpleasant. Antonio's skin smelled scrubbed, unsoiled, whereas her husband always smelled sweaty and unclean due to the physical nature of his work.

When Assunta and Antonio pulled apart, they exchanged not a word. He offered her his pressed, starched handkerchief. She took it, wiped her eyes and blew her nose with gusto then returned it. He shoved it into his pocket and went to see his wife.

That night, Mina slept on a pallet on the floor of Gloria's room while Assunta curled up on the parlor sofa. She had difficulty sleeping, vacillating between concern for Luisa and examining her distaste of her perfectly-decent son-in-law. Why did she despise him so? Was it jealousy that Antonio loved her daughter more openly than Giuseppe did Assunta? Would Giuseppe cry for her? He barely blinked when they were forced to leave Beatrice behind in Longobucco two decades ago, and Assunta never forgave him for that. She knew Antonio would never do such a thing.

As Assunta tossed and turned on the uncomfortable tufted couch, she vowed to try to like her son-in-law better. Love him, even. He made Luisa so happy and was a good father besides. Yes, Assunta would try and do better, to *be* better. Tomorrow, she would go to St. Patrick's, say a rosary for Luisa and for herself, for her own transgressions. She would even go to confession on Saturday too.

Assunta also vowed to try to be more thankful. Though there were lean years following *il Crollo della Borsa*, the older children pitched in, doing odd jobs outside the house to help. Most large construction jobs were halted but Giuseppe did whatever he could—driving trucks, delivering ice—when temporary work became available. He wasn't above repairing a cement stoop or crumbling foundation.

When construction on the world's tallest building began, Giuseppe was among the Italian craftsmen called in to make a rich man's dream a reality. He bamboozled the foremen into believing that cutting and installing Indiana limestone was no different than slate, that setting ten million bricks was "no sweat." Giuseppe and his team lived up to their promises with the Empire State Building. When the builders demanded that they construct one floor per week, this impossible feat was accomplished by the generous bonuses offered to workers. For the first time in their lives, the Tozzis had a bank account, and a fat one at that.

And when the house on Gatling Place went on the market, Giuseppe struck a deal with the owners, whom they'd known since they emigrated to America. He and Assunta were now proud homeowners. They would slowly make improvements, put private bathrooms into apartments, fixing them up as needed. Their American Dream was evolving. 'But what was the sense of all this when one of your own children was suffering,' Assunta asked herself.

'Suffering is a woman's lot,' she concluded, yawning. Losing children in one way or another was a fact of life. Then Assunta drifted off to a fitful sleep on the cramped sofa.

CHAPTER THIRTY

Antonio

On the night Luisa lost the baby, Antonio crept into their room, careful not to wake her. She looked so small and helpless sprawled out on the mattress, the sheet pulled to her chin. There was the faint but distinct odor of sick, of dried blood. He removed his shoes and sat on the bed beside her, trying not to rouse her. But the weight of her body did, and Luisa opened her eyes. They were rimmed with sadness. "*Mi dispiace*," she croaked in a whisper. "I'm sorry," she told him, apologizing in two languages, as though one was not enough.

Antonio bent and kissed her forehead. It was hot against his dry lips and etched with sweaty wisps of hair. "It wasn't your fault," he said. "You did nothing wrong, *amore mio*."

Luisa clasped his hand. "But maybe I should have..." Worked less? Rested more? Antonio wouldn't let her finish the sentence.

"Shhhh," he murmured. "*Basta, basta...*"

"*Piccola Gloria* must be scared," Luisa worried.

"She's sound asleep. Mina is with her. I think she read *The Little Engine That Could* a thousand times until they both fell asleep."

Luisa gave a tiny smile.

"*Credo che posso*," Antonio added. "*Credo che posso.*"
Then in English, he whispered, "I think I can."

"I don't know if I can," Luisa moaned into
his shoulder.

"Of course, you can. You must. For you. For us."

"But what if I can't..." Luisa did not continue but
Antonio knew what she dared not say.

"Have another child?" he suggested. Luisa nodded
hard. "*Piccola Gloria* is enough. More than enough." This
elicited a weak laugh because Luisa knew their daughter
could be a handful, a bundle of energy who often had the
stubbornness of two children. Then Luisa grew serious. "I
don't think I could go through this again," she mouthed.
"Losing a child, I mean."

They spoke in the safety of the dark, then were
silent. When the silence weighed too heavily upon them,
Antonio switched on his nightstand radio. Mercifully,
Chopin played. One of his Nocturnes, Antonio guessed.
Probably his ninth. It soothed them both to slumber.

In the morning, Antonio woke before Luisa. He
watched her sleep for a few moments, her chest rising
and falling, her brow furrowing occasionally, as though
she remembered her lost baby even while she slept. She
looked beautiful, like a fallen angel. Antonio felt his
desire stir for Luisa even now and pushed such foolishness
from his head. Was this what caused the baby to become
untethered? Their vigorous union the night before? This
too, Antonio forced from his mind. It would do no good.

Ah, Assunta was still there with them, cooking a
hearty breakfast farro. Antonio could smell the cinnamon
and brown sugar. She grunted a greeting then went back
to stirring. His mother-in-law had taken a strong dislike
to Antonio from the moment they met. He could feel it
hanging in the air like a disagreeable odor.

Perhaps Mrs. Tozzi's aversion was because Antonio
was so different than her bricklayer husband and her
rough-and-tumble sons, the latter almost men at eighteen

and seventeen years of age. (At eight, Paolo was already displaying a ruffian exterior.) Perhaps it was Antonio's veneration of opera and classical music that made Assunta assume he was *borioso*. Snooty. Or his style of dress. Because of his mother-in-law's unspoken disdain, he held her at arm's length.

But Antonio knew one thing: when he and Assunta cried in one another's arms the evening before, something shifted between them. He hoped it held. After all, they both loved Luisa (and Gloria!) fiercely and this should be reason enough to treat each other with kindness. For Luisa and Gloria's sake, if for nothing else.

When he came home at such a late hour, guilt plagued Antonio because he normally would have been at his wife's side. This would have spared poor Gloria the sight of her mother's lifeless body on the parlor floor, blood pooling at her middle. But Antonio wasn't home because had a clandestine appointment that he'd told no one about, not even Luisa.

The meeting was with one of Mr. Frazzetta's largest customers at a cushy restaurant called Barbetta. It wasn't far from the factory. Antonio had never been to so lavish a restaurant, with its cut-glass chandeliers, heavy damask window dressings, ostentatious floral arrangements and gilded splendor. Antonio was unfamiliar with the rich, cream-filled Northern Italian cuisine and barely touched his risotto; the white truffle sauce caused his throat to tighten.

Although Antonio arrived early, Mr. Mura had already been waiting for him at a corner table he presided over with a sense of ownership. There was affable conversation about the weather and family. Not until the panne cotta and espresso were served did the topic of work arise. "You're a rare commodity," Mr. Mura began. "A man with great talent and the natural ability to lead. I've noticed that you get along with everyone...from janitors to designers to even the most difficult customers."

"Grazie," Antonio nodded uncomfortably, stirring the miniature white china cup with a demitasse spoon. He should have told Luisa about this meeting instead of fibbing that he was working late. But it was only a white lie, no? This was work-related, was it not?

Mr. Mura took a sip of his heavily-sweetened espresso. The diamond on his pinkie finger gleamed in the candlelight. *"Prego,"* he responded then cleared his throat and continued, "I feel that your talent is being wasted in a…a sweatshop, for lack of a better word." Antonio winced at the unfortunate choice of phrasing. True, Frazzetta Limited was no Triangle Shirtwaist Company but it certainly wasn't Chanel. Not by a longshot. "I have something different in mind for you," Mr. Mura proposed.

He went on to describe his vision of creating a high-end tailor shop in Brooklyn which fashioned bespoke clothing for select clients. There were many such individuals moving into Bensonhurst and Gravesend who could easily afford such a luxury, even in the Depression. Somehow these people had not only survived but prospered. Antonio was aware of these swells because he, Luisa and Little Gloria often took Sunday strolls through their well-tended neighborhoods, like Dyker Heights. Occasionally, he even splurged on a decadent cup of gelato for the ladies to share if finances allowed.

Antonio listened to Mr. Mura's proposal, the mushroom risotto curdling in his belly. Could he leave Mr. Frazzetta, who had employed him without hesitation when Antonio first came to America, knowing barely a word of English? "I like the way you carry yourself," Mr. Frazzetta had told him in Italian when Antonio stepped into the factory, nervously fingering his fedora. Antonio recalled that he was wearing a navy pinstripe suit that day, one he'd crafted himself.

Sensing Antonio's hesitation at his offer, Mr. Mura clapped Antonio on the shoulder. "This is business, not personal," he pointed out. "Cristoforo Frazzetta will understand. Give his blessing, even. I will provide the initial investment, refer clients to you and be hands off... as much as you want me to be."

Antonio doubted all of this but still Mr. Mura's offer was tempting. "Let me think about it," he told Mura.

"Take all the time you need," he said.

Walking to the Broadway Local, Antonio considered his options. He would have a shorter commute to work, would be his own boss, could handpick his team and for the first time in his life, truly oversee his own destiny.

Antonio would have to discuss Mr. Mura's proposition with Luisa, only not right now for now was a difficult time. But if not now, when?

1932

CHAPTER THIRTY-ONE

Luisa

As her body recovered from the loss of a child, Luisa's mind struggled to keep step. She didn't know what to do with herself, so she walked off her grief. Luisa trekked all over the borough, pushing Gloria in her pram, sometimes venturing across the Brooklyn Bridge near Anchorage Plaza and into Manhattan.

Once in Manhattan, she would walk the crooked, wet, cobblestoned streets of Chinatown, dipping into Little Italy next door, before venturing home. If she had extra coins in her purse, she might pause for a pork bun from the Nom Wah Tea Parlor or a pastry from Café Ferrara across Mulberry Street, sharing both with her daughter. Gloria's absolute glee at discovering new tastes was tempered by her mother's dolor.

Closer to home, Luisa would push Gloria's buggy past the monumental homes of Shore Road, the long, winding street that hugged the curves of Brooklyn bordering the Narrows and New York Bay. Occasionally she would pause at a bench in Owl's Head Park, the perfect vantage point to watch the ferry journey back and forth from Staten Island. Other times, she would venture into Dyker Heights. Once, she went as far as Coney Island but was so tired that she had to take the trolley back, two strapping men helping to lift Gloria's heavy pram onto the trolley.

As Luisa walked, she thought. Was it her fault she lost the baby? Was it something she did or didn't do? Was she too lustful, letting Antonio take her whenever he desired—and sometimes even being so brazen as to seduce him in the night? Luisa's body, when voluptuous with child, seemed to have no shame. Was this God's will, as her mother told her or just an example of Darwin's survival of the fittest, which she'd read about. Or did it happen because Luisa wasn't sure about the baby at first?

One day, on impulse, Luisa tucked into Georgio's Barbershop and instructed the hairy-armed owner to bob her hair. Incredulous, in Italian, he asked, "*Tuo marido approverebbe?*"

In a huff, in English, Luisa responded, "It's my hair, not my husband's. I don't need his approval." And when Georgio still hesitated, she tagged on, "Do you want my business or not?"

Little Gloria watched with curiosity from her pram as Georgio lopped off her mother's footlong braid at the nape. He grasped it in his fist. "I can get good money for this," he told her.

"Do whatever you'd like with it," she said.

Georgio didn't charge for the cut because he would make a tidy sum from the sale of Luisa's hair. He neatened the bottom and cut bangs so that it framed her face. Luisa barely recognized herself when she looked into Georgio's streaked mirror but immediately felt unburdened, lighter. She remembered reading that in some Indian tribes, people cut their hair as a sign of mourning. This made perfect sense to her.

Antonio didn't complain when he walked into the apartment that night. His initial shock softened into a smile. "You look just like Luisa Brooks," he remarked, Italianizing the first name of the silent film actress who'd made the bob famous.

Work piled onto Luisa's sewing table, but she didn't care. She had no head for repairing torn bloomers, for letting out slacks, for altering heirloom wedding gowns. People began taking back their unmended clothes, but Luisa wasn't bothered by this. She'd grown bored of being a seamstress. Luisa had done it for almost a decade, since she was fourteen, and it had recently become a tedious chore. She had no mind for anything but walking.

Although Antonio didn't grumble about the plain suppers Luisa put before him—rigatoni tossed with fresh tomatoes (not even a proper sauce!) or soups thick with escarole and white beans—Luisa knew they were unsatisfying and left him wanting.

Still, Antonio craved Luisa's body, broken and damaged as it was. And for the first time in their marriage, she turned him away with a tearful, 'Not yet' or 'I'm not ready' or simply by sobbing.

'When will you be ready?' Antonio asked gently. Luisa shrugged in response; she truly didn't know.

Luisa had taken her husband's news of going into business with Mr. Mura as she did most things in the days after losing the baby: with little enthusiasm.

Antonio kept busy setting up shop deep in Bensonhurst. The place was slowly taking shape. Mr. Mura said that money was no object and he meant it. All the machines were pristine, though Antonio initially tried to convince his partner that used machines were more than adequate. But Mr. Mura wouldn't hear of it.

Luisa had the feeling Antonio's *capo* got whatever he wanted and said as much. "He's not *mio capo*," Antonio corrected, "Not my boss, but a business partner."

"And what do you bring to the business?" Luisa posed. "We have barely any savings."

"Mr. Mura brings *soldi,* money; I bring experience," Antonio told her.

If the weather cooperated, Luisa and Gloria would visit the shop on Seventy-Fourth Street and Eighteenth

Avenue, occasionally making a detour to Albano's Bakery to get a *sfogliatella,* a puff pastry that all three would share bits of later.

Antonio was pleased to see his girls at the shop, no matter how hectic the day was. If time allowed, they would stroll to the Seth Low Playground where Gloria would climb and run. When Antonio put her in the metal swings, she would call, *"Più alto!* Higher!" with each push. Afterwards they would unwrap the sandwiches Luisa brought from home, the butcher paper darkened in spots from the olive oil. Afterwards, they'd take turns taking bites from the delicious clamshell pastry, confectioner's sugar dotting their lips.

Making her rounds one day, Luisa stopped dead in her tracks. It was as if she had found an oasis, a lifeline. A new bookstore stood on the corner of Eighty-Third Street and Fifth Avenue. A worker had just finished painting the window sign and was clearing away his drop cloths, brushes and cans. *"Ti piace, signora?"* he asked.

Did Luisa look so Italian that he knew he could speak to her in his native tongue? Yes, she probably did, she decided. Luisa nodded in response then added, *"Si, mi piace molto."* They both stood, admiring his handiwork. *The Avid Reader,* it said.

Although Luisa often took Gloria to the Bay Ridge Free Library on Ridge Boulevard, the young woman no longer read for her own pleasure. She would borrow piles of picture books to share with her daughter at bedtime but never checked out books for herself. Luisa had lost all interest in reading after losing the baby. But seeing this bookstore spring up in her neighborhood like a rose piqued her interest. Did she dare go inside?

Before Luisa could enter, an older woman stepped out onto the sidewalk. She had salt-and-pepper hair that brushed her shoulders, a friendly demeaner and dancing green eyes. "Beautiful, Roberto," she said acknowledging the man's skill. The gold script lettering was ringed in black, making it almost jump from the window and draw the customers in. "What do you think?" the lady asked Luisa. She detected a slight brogue that hinted at County Cork.

"Very nice," Luisa agreed.

Then, as if reading her mind, the woman posed, "Would you like to come inside and have a look?"

Luisa nodded. The air smelled of books, of paper and ink, and of hope. They found a space to park Gloria's buggy near the front of the shop. The girl was sound asleep, so Luisa was free to wander. All the worlds she'd discovered in her childhood were waiting patiently for Luisa to revisit. The glistening streets of Oz, the wide, rolling hills of Massachusetts, the vast cathedral in Paris. All these places and many undiscovered ones.

The woman looked on, delighted by Luisa's expression of wonder. Once or twice, Luisa pulled out a book, examined its cover then slid it carefully back into place. "Do you approve?" the woman wondered.

"Oh, yes," Luisa practically swooned. "Please tell the owner that he did an excellent job choosing stock."

"I don't need to tell the owner," the woman smiled, "because you just did." Then she held out her hand. "Meet Valerie Holson," she added. "Proud owner of The Avid Reader."

Luisa was baffled and stuck out her hand. "Luisa DeMarco, seamstress, I guess, and once an avid reader. Forgive me, but I had no idea that a woman could…"

"Women can do anything, my dear," Valerie told her. Luisa wasn't positive this was true but didn't challenge the statement. "After all, we did get the right to vote. Finally." She paused, "I'm curious, why aren't you an avid reader any longer?"

"I…I don't know," Luisa stammered. "I suppose life got in the way."

"Well, I hope you find your way back to books," Valerie said.

Still in awe of her surroundings, Luisa glanced around the shop. "To me, this is heaven."

Valerie smiled. "What did you like to read? When you read, of course."

Without even thinking, Luisa blurted out, "Tales of faraway lands, places very different than this place. Only, I haven't been reading much lately." Had Luisa already said that? Was she babbling?

"Maybe that will soon change."

Luisa shrugged. "Maybe."

"I know it will," Valerie said. "When my husband died, I had two choices..." she paused for effect. Luisa held her breath in anticipation. "Sink or swim. Douglas had a healthy insurance policy to make sure I'd be well taken care of when he passed. I could either invest it, which would have been the prudent thing to do..."

"...or do this," Luisa smiled, pointing to a bursting shelf.

"Owning a bookstore has always been a dream of mine," Valerie admitted.

"Mine too," Luisa confessed.

Gloria stirred in her pram and sighed in her sleep. She would soon wake, famished. Luisa had to get home. As the two women walked toward the carriage the toddler would soon outgrow, Valerie wondered, "Who's your favorite author?"

Luisa contemplated this for a moment. How could she possibly choose? "Well, I do enjoy Hemingway, but I suppose it's Pearl S. Buck. *The Good Earth* was so wonderful."

"Oh! She's got a new one that's just come out." Valerie went to the fiction shelf where the B's lived. "*Sons.* It's the second book in what will be *The House of Earth* trilogy."

Luisa took the hefty novel in her hands, admiring its bold yellow and red cover, reminiscent of the Chinese flag. "Take it," Valerie told her.

Fumbling for her purse, Luisa calculated what she would need for groceries that week and knew she couldn't afford to buy the book. "Maybe next time," she stammered.

"I insist, Luisa," Valerie said. "It's a gift. You're the first customer to walk through my door. I know you'll bring me luck." Luisa reddened and looked uncomfortable. Valerie pressed, "It's like when a bartender gives you a free drink...he knows you'll order more."

"I...I've never been in a bar," Luisa admitted.

"Why doesn't that surprise me?" Valerie said. She wrapped the book just as Gloria awoke, sweaty and hungry, clamoring for milk. *"Latte, latte, per favore, mama,"* she pleaded. Luisa would have to go home to nurse the child.

Before she left, Valerie had a proposition. "I could use some help around here," she told the young woman. "Someone trustworthy so I could sneak out and do errands and such. Part time for now, flexible hours. I couldn't afford to pay much, in the beginning. So, Luisa DeMarco, do you know anyone who might be interested in this position?" They both smiled.

Luisa continued smiling as she steered Gloria's buggy down Fifth Avenue because she'd found both a job and a friend. She couldn't wait to tell Antonio.

CHAPTER THIRTY-TWO

Assunta

'How could I have raised such a selfish daughter?' Assunta couldn't begin to comprehend how Luisa didn't even seek her husband's permission to start working at that *libreria*. It was as though the thought never even crossed her mind. When Assunta brought this up to her modern, Americanized daughter, Luisa looked at her as though Assunta had a thread of *bucatini* hanging from her nose and barked a short laugh.

"Mama, in *L'America*, women got the right to vote in 1919. That's more than a dozen years ago," Luisa began. Assunta had the urge to slap her insolent daughter but held back. Not in front of *Piccola Gloria*. Assunta's fingertips itched to give Luisa a sharp pinch, at least.

"*Sì, e?*" Assunta pushed. And what?

Luisa gave an annoyed huff and stirred the gravy. "*Più*, please," Gloria said from her highchair, politely demanding another miniature meatball. If only Assunta could slip back and forth between English and Italian as effortlessly as her granddaughter did.

Luisa handed Gloria a tiny meatball from the plate and waited until after Gloria said, "*Grazie, Mama*" before she continued.

"And..." Luisa said. "Women can vote, no? We can think for ourselves. We have our own minds, our own desires. We don't need our husband's permission to do anything. Even cut our hair!"

"Pazza!" Assunta yelled so loud it startled her granddaughter. She stabbed at the pile of meatballs with toothpicks. One for her, one for Gloria.

"It's not crazy, Mama!" Luisa rallied back, exasperated. "Of course, I told Tonio about my day, about the opportunity, and he was glad for me. But I didn't ask his permission to take the job at the bookstore. I'm not a child, Mama."

'No, but you are twenty-three and yet you still call me Mama,' Assunta smiled to herself. She glanced at her eldest, graceful in her own kitchen in her own home, drifting from pot to table to another pot, stirring, searing and feeding her perfect, smart daughter. Assunta felt a wave of emotion flooding her chest. Love? Pride? Ah, it was probably just indigestion. *Agida.* Nothing more.

This was the first time Assunta had seen Luisa happy, truly happy, since the girl's miscarriage. This was another thing that bothered the older woman about her daughter: Assunta had lost babies, both here and in the Old Country, and she didn't mope. Besides, Giuseppe would have slapped some sense into Assunta if his supper wasn't on the table, miscarriage or not. But Antonio was so compliant, so understanding. He cared more about his wife's heart, her happiness, than a hot meal. And he'd *cried!* Cried in Assunta's arms like *un bambino* when Luisa's pregnancy was lost. What man did that?

"Mama, I'm ready for the garlic now," Luisa called from the stove.

Assunta looked at the scattering of cloves on the table before her, still sheathed in their papery jackets. *"Un momento,"* she said, then set to work, smashing each clove with the flat of her palm against the flat of the knife blade, denuding them, then giving them a quick chop on the cutting board Franco had crafted from discarded oak scraps.

She handed Luisa the board, the contents of which she slid into the waiting pan. On the way back to the table, Assunta was overcome by a crippling pain in the right side of her abdomen, just beneath her ribcage. She gripped her belly and staggered to her chair. It clattered to the ground as she hunched over the table. Gloria began to whimper at the commotion.

Luisa wheeled around at the sound. "Mama! What's wrong?" She was at her mother's side in a moment.

Assunta shrugged her off. "Nothing. Just a touch of *agida*." It felt like a knife cutting into her gut.

Luisa righted the chair and guided her mother into it. She ran the tap and gave Assunta a glass of water. "This is much more than *agida*," she said. "You need to see Dr. Lewy."

The older woman shook her head. "And what will he do for me? Eh? Give me a magic pill? Snap his fingers and, poof! All better now." Assunta sipped the water, her hand shaking. "*Grazie, no.*"

In truth, Assunta had been to Dr. Lewy. On her most recent visit, he said that her love of sweets, fried foods and cured meats had finally caught up with her. Her gall bladder was revolting, he explained, after reviewing her test results. 'But what is a life without chocolate, salami and golden, crispy eggplant?' decided Assunta. 'No life at all,' she concluded.

When Dr. Lewy noted her indifference, he tagged on, "This is serious, Mr. Tozzi." Then he told her the Four F's, counting off on his stubby fingers: she was female, over forty, fertile and fat. High risk for gallbladder disease. Dr. Lewy suspected Assunta had gallstones and it was highly likely that a specialist would opt to remove her gallbladder.

Assunta didn't even wince at being called fat; she'd been called worse. Instead, her mind tackled weighty words such as "specialist," "surgery" and "serious." She knew an operation of this sort would be expensive. How could they afford it with the house? And who would look after Giuseppe and the children while she was in the hospital? These days, Luisa had begun to depend on her more and more, especially now with her silly job. But the reality was that all these people could look after themselves—and they were perfectly capable of looking after Assunta while she convalesced. But Assunta was hesitant to take a step toward her own care.

If it had been Giuseppe or one of her children, Assunta would have forced them to see a specialist. But Assunta would permit no one to force her to do the same thing, for she would tell no one of her illness.

Dr. Lewy had sensed his patient's reluctance. It was common with immigrants who had sacrificed so much, who had left behind so much to come to a new land. In this new land, they believed they were invincible. He suspected this was the case with Assunta. "Mrs. Tozzi, left unchecked, gallstones could lead to gangrene, sepsis, or worse," he warned.

Cowboys were constantly getting gangrene in the Western pictures Dominic and Serafino dragged Assunta to at the Harbor Theater, but it was usually from a gunshot wound. Dr. Lewy took the care to explain sepsis to her—a serious condition resulting from the presence of harmful microorganisms in the blood.

Assunta succeeded in ignoring her symptoms, except when they overtook her like a freight train running through her belly. When that happened Assunta struck deals with God, prayed without ceasing and swore she would call the specialist—the gastroenterologist, what an unwieldy word—whose name Dr. Lewy had written on a scrap of paper. But when the pain passed, Assunta forgot about her promises to *il Signore* and seeing this special doctor.

Back in Luisa's kitchen, Gloria watched the exchange between her mother and grandmother, lines of concern furrowing her little forehead. Nonna crying out had startled her almost to tears. Assunta read fear on the toddler's face and rubbed the girl's pudgy, dimpled hand to assure her that Nonna was all right. *"Fa bene, fa bene,"* she cooed. But the child didn't seem convinced that her grandmother was okay.

An acrid odor filled Luisa's kitchen. *"L'aglio!"* she cried. Luisa left her mother's side and ran to stove, the garlic blackening in the pan.

Assunta dashed to the bathroom and turned on the tap full blast so her daughter wouldn't hear her vomiting into the toilet.

CHAPTER THIRTY-THREE

Antonio

L ong ago, Antonio realized that people's dreams were different. What might be paradise for one could be hell for another. For his brother Franco, coaxing bits of wood into a cradle or a bookshelf was a source of joy. Antonio gleaned pleasure from the satisfaction of turning bolts of material and lengths of thread into a superb suit of clothing. For Franco, this would be sheer torture, just as wielding a hammer and a bevel-edged chisel would be for Antonio.

So had sewing become for Luisa. Agony. A chore. Since losing the baby, Luisa had difficulty sitting still. She suddenly found the repetitive nature of being a seamstress maddening. Luisa took to walking, walking all over the city, as though this might rid her of her grief. Antonio had lost count of how many times she'd taken her shoes to the cobbler for soles.

And now, this new job. It clearly brought Luisa joy: matching the right person with the right book. She spoke of this breathlessly as she prepared dinner in the evening, how Mrs. Flynn had come back to gush about how she loved Jane Austen and wasn't that Emma such a troublemaker?

At first, Assunta balked about watching Gloria when Luisa had to work at the bookshop, but it was easy to see this was a flimsy front and that his mother-in-law loved being in her granddaughter's presence. Especially now that her own children were growing older and her serial childbearing had mercifully stopped. (Truly, the woman seemed exhausted.)

Although Antonio had worked in tailor shops since he was thirteen, he had no idea how much work went into setting one up. Mr. Mura seemed to have no bounds as to expense—he required the best machines, the best materials. Antonio began to worry that this relationship was too good to be true and that perhaps his benefactor might try to cheat him, to squeeze him for money. But Antonio soon saw that Mr. Mura gained satisfaction from doing the right thing, from helping others and witnessing his labor bear fruit.

When Antonio began partnering with Mr. Mura, Assunta, who tended to see the dark side of the coin, was convinced he was a mafioso, a member of the Black Hand, if there were such a thing. But Charles Mura soon won over Assunta as well. There was no ulterior motive in anything the man did, just pure decency.

The renovations of the long, narrow workspace underway, Antonio began to interview men and women from the community to come work for him. Usually, tailor shops employed just men or just women, but Antonio sought to utilize the skills each possessed. In those days, it was rare, if not unheard of, for the two sexes to work side by side. By blending the two, Antonio hoped they would learn from one another: the females' delicacy of stitching and the males' rugged needlework. Top of mind was how Antonio had enjoyed working at home with Luisa, how he'd learned from her. And vice versa. He planned to replicate this feeling of satisfaction in his shop.

Antonio was conscious of the things he disliked about working in a large factory: the poor lighting, the inferior ventilation, the crowded conditions. In kind, he asked Mr.

Mura's construction workers to uncover sealed skylights, to scrape layers of paint so that windows could be opened to let in fresh air and natural light. In addition, they purchased big, whirring overhead fans for when it grew too hot.

"A happy worker is a good worker," Mr. Mura agreed. "And it's the right thing to do," he tagged on, recounting his mother's ill health and failing eyesight from years of factory work in badly-lit, dank (or sweltering) sweatshops. Mr. Mura had told Antonio this story that evening at Barbetta when the man unfolded his plan across the linen tablecloth. Mr. Mura was determined not to repeat the sins of those who came before him but to create a healthy work environment.

It troubled Antonio how many of the women he interviewed alluded to being manhandled by their bosses and shop stewards. Some of these fellows wore skullcaps and were supposedly pious family men. The ladies were resigned to the fact that they must submit to a pinch of the buttocks here or a squeeze of the breast there (sometimes more) to keep their jobs. Antonio was clear that this would not happen at Chatonio's Haberdashery, either from bosses, coworkers or customers. Though a couple of ladies hinted that it would be all right with them if it did, Antonio ignored these remarks.

Were they flirting with him? Luisa made a point of telling Antonio what "a real looker" he was but Antonio didn't see it. He was beginning to gray at the temples and had begun to thicken slightly in the middle from his wife's superior cooking. Did women think him attractive? He only had eyes for Luisa, who he still saw as the mature, serious, comely teenager he'd met in Cannonball Park what seemed eons ago. The years, their struggles, weathering the Depression, hadn't jaded her. Luisa's laugh, like the prelude to his favorite aria, colored his days.

Before long, the shop was ready to open. Mr. Mura said there was already a list of potential customers waiting (somewhat impatiently) for appointments. Many were Calabrese like him and knew the legendary talents of Calabrian tailors and seamstresses. Some gentlemen even had bespoke suits cut by Gennaro Pucci, whom Antonio apprenticed for in the Old Country, making the pilgrimage to Calabria to be outfitted once or twice a year. (A few were certain they even had clothing stitched by Antonio himself.) Others went to Hong Kong or Singapore for their wardrobe. Visiting a shop in Bensonhurst would be considerably less costly.

Antonio hoped Mr. Pucci would be proud of him. But he knew Luisa was, and that's all that mattered.

He came home from the shop every night tired but content. Antonio was determined not to work his people to the bone and swore he wouldn't keep late hours himself. Having a good home life was as valuable as having a good work life. Having enough energy to play with your children, to cuddle with your wife, was of great worth. The customers would have to wait.

CHAPTER THIRTY-FOUR

Luisa

It still thrilled Luisa to see her husband's weary but glad face appear in the doorway each evening. He was doing something important, something that mattered. It gave Antonio satisfaction to create fine garments that, in turn, gave others pleasure. This was a feeling Luisa herself had lost in her former trade but had rediscovered in her new career.

Could working in a bookshop actually be a calling instead of just a dalliance? Valerie couldn't afford to pay Luisa a lot, but the wages were fair, the work was pleasant and the hours flexible. Besides, Luisa didn't feel drained at the end of the day; instead, she felt invigorated. She didn't return home in the evening bleary-eyed or with an aching back. Instead, she came home energized, excited, eager to tell Antonio what she had read or sold. He enjoyed the stories she shared about the amusing, quirky customers she served. "You're better than Jack Benny," Antonio would laugh. (Like most Americans, they listened to "The Jack Benny Show" on NBC Blue Monday nights.)

On the days Assunta was too fatigued to mind her granddaughter, Valerie welcomed Gloria into the shop. At four, the girl shared her mother's reverence for the hallowed hall of tomes. When permitted to look at a picture book, Gloria did so carefully, turning the pages gently.

During slow times, Luisa began teaching her daughter to read, first introducing her to each letter and pronouncing them painstakingly. Gloria repeated them as best she could, making the connection between sight and sound. Valerie looked on as she busied herself about the shop, smiling vaguely at the interaction.

Both she and Luisa marveled at the fact that the child could speak, and now, read, so effortlessly in two languages. She was able to differentiate between the long American "aaa" and the sigh-like Italian "aah." Soon, Gloria was reading easy stories aloud, plodding ahead just as the Little Engine that Could, one of her favorites, thanks to Zia Mina.

The child had taken to the bookshop keeper as though she were family. Without urging, she called Valerie "ZiaVal," as though her name were one word, with no space between. Neither Luisa nor Valerie corrected her. "ZiaVal" seemed just right.

Luisa had a knack for bringing in customers (mostly women) in the most creative of ways. Valerie never turned down one of Luisa's ideas, saying, "Let's see how it flies. It won't cost a cent to give it a try, will it?" In this manner, Luisa introduced knitting classes where the ladies would sit in a semicircle resembling a dozen Penelopes, learning a new stitch each week. As they practiced, instead of gossiping, Luisa would read to them from the most popular releases. *Brave New World, Little House in the Big Woods, Tobacco Road...*

The knitting circle was always hungry for more. This gave Luisa the thought that The Avid Reader might offer books on credit where the buyer could pay, say, ten cents weekly (at no interest). In no time, the book would be paid off and the reader would be ravenous for another. Valerie quickly did the math in her head and declared this a tip-top idea.

When a couple of the knitters confessed that they struggled with reading, Luisa suggested they hold informal reading classes in the bookshop. Both she and Valerie taught them the basics, taking turns between serving customers and gliding over sliding vowels or explaining the concept of silent consonants. The instructors were patient and thorough while the students mastered phonics and sounded out syllables without shame, much like Little Gloria did

When Valerie called Luisa "innovative," the young woman was taken aback. While her employer was using the washroom, Luisa slinked off and looked up the word in the huge Merriam-Webster they kept on a stand near the counter. There, Luisa culled that being innovative was indeed a good thing—it meant that Luisa was inventive and pioneering. She flushed and shut the dictionary. No one had ever called Luisa anything that nice before. Not even Antonio, who was always saying nice things to her.

Valerie kept a small hotplate in the storage room so they could brew coffee and such. Soon Luisa began making them lunches on the burners. Nothing fancy, just one-pot dishes like escarole and beans or else Luisa toasted sandwiches in a cast iron frying pan beneath an errant brick covered in tinfoil to flatten the bread into paninis. Valerie ooh-ed and aah-ed as though she'd never had such deliciousness, but to Luisa, these lunches weren't fancy. *Semplice.* Simple.

"She's Irish," Assunta told Luisa instead of complimenting her daughter's prowess in the bookstore kitchen. "The Irish boil food to death and call it cooking." Luisa was taken aback by her mother's blanket prejudice against Gaelic cuisine. But Assunta had been feeling poorly again and was cranky about life in general lately. She sometimes even lost patience with *Piccola Gloria* and she loved the child dearly.

Perhaps Assunta felt a tinge of jealousy about Valerie's appreciation of her daughter's cooking. Just so Luisa was aware of it, Assunta tagged on, "And remember, I taught you everything you know *nella cucina.*"

Luisa assented. "Yes, you and Zia Claudia."

Valerie, on the other hand, was blossoming with praises for Luisa. She marveled at how the young woman could create such flavorful meals on a two-burner hot plate. Valerie swore it brought more customers into the bookshop, especially when weather permitted and they propped the front door open. They began keeping extra utensils and palm-sized Pyrex cups on hand so curious customers could have a taste. Luisa didn't mind doing extra dishes in the back room's enamel slop sink. "Maybe we should begin offering cooking classes," Valerie mused.

Cooking classes! What did Luisa have to offer anyone? But then she remembered that she'd taught Little Gloria to read (in two languages). Plus, there were those informal reading classes the shop held. And she'd taught all those leaden-fingered ladies—and one boy!—how to knit. Luisa surprised herself when she told Valerie, "I think cooking classes are an excellent idea."

Together, they brainstormed about how this could be accomplished. Maybe Silvio, the greengrocer, would give them a break on bruised vegetables. Maybe Joe the Eggman, would give them a discount on his wares. Maybe, maybe. These men ended up giving the bookshop ladies their goods free of charge because they felt it was a grand thing they were doing for the community. And in turn, it brought them more business, for after each class, the culinary students tried making these dishes at home.

Of course, Assunta was skeptical, but then she was doubtful about everything. How would they make money from giving free cooking classes? How would this cause people to buy books?

Yes, Assunta's disposition was more dour than usual. She arrived at the bookshop one day, holding Gloria's hand, out of breath after only a few blocks, perspiring lightly. Valerie made her sit, daubed her damp forehead with a hankie then fetched her a cup of water, which Assunta sipped gingerly. She waved off Luisa's concerns.

"Basta, basta, é solo agida," Assunta told her daughter once more.

"It's not *agida*, Ma," Luisa said, exasperated.

"Honestly, I don't think it is either, Mrs. Tozzi," Valerie echoed.

Although Luisa felt helpless where her mother was concerned, never had she felt more useful in other aspects of her life. Not that being a mama and a housewife didn't have their own sense of merit, but working in The Avid Reader was different. This was helping strangers. Luisa had the power to make people happy. She had the power to make a difference, to feed empty bellies. It didn't even matter that some came back for more than one taste of whatever Luisa happened to be cooking on the bookstore's burners that day. True, they might never purchase a book. And that was all right. It was all right if it filled the needs of the hungry. And so many hungered in those days.

CHAPTER THIRTY-FIVE

Assunta

'**D**o we ever stop worrying about our children?'
Assunta wondered. 'Even when they are
grown? Perhaps this is when we worry about
them most of all.' Assunta remembered their neighbor
Willie Larette saying, "Little children, little problems. Big
children, big problems." And it was true.

As Assunta walked down Fifth Avenue, she offered
a prayer with each small, tentative step. She seemed to
get so winded lately. Did anyone notice the short, stout,
graying woman who moved as if on eggshells? Probably
not. Everyone went about their own business, stocking
crates of potatoes, delivering cartons of macaroni,
gazing into shop windows. No one seemed to realize
that Assunta stopped nearly every block, clutching a
lamppost or a Johnny pump to catch her breath, then
proceeded tenuously.

'Did Serafino drink too much?...Will Barbara be a
good wife?...Will Dominic's roving eye lead him into
another woman's bed? (And was he unfaithful to his
devoted, thick-ankled wife even now?) Will Mina ever
learn to sew?...Will Paulo's temper get him in trouble?...
Will Giuseppe's back hold up?...Or will he get hurt on
the construction site again?...' These thoughts fluttered

through Assunta's mind, an unruly flock of birds, winging this way and that.

And Luisa, her Luisa still worried Assunta most of all. True, she was nicely settled, and the serious, bookish girl had somehow nabbed herself a respectable husband. Together, they seemed to get by, even though Antonio had left a perfectly adequate job to chase the cockamamie dream of owning his own shop. And that Mr. Mura, his partner... Why would he put his faith into a lowly seamster and sink God-knows-how-much into a new business. Was Mura a mafioso? Was he *pazzo*? Or a saint?

But her Luisa, always with her head buried in books. Now she was teaching Glorina to read in not one but two languages. What four-year-old needed that? Now Luisa worked in that ridiculous bookshop and Antonio seemed pleased about it, proud, even. Being a bookstore clerk wasn't a proper job!

Still, Lu seemed content. Had Assunta ever been content? She couldn't recall. Even her glad moments seemed tinged with sadness. Shadowed by Beatrice, the girl she abandoned in Longobucco. The girl who died crying for her mama, Assunta's own mother had written to her. Or more closely, Virgilio, the town scribe, had written to Assunta because her mother was illiterate.

Whenever Assunta visited Luisa at the bookshop, however, her fears about her daughter were quelled. The girl, at twenty-three, a woman really, seemed so capable, so in control. With her agreeable manner, she could show a clumsy woman a complicated stitch without making her feel foolish. She could feed a famished child without the means to buy a book without making them feel like a beggar. She could choose the perfect read for a clueless husband to give his wife after hearing only a sentence or two about the woman. Assunta realized that this was truly a gift. And Luisa had other outstanding qualities. Her compassion, her perseverance, and lastly, her beauty, which shone like a pearl, from within.

It was Luisa who would take over as matriarch of the Tozzi family when Assunta was gone. She would look after her father and all the rest. Giuseppe would be all right, Assunta decided. Though he would miss her, maybe he would remarry. Most likely, he would miss Assunta's cooking more than he would actually miss *her*. But other females could cook. However, you don't share a bed with a woman for more than twenty-five years without feeling a sense of loss, an empty space, do you?

Perhaps Assunta would miss *Piccola Gloria* more than any of them. The relationship was so new, the bond just forming. She would miss the feel of the girl's tiny, warm hand in hers as they walked to and from the bookshop, to and from the apartment. Recently, Gloria had rejected even the upright stroller in favor of walking. Luckily, the girl's diminutive legs carried her at a pace that matched her ailing grandmother's.

Assunta truly took enjoyment in Gloria's company, studying her bright eyes that sparked with wonder upon seeing a grasshopper on the concrete. Hearing her high-pitched squeal of, *"Nonna, guarda!"* (And Assunta looked, even if it was just a twig.) She enjoyed the company of her granddaughter more than she had any of her own children, for Assunta had always been so busy, so tired dealing with her own offspring. But in a different way than she was tired now. And there were so many of them. Why did Assunta have so many kids?

Would Little Gloria miss her? Would she even remember her? What would Assunta be remembered for most? If she were to be remembered at all. Her sharp tongue? Her incendiary temper? Her gruff manner? Surely, there was some goodness in her. But where?

St. Patrick's church loomed, only a block in the distance, but it seemed miles. Assunta could see its square bell tower soaring high above the streets. Its comforting red brick façade called to her. Ah, it would be a relief to cross herself with the cool holy water that waited in its marble cup, to rest a few moments in one of its polished wooden pews, to bathe in the light of its splendid stained-glass windows.

Choosing the middle staircase, Assunta climbed the granite steps with difficulty, using the wrought iron railing as a crutch. She entered the church through the center set of double doors. Immediately, she was engulfed by a sense of peace. Was it the presence of *il Signore* or something else?

To Assunta's left was the marble baptismal font, caged behind iron latticework, cloaked in darkness. Her youngest, the ones born in America, had received their first sacrament here (though in the previous version of this church). Her first grandchild was the first to be baptized in the new church. Assunta's eldest living daughter had been married here. Had it been five years already? Where did the time go?

After dipping her finger in the chilled holy water and tracing the sign of the cross into her forehead, Assunta slowly worked her way along the aisle to the front of St. Patrick's. There was no one else inside at this hour. She never sat this far up during mass, always careful to tuck herself near the back so the other congregants couldn't judge her shabby clothing—or her unruly sons. But *il Signore* knew she was in church, didn't He?

Assunta slipped into the second row on the lefthand side. The bride's side. Would she live to see another daughter married off in this church? Assunta sighed deeply as she sat, the firm wood supporting the backs of her thighs. Her entire body ached but her heart especially. There was a heaviness in her chest, worse than ever. Was it wistfulness? Longing? Or something more? Dr. Lewy had warned her to take these pains seriously. Could a bad gall bladder really affect the heart? Had Assunta remembered to put that vial of pills he had prescribed into her purse? Those miniscule, white pills with the sugary, burning taste. No matter.

Assunta crossed herself again, too weary to kneel on the tuffet. She took in the beautiful altarpiece housed within a marble arch: Jesus on the cross, His mother Mary on the left, Mary Magdalen on the right and someone else at His feet. Assunta had never been sure if this was a man or a woman gazing up at Him. But what difference did it make? She was struck by the mournful expression on Mary's face, delicate hands folded in prayer, studying her broken son. How horrible it would feel to see your child posted to a cross!

But then there was the beauty of the stained glass, the rosette behind the choir loft. Colors danced on the pews and the marble floor of the empty church, cast from the tall, arched colored glass windows. The wedding at Cana. The Sermon on the Mount. All the different shades shimmering in the late afternoon sunlight. The blues were the ones Assunta liked best; she favored the deep sapphires.

Assunta dug through her purse. She came out with the string of rosary beads Antonio had brought her from San Vincenzo, a gift she would never admit she treasured. She sighed, sat back and fitted a prayer onto each pink bead. A shadow appeared near the altar, in the vestibule beside the confessionals. It seemed to be a woman, draped in a shawl. She seemed strangely familiar. But who was it? Her mother? Her daughter Beatrice? This was impossible because both were long dead.

When Assunta looked again, the figure was gone. She heard a creak and felt movement on the bench beside her. Someone grasped her hand. Was it the shrouded woman? Her mother? Beatr...

Suddenly, there was a bright, blinding light. Then nothing but darkness.

CHAPTER THIRTY-SIX

Antonio

The adage, "If something is too good to be true, it usually is" rang through Antonio's head as he fastened the knot of his necktie. The shop was running smoothly. His workers were dedicated and skilled, and there was no shortage of customers. When they turned a profit, Mr. Mura said he would begin taking a small percentage to start paying back his initial investment, exactly as his contract with Antonio stated. Then Charles would draw a small salary as the business grew. It was all on the up-and-up, the paperwork drafted by a lawyer.

Then why did Antonio feel so uneasy? The face that stared back at him in the mirror showed fine lines bracketing his eyes and a double furrow in the center of his forehead, just above his proud Roman nose. When had Antonio begun to get so gray? He would have to ask Luisa. The dusting of silver around his temples caught in the harsh bathroom light and glared back at him.

'Everything is fine,' Antonio told himself. Gloria was growing up smart and strong, a unique sapling he helped cultivate. Luisa was the perfect partner: attentive, caring, attractive and supportive. The pleasure she took working at the bookshop overshadowed her recent sadness. And who could blame her for feeling blue after losing a pregnancy. But Luisa didn't let her sorrow overtake her, though in the months after it happened, he'd heard her weeping beside him in the night. Antonio let his wife have her tears because tears were necessary. She needed to get beyond her grief. He would rub her back, say nothing, but his silent touch let Luisa know she wasn't alone.

Antonio's brother Franco had a nice place in Williamsburg with his wife Rosa and they were expecting the arrival of their first child. Luisa's string of brothers and sisters were all doing well, each in their own way. And Luisa's employer Valerie had become a dear friend, a surrogate mother to them both. Mr. Mura, or Charles, as he insisted on being called now, and his wife Antonella had become family. 'So, what is the problem?' Antonio asked himself.

The problem was, he wanted more. Was Antonio wrong for wanting more? He wanted to give Luisa and Gloria their own home. A house. He wanted them to live in a place where no one walked above their heads, where they didn't have to fear they were making too much noise for the neighbors. Where they didn't share a party wall on either side. In their own home, there would be no shop beneath, no upstairs neighbors or neighbors on either side, just them.

Perhaps the DeMarcos could even have a garden, a place for Gloria to dig in the dirt, for them to plant fragrant flowers and grow vegetables. And a sunny corner for a fig tree to stretch its arms. And roses. Roses of every color. Besides longing for a real home, Antonio also wanted another child, maybe two if they could manage.

With so much suffering in this Great Depression, Antonio felt guilty for desiring more. So many had holes in their shoes or no shoes at all. So many dressed in rags, lived in filth. So many went hungry, even people in Bay Ridge. Why, he'd read that a ramshackle shantytown had sprung up in Central Park's newly-drained reservoir. Hundreds of crude campgrounds were being built across America. Hoovervilles, they were called, after the president who didn't do nearly enough.

But Antonio and his family had enough, more than enough. And for that, he was grateful. He couldn't imagine what it would be like to watch your child starve before your very eyes. He knew he wouldn't be able to bear it.

That morning, waiting for Antonio on the kitchen table was a steaming cup of black coffee, his two newspapers and a fresh loaf of bread, still warm from the bakery. In her highchair, Little Gloria fed herself oatmeal and managed to get some into her mouth. "Papa!" she cried as Antonio sat and shared a spoonful of mush.

Luisa smiled when she saw her husband. It marveled Antonio that whenever he laid eyes upon his wife, his heart felt full and glad. Still. After six years of being her companion, Luisa made Antonio happy in so many ways. He prayed it would always be so, even fifty years hence. He couldn't imagine being one of those couples who sneered and sniped at one another, rolling their eyes and sighing with disdain. "No matter what happens, I hope we can always be kind to each other," he'd once told Luisa, masked in the cover of night. Thus far, they had.

Luisa carried her own cup of coffee to the table and sat across from Antonio. She ripped the heel from the bread and gave it to Gloria. "*Pane,* thank you," she lilted.

Then Luisa tore another piece for her husband, and lastly, for herself, slathering both with butter. It melted upon contact, dripped into the plate. "Is today the day you tell him? Luisa wondered. Antonio nodded, his mouth full. "How do you think he'll take it?" she asked, tearing off more bread.

Antonio swallowed, shrugged. "We'll see." Luisa kissed him firmly, tasting of sweet butter, yeast and possibility.

"Going to the bookshop today?" Antonio wondered.

"Tuesdays are usually slow, so Val doesn't need me," she said. "I was thinking of taking Gloria to Green-Wood."

"The cemetery? Again?" he sighed.

"Again," Luisa told him. "I like the peace and quiet, and Gloria likes running on the hills."

"And the flowers," the child added. *"Mi piace fiori."*

Although it took longer to get to the shop by trolley, it was Antonio's preferred mode of transportation. The tracks sliced down Eighty-Sixth Street to the higher avenues and past the golf links. Just before the curve of the El, Antonio clanged the trolley bell and stepped off.

Contrary to most tailor shops, Chatonio's Haberdashery was brightly lit and airy, the windows flung open to the sun and breeze. This was deliberate and purposeful, for it brightened the workers' moods. From a young man named Tommaso, small oil paintings were purchased depicting tools of the trade: a needle pricked through a spool of thread, a pair of black-handled scissors, silver thimbles, a red pincushion looking ripe as a tomato. These prints decorated the walls. Anna, the cutter, brought roses from her garden by the armful and popped them into Mason jars that were scattered about the shop. Yes, Chatonio's was a good place to work; everyone seemed to like being there, from the workers to the bosses.

There was even a writeup in *American Gentleman and Custom Cutters' Exchange,* the leading men's fashion journal of the custom tailoring trade. The reporter made the journey into the heart of Brooklyn from his office on West Thirty-Ninth Street in the heart of the Garment Exchange. Mark Murray, the writer, was impressed with Chatonio's operations, wholesome environment and stellar product. He wrote a glowing report, complete with a photograph of the personnel, all of whom grinned uncomfortably for the camera. This write-up brought in even more business.

While Antonio was chalking a dress pattern, Charles arrived. Every week, he looked over the books, nodding with approval, smiling. Sometimes he would stop in just to say hello or to drop off a box of pastries from Alba's. ("The best!" he'd grin.) Once, he balanced a stack of pizza boxes from Di Fara's, which was also the best. Charles was fascinated watching people create garments from scratch and asked pointed questions regarding technique, not to be critical but to learn. He remembered the names of spouses, children and even pets. Antonio noted this with pleasure.

When they started the business, Charles stressed that he intended their venture to be more of a partnership, though the startup funds invested were all his. Antonio remembered how the pair had politely argued about the name of the shop. Though they agreed it should be a combination of their two names, Charles wanted Antonio's to come first. Antonio finally won after pointing out, "Toniochar just doesn't roll off the tongue."

Antonio gave Charles time to settle at his desk in a glass-walled corner toward the back of the work floor, far from the tsk of the sewing machines. Charles looked up from the ledger when he heard footsteps stop in the doorway. Antonio sighed, trembling. Why was he so nervous about talking to his friend? "How does it look?" Antonio inquired, trepidation creeping into his voice and teasing it an octave higher.

"How it always looks," Charles admitted, pausing with purpose. "Excellent." Antonio allowed himself to exhale. "You've built something grand."

"You mean, *we've* built…"

Charles interrupted Antonio. "It was all you, my good man. The ideas, the expertise, the workers. All I did was supply the cash. That's the easiest part. Everything else is you."

Well into his thirties, Antonio still didn't know how to graciously accept a compliment. He reddened and stammered, "I couldn't have done it without you."

Charles didn't know how to take a compliment either. Instead, he deflected. "Tonio, you look as though you're going to the guillotine. What's on your mind?"

Again, the stammering, the words sticking like dry bread crust in his throat. "You know I'm very pleased with things here," Antonio began.

"Don't tell me you're jumping ship!" Charles said.

"No," Antonio told him. "No, it's just that…I have an idea."

"Yes?" Silence. "Well? Out with it."

"I don't think we should cater just to the wealthy," Antonio blurted.

"But the poor can't afford bespoke garments," Charles pointed out. Antonio visibly deflated but his partner allowed him to continue. "Go on," he coaxed.

"That is true," Antonio conceded. "But what if we introduce a line, not bespoke, but for the everyday customer? The common man and woman."

And there it was, a trickle that turned into a torrent. "We could begin with a few patterns. Simple lines, timeless designs. We could use less expensive yet durable cloth in colors and patterns that never go out of style. Navy blues, pinstripes, polka dots."

"Hmmm," Charles said. It wasn't a wave of enthusiasm, but at least he didn't out-and-out refuse.

Antonio took this as a sign to continue. "So many are without jobs but how can you get a job without a decent suit of clothing, without a proper dress?" Charles nodded. "We could make them in the most common sizes, have belted or buttoned waists and then…"

Charles cut in. "First, you wanted to introduce a women's line. And I said sure. Now this!" He paused. "Do you know what I think?" Antonio held his breath, shook his head. "I think it's an excellent idea!" Charles pushed out a chair and invited his partner to sit. He turned a fresh page in a yellow pad and together, he and Antonio sketched out a future that darted off in a different direction.

After about an hour, their shirtsleeves were rolled up and several pages in the yellow pad were full. Charles smoothed his brush-like mustache as he thought, then added, "And we could do a giveaway. Win a suit or dress simply by entering."

"You mean, a raffle," Antonio added.

"No, it wouldn't cost them a thing. They wouldn't have to buy a ticket. We would just give the clothing away."

"But how would we turn a profit?" Antonio wondered.

"Our goodwill gesture will bring even more people to our door," Charles said. "You wait and see."

Charles pulled open one of the desk's cavernous lower drawers. From it, he produced an almost-full bottle of blackberry brandy and two carved, lead-crystal cordial glasses. "A toast?" he proposed, though it was barely ten in the morning. Antonio nodded; Charles poured. "To new beginnings," he said. They clinked glasses and sipped.

The deep purple fluid burned slightly but warmed Antonio's throat. Liquid courage, he'd heard it called. He took a deep breath and asked, "Why do you do this?" Antonio gestured to the sewing machines and racks of apparel surrounding them. "There are easier ways to earn a living."

Charles gazed off wistfully and downed his brandy. Then he poured another glass. "Ah, Tonio, it's not about making money. It's about doing what is right. And helping others..."

The sound of women's laughter rose from beyond the office. It came from Raquel and Mayda, two friends from Cuba and Puerto Rico, respectively. They worked Singers side by side and gossiped all day long, slipping easily back and forth between Spanish, Italian and English. Remarkably, they managed to produce more pieces than anyone at Chatonio's. Raquel glanced toward the office and covered her chuckles. "*Scusi,*" she apologized to her bosses.

"Non scusarti mai per la musica delle risate," Charles scolded, instructing her never to apologize for the music of laughter. *"Capire?"*

"Si, capisco," Raquel smiled, reddening.

Charles turned back to Antonio. "I do it for this. For the laughter. To make the world a better place. One person at a time," he tried to explain. Antonio didn't seem to understand at first. "When my father came to this country, he had to fight for everything. He had to fight to get a job. He had to fight to be accepted. Did you know that some help wanted ads used to read: 'No Coloreds or Italians need apply'?"

Antonio shook his head. Charles continued, "He named me Carlo, but insisted I be called 'Charles,' like a *'Mericano.* He didn't want me to be hated because of my nationality or called a Guinea, like he had been."

Charles, born "Carlo," took a gulp of brandy and continued. "I grew up, watching my old man with his head bowed, his hat in his hand, begging for employment. He was a terrific guy, honest, a solid worker, could fix anything. But that wasn't enough. He died poor and broken." Charles's voice cracked when he began again, "Well, I promised myself that when I got rich—and I knew I would get rich!—I would help people like my father get a better life. Hard workers, good people. People like you. People like Raquel," he said, gesturing beyond the glass wall.

"Your father would be proud," Antonio said.

"Yours too," Charles told him. Antonio doubted this but said nothing.

He couldn't wait to tell Luisa his news when he got home from work. But little did he know that his wife had news of her own.

CHAPTER THIRTY-SEVEN

Luisa

Sleep eluded Luisa. Whenever she closed her eyes, her mind painted a portrait of Assunta slumped over in the church pew, cold as dried candlewax by the time the altar boy found her. Like some lesser saint in a fresco by a long-forgotten artist in a back-alley chapel. Assunta's pale pink rosary beads from her homeland had slipped from between her fingers and onto the bench beside her. Luisa wondered, had anyone heard them clink onto the shining wood? Anyone besides the angels?

Luisa, her father and her siblings arrived at St. Patrick's as quickly as they could, word of Assunta's collapse traveling fast through Bay Ridge, neighbors with telephones reaching out to those who didn't have them. The Tozzis and former Tozzis appeared from different corners of the community like scattered stars. Luisa was contacted at the bookshop. Valerie ordered her to leave Gloria with her and go.

By the time the family got to St. Patrick's, Assunta had already been laid on the pew as per Dr. Lewy's instructions. (He had been in the area, attending to a feverish child on Ninety-Fifth Street, so he arrived quickly.) Someone had placed Assunta's purse beneath her head like a pillow. One arm dangled toward the floor. Her feet looked tiny, like doll's feet in her strapped shoes, her stocking sagging and wrinkled, making her look especially vulnerable.

Luisa and her father were the first family members to arrive. They rushed in, hailing from their separate workplaces at the same time, wordlessly grasping each other's hands as they threw open St. Patrick's double doors and streamed down the middle aisle to where a small crowd had gathered. Dr. Lewy, priests, altar boys and two nuns. Giuseppe's breath caught in his throat when he saw his wife. *"Se n'é andata,"* he howled. *"Posso sentirlo."*

"Yes, I think you're right, Papa," Luisa admitted to him sadly. "She's gone. I feel it too." Giuseppe sunk onto the pew beside his wife's immobile body, wringing his hands. All her life, Luisa had never seen her father cry. Not when he heard that his daughter Beatrice had died back in Longobucco, not when the stock market crashed, not when he heard that his own parents had passed. But now, he sobbed inconsolably. 'There is a first time for everything,' Luisa decided.

She slipped into the pew behind her parents and placed her hands on her father's heaving shoulders. Squeezed. Hard. Then harder still. He put his work-rough hand on top of hers then let it fall like a bird to earth. Giuseppe removed Assunta's purse from beneath her skull, gave the pocketbook to Luisa, then wedged his wife's head onto his lap. Held it there. *"È così fredda,"* he said. Giuseppe wrestled his arms out of his worn jacket. Covered his wife with it to warm her. For once, Luisa didn't pester her father to speak English. At a time such as this, only Italian would do; it was the language of poetry and misery.

Then Giuseppe pulled the jacket over Assunta's face, a makeshift shroud. "She never did like being the center of attention," Luisa sighed.

Dr. Lewy spoke to a man she didn't recognize, then shook his hand. They looked at Luisa and nodded. Dr. Lewy joined her on the bench. "I'm so sorry for your loss," he said with true sorrow. "Your mother…was a force of nature."

Luisa nodded. It was true. "She liked you. Very much."

"And I, her," the doctor confessed to Luisa.

"We knew this was coming," she said, shaking her head. "If only she…" Luisa allowed one tear to fall, just one. "She was so stubborn."

Dr. Lewy shook his head. "She was Assunta. No one could tell her what to do."

"Not even her doctor."

"That man…" Dr. Lewy gestured to the fellow leaving St. Patrick's. "He's from Brizzi's."

"Ah, the undertaker."

"I assume you'll want to wake her in the house." Luisa nodded once more. "Ralph will prepare her body, transport her. Assunta's in good hands. I promise. He's just gone to get the paperwork."

Rising out of his cloud of grief, Giuseppe finally noticed Dr. Lewy sitting behind him and shook his hand. "I'm sorry we have to meet like this," the doctor said to the widower. *"Le mei condoglianze,"* he added in horribly-accented Italian. But his effort was appreciated.

"You understood her," Giuseppe told him. "You were good to her."

"She was good to me too," Dr. Lewy admitted, patting his belly. "Making me biscotti, fig cookies. But seriously, I will miss her."

Giuseppe nodded. "And please, tell that man Brizzi to take care of Assunta and then bring her home."

In those days, family members were waked in front parlors. All furniture was pushed against the walls or else stored in another room. Chairs were either borrowed from funeral homes or from neighbors and lined up in front of the casket so family and friends could pay their respects. Because of this home waking tradition, many tenements were built with niches cut into walls around staircase turns. They were known as "coffin corners" and were created so the box could easily round the narrow space around a turn in the stairs. The Tozzi home was no exception. To anyone's knowledge, this would be the first time the niche in their wall was used for a coffin to round the tight curve.

At Brizzi's funeral parlor, Giuseppe selected an unadorned pine box which Antonio's brother Franco helped him choose. The woodworker suggested a particular coffin of superior, uniform grain that was well-crafted and carefully sanded. Giuseppe agreed that it was a fine piece of workmanship. The interior was lined with linen, the same material with which they wrapped Jesus's body when they took Him from the cross. The pillow was stitched by Brizzi's daughter Erica by hand. Franco asked if he would be permitted to carve flowers into the coffin's sides and lid, to which Giuseppe agreed. "Assunta loved flowers," he said.

Franco stayed most of the night etching the blossoms, a serious expression on his face, honored by the weight of his task. Curls of pine decorated the funeral parlor's carpet, which would be swept away by Erica with a whisk broom and dustpan. When Franco was finished, Assunta was placed inside, then the box was delivered to the Tozzi home.

It was customary never to leave the deceased unattended, so someone always sat with Assunta in the parlor. First, Luisa, then each of the deceased's daughters and sons took shifts. Giuseppe couldn't manage the task, even accompanied. That first evening before the wake, Antonio stayed at home with Little Gloria during the vigil. The child would prove to have a difficult time understanding what had happened to her best friend, her Nonna.

The three days of Assunta's wake passed slowly, as if stuck in molasses. The family was emotionally exhausted, tending to the stream of visitors who arrived to pay their condolences. Neighbors, colleagues, far-flung friends, mere acquaintances, cherished family and those who were barely tolerated came by. The story of Assunta's demise was repeated for everyone's benefit. The church, the altar boy's discovery, Father Kent's arrival, the shock of it all.

Zia Claudia was heartbroken, her eyes perpetually red and swollen. "She was so stubborn," Zia lamented to Luisa. "And in the end, it was stubbornness that killed her." Then, she softened, "Assunta was like my sister. Closer than a sister because we chose each other."

Luisa's eyes kept straying to her mother, stiff, inert, her face heavily painted with powder and rouge that she never wore in life. Her frozen fingers clutched the pale-pink rosary beads. Assunta seemed carved of pale wood, no hint of the woman with chapped fingertips that had once smoothed the hair from her granddaughter's face so lovingly, no trace of the reluctant laugh that illuminated her face whenever Serafino told an off-color joke. Luisa wanted to protect her mother from the prying eyes, from the judgmental mouths which announced in whispers, "She looks awful" or "She looks wonderful."

To Luisa, her mother didn't look good or bad; she looked dead. Luisa ached to slam shut the coffin lid to shield her mother so that all people could do was admire Franco's carved roses and peonies. But Old-World Italians expected to see a corpse and that's what they got.

Sensing his wife's struggle, Antonio stood beside Luisa, his hand pressed to her lower back an anchor, giving her strength when she feared she had none left. *"Finirà presto,"* he breathed to her. But for Luisa, it couldn't be over soon enough.

Food was carried in and empty plates replaced. Platters washed, filled and washed again. People ate, drank, smoked and spoke in whispers. Occasionally, there were short bursts of laughter that were quickly hushed with a withering glance.

The church service was a blur, the family solemnly following Assunta's casket up the middle aisle of

St. Patrick's. Eyes couldn't be stopped from wandering to the pew where Assunta had taken her last breath. It had conspicuously been left empty.

Ralph Brizzi supplied several cars to take the family out to St. John's Cemetery way out in Middle Village, Queens. Nearby Green-Wood and Holy Cross Cemeteries were deemed too expensive by the frugal bricklayer widower. The funeral cars followed the hearse in a solemn queue, first passing the house on Gatling Place where Assunta had spent the bulk of her life then venturing onto the parkway.

Mercifully, the sun shone and the air was warm. Section Fifty-Four was in the uppermost corner of diamond-shaped St. John's Cemetery, bordering Furmanville Avenue. The headstones stood like uneven soldiers, the surrounding trees and bushes bare, bleak. 'It will look better when spring finally comes,' Luisa decided. But it didn't.

None of the family would remember a word of what Father Kent said that day. But at least he'd known Assunta, had often heard her confession and had placed the communion wafer onto her waiting tongue too many Sundays to count. He'd married Antonio and Luisa, baptized Gloria, and now, he laid Luisa's mother to rest. It seemed fitting that he pray over Assunta's open grave.

That evening, the apartment was unusually empty and still. There was no aroma of garlic browning or red peppers roasting. The Tozzis' thoughtful neighbors had put the furniture back into their original places in the parlor, folded the folding chairs and returned them to their rightful owners. There were plenty of leftovers from the condolence platters people had brought, but no one felt like eating.

When it was time for her to go home, Luisa couldn't find her father. She'd looked everywhere in the railroad apartment's rooms, even on the fire escape, where he relished smoking the occasional cigar. Now, with Assunta gone, Giuseppe could smoke anywhere he wished.

Finally, Luisa realized that the trap door to the roof was slightly ajar. She climbed the rungs of the ladder, careful not to step on her skirt. Sure enough, Luisa found her father sitting on the tarpaper roof. She scooted beside him wordlessly and laid her head on his shoulder. "I really did love her, you know," Giuseppe said in faltering English.

"I know," Luisa told him.

"But did she?" he wondered.

They studied the stars in silence. That night, there was no moon.

Part Two
1940

January 1940

Luftwaffe Commander-in-Chief Hermann Göring assumes control of most of Germany's war industries.

The blockbuster film Gone with the Wind *is released throughout the U.S.*

Three gasoline-powered trains carrying factory workers crash and explode approaching an Osaka train station, killing approximately 181 and injuring 92.

These days, Luisa worried even more. Worried about everything. If someone were keeping track, her change in demeanor began suddenly on September 2, 1939, the day after war was declared in Europe. That's when Luisa decided to stay bed and pull the covers over her head. The voices of her children drifted up the staircase, shushed by Antonio who struggled to give them breakfast. There was the aroma of charred oatmeal, the sound of pots banging. But Luisa paid no mind. She rolled over and hid beneath the blanket.

It wasn't until Gianni cracked the door to her room and tiptoed inside (as quietly as a four-year-old can tiptoe) that Luisa opened her eyes. When he saw her looking at him, the child's worried face dissolved into a smile. Halfheartedly, Luisa smiled back and parted the covers. Gianni crawled in, curving his small, warm body into hers. She took his chubby hand, kissed it.

Antonio was moments behind Gianni. "*Figlio mio*, your mama doesn't feel well," he said gently. "*Vieni qui.*"

The boy's unbrushed curls grazed Luisa's chest through her nightgown as he shook his head. "Papa, no," he whispered. "I make Mama feel better."

Luisa smiled again, then saddened. 'There's nothing I can do to protect my children,' she thought dolefully. 'Not from war, not from anything.' She felt Antonio sit on the edge of the bed and turned toward him. Gloria appeared in the doorway, already dressed in her plaid school uniform and thick woolen tights. "I'm leaving now," she said. "I don't want to be late."

At almost twelve, Gloria was permitted to walk the three short blocks to St. Anselm's with her friends. Luisa had packed the girl's lunch the evening before as she listened to the kitchen radio. That's when she heard the terrifying news of September 1, 1939—Adolph Hitler's troops had invaded Poland. Luisa knew that the world would be forever changed. Her world too.

"Take your brother downstairs, please," Antonio asked of his daughter. The normally argumentative almost-teenager complied. Though Gloria showed no outward empathy for her mother, inwardly, she feared that her rock, that the pillar of the family, was crumbling. Gloria complied. She set her brother in front of his beloved Lincoln Logs on the parlor floor and kissed the top of his head, which always smelled sweaty, no matter the season.

Gloria liked their new home. It wasn't as cramped as the railroad apartment above Heffernan's Confections. She liked the wide windows that faced Holy Cross Greek Orthodox Church. She liked the bells that announced each hour. She liked her uncomplicated, happy life.

Gloria grabbed her bookbag, her brown-paper-sack lunch and went outside to meet her friend Siobhan, who was already waiting for her on the sidewalk.

On the first floor of the DeMarco home, Gianni tried to build a barn. Upstairs, Antonio pushed his wife's hair back from her forehead, trying to smooth out the furrows. It didn't work. "What's wrong, *belia*?" Antonio asked in a soft voice.

"Nothing. Everything. I don't know." Luisa began to silently cry. "I feel like everything is out of control. I...I can't protect our children."

He smiled. "You just realized this?"

Luisa elbowed him. "You're not helping."

"The truth is, we never have control over anything. Ever."

"Then what do we have?" Luisa pressed.

"We have one another. We have faith. Isn't that why you go to church? *Fede.*"

Luisa sighed and sat up. "I don't know anymore."

"I don't either," Antonio admitted. "But I do know one thing." Luisa raised her eyebrows and held her breath, waiting for her husband's revelation. He continued, "I know that if you take to your bed, then they've already won."

Luisa stared into her husband's earnest eyes. "But there's so much suffering in the world. They're sinking British battleships left and right. Italy invaded Albania this April. That boat of refugees was sent back to Europe, meaning certain death. And a five-year-old girl in Peru gave birth! This means that a man had to..."

"Ah, not Lina Medina again..."

In spite of herself, Luisa cracked a smile. "It's not funny, Tonio."

"I'm not laughing." Then he laughed; they both did.

"The war..." Luisa began

"It's not in America.

"But it will be," she countered. "How could it not come here? I'm so afraid we'll be attacked. I'm worried. For my children. For my brothers."

"But there's no conscription," Antonio pointed out.

"Not yet," she countered. "And you know them. They'll enlist. *Idioti...*"

"I understand your worries, Lu. But what purpose does worry serve? What does fear accomplish?"

Luisa knew Antonio was right. She groaned, pushed back the covers and got out of bed.

For the three or so months since her brief sleep-in, Luisa continued to worry. (But internally this time.) And pray. And light candles at St. Anselm's, which was nearer to their new place than St. Patrick's. She scrubbed the woodwork of the home they'd had the good fortune to purchase just before their son Gianni was born. The house was closer to Luisa's father on Gatling Place, closer to her brothers and sisters, closer to The Avid Reader. And there was more room, two floors, more space to stretch out and grow as a family. But most of all, there was a large backyard, and a front garden with a cherry blossom tree.

Already, *Piccola Gloria* was in sixth grade and Little Gianni (or Johnny, as he sometimes demanded to be called) was in nursery school. They had begun the new term the day after Labor Day that past September, two days after war had begun in Europe. Where had the time gone?

'Life is good,' Luisa mused, as she took the few blocks to The Avid Reader. '*Grazie a Dio,*' she tagged on as a benediction. Then why did Luisa feel so guilty? Because life wasn't good for the countries that had recently been invaded, for the shopkeepers in Munich whose windows had been shattered in *Kristallnacht,* and more recently, for the earthquake victims in Turkey with almost thirty-three-thousand dead. How could Luisa dare be cheerful when other people's lives had fallen apart?

Seeing Valerie's sweet, plain face made Luisa glad. Her warm smile was waiting for her when Luisa pushed through the shop's front door. Valerie always smiled upon hearing the brass bell ring; it meant that a potential customer or a friend had arrived.

Luisa and Valerie shelved an order from Macmillan later that morning. *Between Heaven and Hell* had topped the bestseller list for fourteen weeks the year before, battling *The Grapes of Wrath* for the top spot. Luisa couldn't wait to read Lucille Plain's scandalous book aloud to the knitting circle—who would be amazed that their next title was written by a woman. Often, the knitters' interest was so piqued that they couldn't wait until the following week to hear what came next and ended up buying the book.

"A beautiful governess, a dashing employer, a jealous wife," Valerie gasped in mock drama. "Passion! Murder! Intrigue!"

Despite her gloomy mood, Luisa laughed. "I hear it was based on a true story," she said. "About the author's great-aunt Colette."

"And I read in *Screen Guide* that they're making it into a picture starring Joan Crawford and Cary Grant," Valerie continued. "Won't that be something? Maybe we'll go see it together at the Alpine when it comes out."

"Maybe," Luisa conceded.

Valerie paused and considered the watercolor on Lucille Plain's book jacket: a tall-masted ship in a quaint harbor, workers huddled round a fire and a dark-cloaked woman, chin up, eyes forward, bracing herself to face a storm. Colette reminded the bookshop owner of Luisa, but Valerie didn't say so. At any given moment, Luisa seemed ready to brave the world, whether it be her son's skinned knee or the death of her mother, which Valerie knew still wounded Luisa eight years hence.

Valerie fit the book onto the shelf. "We do important work, you know," she began. Luisa looked at Valerie, hard and steady, wordlessly asking how. "We make a difference. We give joy. We give people a chance to escape, at least for a little while. Especially in these hard, unstable times."

Luisa huffed, "You sound like a book jacket!"

"Maybe," Valerie told her. "But I truly believe this. Books bring happiness. Even to those who can't read. We read to them. That's important."

Luisa didn't look entirely convinced, so her friend and employer plowed ahead. "We can make the world a better place, in small ways. True, we're not writing letters to Hitler like Gandhi or scuttling the *Graf Spee* but we're all doing our part. In tiny kindnesses. We do the best we can."

The housewife/book clerk considered this for a moment. "Tiny kindnesses. I like that," Luisa said.

"It's the tiny kindnesses that make all the difference," Valerie declared emphatically. "Now let's gather the chairs for the knitting circle."

Almost on cue, Luisa's father appeared, setting off the door's wee brass bell. Although it was well before The Avid Reader opened, Giuseppe knew the two women would be already there, setting up for the sewing and reading event, which occurred weekly on Monday mornings while the attendees' children were at school.

Guiseppi's eyes brightened upon seeing Luisa and Valerie. He kissed his daughter on the cheek, his brushy whiskers grazing her skin. Then he kissed Signora Valeria's hand as he normally did. Was that a blush upon the shopkeeper's cheek?

Though the man had suffered deep grief following Assunta's passing, he was recovering. He was slowly burying his guilt and the fear that he hadn't treated his wife as he should have. Giuseppe regretted neglecting

Assunta as though she'd been a piece of solid, dependable furniture that would always be there. In Assunta's absence, Giuseppe realized that nothing remained constant, that stalwart furniture eventually broke, that people died.

Giuseppe's daughters taught him how to fix simple meals, how to work the washing machine and the proper way to hang laundry. These were valuable skills for a man to have, they argued, even though Mina, at age fifteen, still lived at home. (So did seventeen-year-old Paolo.) Mina would be married soon enough, as would Paolo, though that boy was a wild one. Giuseppe needed to know how to fend for himself.

After marathon Sunday dinners at his elder children's tables, there were plenty of tinned leftovers for Giuseppe to heat for his solitary lunches at the battered kitchen table. He was self-sufficient in a manner of speaking; he could fend for himself when Mina and Paolo were working or off galivanting with their friends. Although his life was full, Giuseppe was often lonely.

Mina joked that in his retirement, Giuseppe was better at being a *nonno* than being a papa. Reluctantly, Luisa had to agree. It was a sad truth. Giuseppe had no trouble showing affection to his grandchildren, taking them sledding at Owl's Head Park, donning a bedsheet to play the bogeyman and chasing them through the house. "He was too busy working when we were kids," Luisa reminded her sister. "And there were so many of us."

"I suppose," Mina said.

Now the man had learned to master the art of making franks and beans and grilled cheese. (With mozzarella, of course.) And pushing Gianni at the perfect pace on the metal swings, ensuring that the boy's little fingers didn't get caught in the guard bar. Giuseppe was available to fix a wonky banister post or to right a wobbly kitchen drawer. He also had a knack for knowing the precise time "the Girls" (as he called Luisa and Valerie) were setting

221

up for their knitting circles and always happened "to be in the neighborhood" to pop by and help.

Luisa noticed that his hand brushed Valerie's as he passed her a chair. Was this on purpose? Was Val blushing again?

Giuseppe stayed to listen, hanging in the shadows, as Luisa and Valerie took turns reading the book. His face was rapt, his eyes aglow. Luisa glanced at her father and thought, 'Papa's not a bad looking man.' Then she returned to the page, to the knitters, exposing one of the most notorious murders in French history.

The clicking of the needles lulled the room as Valerie took the book from Luisa and began the second chapter. She cleared her throat.

> *Monsieur Le Monde's home, one of a row of sorrowful houses in the passé part of Castellane, was one not easily distinguished. Half rooming house, half school, its long, sprawling bed-quarters and stuffy salons had for several decades housed a parade of students from numerous lands and other transitory travelers to Marseilles as...*

Luisa wove her way through the semicircle of seats, loosening someone's grip on the needles, offering words of encouragement and refilling coffee cups. Her father accepted another home-baked butter cookie from the plate, not taking his eyes from the reader. Did Luisa detect cologne on the man? Was that a new waistcoat? Soon, it was Luisa's turn to read again. She handed Valerie the cookie dish and took up the novel.

> *Colette marched to greet her destiny in the Castellane as if summer itself were nipping at her feet.*

Giuseppe lingered until the very end then helped them store the folding chairs. "Thanks, Joe," Valerie demurred. "You're such a help."

Now it was Giuseppe's turn to redden. "*Prego!*" he said.

"*Grazie molto*," Valerie nodded.

Luisa started slightly. Since when did the Irishwoman speak Italian?

When the last chair was stowed, Giuseppe kissed Luisa on the cheek. "See you later," he said.

"What's later?" she wondered. Her father didn't answer but instead, winked. Valerie giggled. Giggled? Were they keeping secrets? Secrets that caused Val to laugh like a nervous teenager? What was happening?

Luisa was surprised to see Antonio already home when she brought the children back from school. "Do you feel well? Is everything all right?" she worried.

"Everything is fine," he said.

"I was going to cook *pasta fagioli* tonight," she told him.

"Make it tomorrow," Antonio suggested. "Your father will make Beanee-Weenee for the kids tonight." To which Gloria and Gianni cheered and surreptitiously snickered between themselves; the way their dad pronounced "Beanee-Weenee" was comical. Luisa found his attempt at embracing this American colloquialism endearing.

"My father?" Luisa wondered. "Why is he coming by?"

"You and I are going on a date," Antonio announced. "I've already freshened up," he added, giving her an affectionate swat on the bottom that made her jump. Gloria rolled her eyes, unaccustomed and uncomfortable with seeing her parents behave like this.

Giuseppe arrived to much hubbub, toting a grocery bag which contained a package of Hebrew National frankfurters, two tins of Van Camp's Pork and Beans (in his opinion, *il best*) and two bottles of Rheingold. Plus, a green box containing Ebinger's famous blackout cake. Gianni practically did backflips upon seeing his grandfather at the front door. Antonio smiled and clapped his father-in-law on the shoulder, taking the paper sack from him. It clinked. "Thanks for coming," Antonio said. "But this time, go easy on the beer, *se tu per favore*."

"*Ma, é il mio ingrediente secreto*," Giuseppe mock protested. "Plus, I make it from scratch," he added, proud that he could slice Hebrew Nationals and add them to cans of baked beans.

"In English!" Gianni complained.

"Secret ingredient or not, less beer in the Beanee-Weenee, Papa, eh?" Luisa said, leaving the room. "We don't need them being hung over for school tomorrow."

Minutes later, she reappeared in the doorway, awash in Evening of Paris, afloat in a raspberry taffeta frock Antonio had designed and sewn. She even wore black kitten heels. When Giuseppe gave a wolf whistle between his teeth, Luisa turned almost as pink as her dress.

Antonio held out her coat; a black wool A-line with a rabbit collar dyed to resemble ermine. "Where are we going?" she asked.

"You'll see," he told her.

It was already dark when Antonio led his wife toward Fifth Avenue. The leftover holiday lights of December still lit the January night. The wide windows of Leo's Casa Calamari beckoned them. The glorified pizzeria looked warm and welcoming inside. Leo's was their favorite eatery in Bay Ridge. Antonio held out his hand and beckoned Luisa into the humble establishment as though she were a queen.

The Formica-topped tables were occupied, all except for one, which was set with a tablecloth, polished cutlery and shiny, bone china plates. There was also a bud vase with a single crimson rose and a "Reserved" sign. Odd for a pizza place.

Leo himself was behind the counter, rotund and jovial as ever. He truly loved feeding people, especially with his family's treasured recipes. On Sundays, he brought in his mother and *zia* to make a *ragù* and perhaps a couple of trays of eggplant parmigiana or lasagna if the mood struck them.

He showed the couple to the elegant table, first pulling out Luisa's chair for her. "*Buon appetito,*" Leo said, and left.

Luisa folded her hands on the linen. "No menus," she remarked to Antonio.

"None needed," he told her. She snapped a napkin into her lap; it smelled fresh and starched.

A moment later, Leo was at their table with a glistening, steaming platter of calamari, breaded and fried to a golden brown. "Your favorite," Leo said, setting down the plate.

Antonio took the lemon wedge. "*Permisso?*"

When Luisa nodded her assent, he squeezed fruit juice over the dish. "You're a sly one, Antonio DeMarco," she informed her husband. He feigned innocence. They ate.

Next came Zia Julia's eggplant parmigiana, which Leo had set aside the day before, perfectly complimented by a small portion of spaghetti on the side. Finally, there was a tiramisu, which Antonio and Luisa shared, because they were stuffed, and two espressos, so they would stay awake for the movie, Antonio explained.

"Movie? What movie?" Luisa gasped.

"It's a long one," Antonio said. "I want to be sure we don't fall asleep."

Since she'd read about its completion in *Modern Screen,* Luisa had waited patiently for *Gone with the Wind* to come to the Alpine. Now it had finally arrived. She fretted about how they'd be able to manage almost four hours to sneak off to watch the film, and here Antonio had orchestrated it all on his own.

"Come, we shouldn't be late." Antonio paid the bill, they donned their coats and dashed.

The movie was a dream, from start to finish, to Luisa, it didn't even feel like two-hundred-and-thirty-eight minutes. While some swooned for Clark Gable, Luisa preferred Leslie Howard, whose quiet good looks reminded her of a paler version of her own Antonio.

They walked home hand in hand in the biting cold, well past either of their bedtimes. "Thank you," she told her husband, "For all of this."

"*Prego*," he nodded. "You needed a night off. Deserved it. You work hard. At the bookshop, at home."

"When you love something, it doesn't feel like work," she said. "Tell me, how are the shops doing?" Chatonio's had two locations now, one in Bensonhurst, the other closer to home in Bay Ridge.

"Fine," Antonio said, a bit too quickly.

In truth, business had fallen off sharply. Not the less expensive, ready-to-wear items but the costlier bespoke pieces. It seemed the war in Europe had affected the spending patterns of the rich. Or was it the activities of Mussolini sparking anti-Italian sentiments? Antonio wasn't certain, but his business had clearly suffered since the stubborn-chinned Benito had taken office. At first, the decline in earnings was almost imperceptible but now it was undeniable. Even Charles Mura expressed concern. "Business is fine," Antonio lied to Luisa. It was the first time he had ever uttered an untrue word to his wife.

At home, the children were safely tucked away in bed while Giuseppe nursed the last sips of his Rheingold. Alongside the Ebinger's cake were the remnants of a cream-cheese topped Guinness cake, which happened to be Valerie's specialty. *Hmmm,* Luisa thought to herself. Hmmm indeed.

February 1940

In the Altmark Incident, a British destroyer pursues a German tanker into the neutral waters of Jøssingfjord in southwest Norway and frees the 290 British seamen held captive aboard.

Four-year-old Tibetan Tenzin Gyatso is proclaimed the rebirth of the thirteenth Dalai Lama.

At the University of California Radiation Laboratory in Berkeley, chemists Martin Kamen and Sam Ruben discover the synthesis of the radioactive isotope carbon-14.

The world was changing rapidly, to be sure. Too rapidly for Antonio's taste. Here he was, a man of forty, yet some days he felt ancient. It seemed as if he'd been working his whole life. Though running a shop—two shops, actually—was different than pushing out piecework, it was still stressful. In some ways— paying the business's bills, seeing that the machines were maintained, choosing fabrics that were hardy yet fashionable and reasonably-priced—was more taxing than working on clothing.

Not to mention the stress of dealing with people! Staff and customers alike. Who needed a day off...

who called out sick because of a sniffle…who didn't get along with that *strega* at the machine next to her. Not to mention appeasing a customer who was rude because their intricately-beaded evening gown would take just a day longer to complete. And another who was indignant because Antonio refused to fulfill an order until the previous order was paid. And another who flew into a rage because a suit was too snug. (When in truth, the client had put on a few pounds.)

Antonio learned to take all this minor abuse with a nod and a smile, just as Luisa had taught him. "They put food on our table," she reminded him when he became frustrated. "Both your workers *and* your customers. Just smile and nod but on the inside, you can be thinking, *Va Napoli!"* (For most Italians, except Napolitani, telling a person to go to Naples was the equivalent of telling them to go to hell.) 'Luisa is always right,' Antonio admitted to himself. 'She's *molto* level-headed and calm.'

So, Antonio smiled and nodded until his face ached and it felt as though his head would fall from his neck. He smiled and nodded as Mrs. Herlihy demanded he let out her silk dress (for the third time in as many months) for free. He nodded and he grinned like an organ grinder's monkey.

Even at only eleven and a half years of age, there were some things Gloria knew she couldn't divulge to her parents, as kind and understanding as they were. For instance, ZiaVal often came to visit, bearing treats, on the nights that Nonno Giuseppe babysat. Gloria looked forward to the sweets, especially the creamy black and white cookies from Leske's Bakery. There was no doubt that Gloria loved ZiaVal and the black-and-whites but the child felt she was old enough not to require a babysitter, let alone two! Gloria was confident she could look after her annoying brother as well. But no matter how fervently she presented her case to her mother, Luisa wouldn't hear of it. Gloria suspected this was because her mother wanted to keep her father occupied.

At four, Gianni was fascinated by the concept of keeping secrets. It reminded him of "Lights Out" which Nonno let him listen to. This was a program that never ceased to frighten the boy, so much so that he was known to wet the bed after hearing a particularly scary episode. Though Nonno and ZiaVal's antics were pale compared to skullduggery and haunted jail cells. Gianni could keep a secret for a cookie...or two.

Another thing Gloria couldn't tell her mother was that sometimes the boys at St. Anselm's taunted her and called her a "skinny Guinea with ravioli eyes." She bit her lip to keep from blubbering the first time this happened, even though she didn't know what a Guinea was. But it sounded bad.

When Gloria asked Luisa in the kitchen later that afternoon, she told her patly, "Guinea is a country. In Africa."

Gloria kept doing her math homework, not daring to look into her mother's eyes as Luisa squished chopped meat with her bare hands. "Not that kind of Guinea," Gloria pressed.

"Well," Luisa said, "It's also a type of animal. Like a hamster, only bigger." She brushed a shock of hair from her face with her forearm. "A Guinea pig."

Gloria pushed her pencil into her composition book, making a dent in the paper with the lead tip. "No, not an animal," Gloria qualified. "A person." Luisa added the chopped garlic to the bowl of raw meat. She squeezed it through her fists to thoroughly mix it. Gloria held her breath and continued, "What if someone called someone else a Guinea?"

Luisa looked up with a quick jerk of her head. "Who called you that?"

"No one!" Gloria lied, pressing the pencil so hard that the tip broke. "I just heard it."

Luisa fumed. "Why, I'll go straight to the principal's office and…"

"No one called me that, Mama! No one! I swear." The vision of Luisa marching into the school on her thick, little legs and demanding a meeting with Sister Gertrude Ramilda was too much for Gloria to bear. It would only make matters worse. She closed her marble notebook and left the table just as her father came into the kitchen.

Later, when Luisa was putting Gianni to bed, the girl had the courage to ask her father, who had caught the tail end of the "Guinea" kitchen conversation earlier. They were in the parlor. It was during a commercial break as "The Jell-O Program Starring Jack Benny" aired. "Ah," Antonio nodded thoughtfully. He lowered the radio's volume. "A Guinea is a bad name that people sometimes call Italians."

"Why?" Gloria wondered.

Sitting beside his daughter, Antonio stroked her hair. *"Non lo so,"* he said. "I don't know. I can never understand why people say things that hurt each other's feelings, *bella*."

"Neither can I," Gloria admitted.

"Ma," he corrected himself, shifting back to English. "But…a Guinea refers to the people of Africa. Perhaps they compare us to them because of our dark complexions. *Non lo so*."

Gloria was momentarily satisfied. Sad but satisfied. She decided not to ask her father about the "ravioli eyes" part of the slur. Gloria dipped her head onto Antonio's shoulder and admitted, "Sometimes the boys call me that."

His lips brushed the crown of her head. "Boys can be *molto stupido*, especially at this age. Don't pay them any mind."

"I'll try," she said.

Gloria also chose not to share with her father how she was teased because she wasn't developing as quickly as the other girls. Often, her flat chest was publicly compared to two fried eggs, then accompanied by hearty laughter. She doubted her dad would understand.

Luisa came in, weary from the day and bleary-eyed from reading *The Tale of Peter Rabbit* too many times in rapid succession to Gianni. She dumped into the ottoman and lifted her legs with a sigh. "Tell me, will Mrs. McGregor ever put Peter's father into a pie?" Antonio wondered. His wife always edited out that traumatic part about the mischievous rabbit's papa's fate.

"Not while I'm reading it to Gianni," Luisa smiled sadly. "The world is difficult enough. Why spoil the story for him?"

"He'll learn the truth one day," Gloria said.

"Yes," Luisa agreed. "But not from me."

In the evenings, after their busy days and after supper, the DeMarco Family usually took refuge in the radio. Antonio made a point of avoiding news stations which discussed events like the Mechelen Incident, where a German plane carrying secret plans for the invasion of Western Europe crash-landed in Belgium. Then there was the sinking of the British submarine Starfish. It was advisable for the DeMarcos to avoid these horrors, especially at bedtime. Otherwise, there might be nightmares to contend with, and the family deserved a good night's sleep.

Of the wicked ways of the world, Luisa often commented, "The children will learn soon enough. Let them enjoy the peace a little while longer."

Though Antonio considered it similar to perpetuating the lie of Santa Claus—or Pietro Rabbit—he complied. Ignorance was bliss.

Gloria, also a voracious reader, basked in the disturbing headlines she read at the newsstand going to and from school. About the beginning of food rationing in the United Kingdom. About the Olympics being pushed back. Gloria was scared. Scared of being blown up. Scared of going hungry. But she said nothing. She did her schoolwork, filled her belly and tried to be an obedient girl. Though she often failed. At least in her own eyes.

But the radio, the big, honey-brown, wood-cabineted Philco in the parlor provided escape. From the screaming headlines. From the bullies at school. From everything. Mama, Papa and Nonno were the only ones in the household permitted to work Philco's dials and they did so slowly, with reverence until the hum of the desired station came in. Then there was the customary "aaah" when the channel was located, as though the family feared the stations would disappear when the radio was not in use.

This particular late winter afternoon, the DeMarcos listened to the Philco before dinnertime. It was an exception to all the rules, but rules were made to be broken on momentous occasions such as this. "The Adventures of Superman" bounded into the living room, into all living rooms in the country for the very first time. The inaugural episode aired on WOR on the twelfth of the month. All four DeMarcos gathered in their parlor to listen.

Luisa put the pasta water on a low boil, dried off her hands and sat. Antonio left early from the shop for the occasion. Gloria had her homework done before five so she had enough time to get settled before it aired at five-fifteen.

The Superman show was all Gianni talked about for weeks. He was a fan of the comic strip and begged his sister to read it to him at breakfast every morning as soon as the paperboy delivered *The Daily News*. (But Gianni insisted on calling it *The Daily Planet.*)

The boy shushed his family as soon as the thrilling opening began. His parents grinned instead of reprimanding him. Gloria just rolled her eyes, as almost-twelve-year-olds do. After a brief note from the show's sponsor, Kellogg's Pep Cereal, the parlor filled with the aeronautic sound effects of Superman zooming through the clouds. Then:

Up in the sky. Look! It's a bird! It's a plane...

Gianni looked up at the plaster ceiling before finishing, "...it's Superman!" in unison with the broadcast. For the others in the room, the child's delight was just as profound as listening to the show itself.

The fifteen minutes flew by and life in the DeMarco household returned to normal afterwards. Luisa added spaghetti to the boiling water and stirred the sauce on the opposite burner. Antonio read *Il Progresso* and Gloria set the table.

At supper that night, all talk turned to Superman. From the opener where the El family must flee their doomed planet—which made Luisa think of Europe's Jewish folk fleeing the Nazis—to "Clark Kent, Reporter" which would air two days later. Superman had a permanent yet invisible seat at the DeMarco dinner table.

Luisa promised to buy Kellogg's Pep ("the Sunshine cereal") at the A&P the next day, even though it was advertised as being "mildly laxative."

Giuseppe's supper table was tranquil on the rare evenings he ate alone. He savored the occasional silence. Mina tended to chatter throughout the meal and tonight, she was out at the movies with school friends. Paolo was working. Dinnertime at Giuseppe's children's homes was unintentionally raucous with so many crowding the table.

It reminded him of days past with Assunta. She would throw together a satisfying meal with no more than a wish and a hope and a handful of cornmeal.

Supper at Valerie's was more reserved. Fine crockery as opposed to well-worn, mismatched earthenware. Giuseppe was growing used to roasts and boiled meats. He had even found favor with buttery potatoes versus pasta. And the company was pleasant, especially when he and Valerie listened to Lux Radio Theater. Giuseppe liked the weight of Valerie's head on his shoulder, of her presence beside him on the sofa. Of her presence in his life.

But how could he divulge this to his children? Would they think he loved Assunta any less? Or not at all? Giuseppe didn't like keeping secrets, but certain things were better left untold.

March 1940

At Promenade, nearly four-hundred women are hosted at the Yale freshman dance.

John Steinbeck, Ed Ricketts and six others leave Monterey for the Gulf of California on a marine invertebrate collecting expedition.

Mussolini agrees to bring Italy into the war "in due course" when he meets with Hitler at Brenner Pass in the Alps.

"Mama, look!" cried Gianni in the soapy tub. "My *pishi* is a boat!" Named to honor Antonio's father Giovanni, who had passed quietly in San Vincenzo all those years ago, Luisa wondered if the father-in-law she never met would find her son's aquatic antics funny or horrifying.

She never knew how to respond when her son proudly boasted about his bathtime erection. All Luisa knew was that Tenzin Gyatso, who, last month in Tibet, had been proclaimed to be the rebirth of the thirteenth Dalai Lama, probably didn't do this in the tub. Or pick his nose. Or...

Gloria barged into the bathroom to brush her teeth but immediately thought better of it. "Ewww, gross!" she said, then stomped out. The girl had less and less patience for her brother's silliness lately.

Thinking back, Luisa realized that she had been the same way with her own brothers. Except there were two of them; Luisa was outnumbered. As kids, Sam and Dom were always getting her in trouble because Luisa was held responsible for their mischief. (Paolo, so much younger than she, was innocent since he was Gianni's age when Luisa and Antonio married.) However, in the end, it was family who would stand up for you. It was family who had your back, no matter what.

Luisa tried to figure out why Gloria was so ill-tempered recently. Maybe something had happened at school. Compared to her friends, Gloria was much smaller and slower to develop. She begged for a brassiere, although she had almost nothing to fill the cups. Should Luisa relent? Was the girl too old for cotton camisoles? Was Luisa built the same at Gloria's age? She couldn't recall. Luisa had been too busy looking after her siblings, wiping bottoms, scrubbing the linoleum and preparing supper. Although Gloria—and even Little Gianni— helped around the house, Luisa didn't want the same sort of life for her children as she'd had. Didn't most parents want this for their kids?

Gloria shut the door to her room, a bit harder than she should have. Her chest was hurting again. More specifically, her *capezzoli*. They felt swollen, tender. Did this mean that her breasts were growing? Gloria was too embarrassed to ask anyone, even her friend Siobhan, who she could ask anything.

There was no privacy in the house, no place where Gloria could truly be alone. Why, her bedroom door didn't even lock! Gloria propped a chair under the glass doorknob so Gianni wouldn't barge in. She sat on the edge of her bed. As Gloria unbuttoned her blouse, her fingers shook. They were moist and sweaty. She slid down her camisole's straps, exposing her almost-flat chest. Gloria bet her chubby little brother had more meat on his ribs than she had on hers. Except for her nipples, which were rather pronounced.

Sure enough, Gloria's nipples were sore again. Puffy. Pink. Was this normal? Did she have some horrible disease? Cancer like her Aunt Grace had? Gloria grabbed the bottle of lotion. Just the pink of the cream alone was comforting. She tapped a dollop into her palm, rubbed it into one side of her chest, then the other. Her nipples hardened, darkened. Was this supposed to happen? Gloria pushed the question from her mind. It felt so soothing. It calmed the itch. That's what mattered.

But from between Gloria's legs came a curious sensation. A throbbing. A glowing. It stopped when she stopped applying the cream. Only Gloria didn't want to stop. That was the problem. Somehow, she knew it was a problem. Somehow, she knew this behavior was shameful and should be revealed to Father Kent at Saturday afternoon confession. But Gloria opted not to. Because to confess meant she had to stop doing it or at least try to.

There must be something wrong with her, Gloria decided. Something terribly wrong. Gloria hoped no one would find out, last of all, Father Kent. When the other girls were swooning over Clark Gable or Humphrey Bogart, Gloria was more interested in Claudette Colbert and Rita Hayworth. To see the fiery redhead lifting her skirts and dancing on a tabletop in *Music in My Heart* made Gloria breathless. She wondered if anyone noticed.

And oftentimes, when they sat close, paging through *Life* or *Silver Screen Magazine,* Gloria fought the urge to kiss Siobhan on the lips, like men and women did in the movies. What would happen if Gloria did this? If she gave into her yearnings? Gloria didn't have the courage to find out, though she had the desire. But her trepidation outweighed her longing. Would this always be so?

Antonio tried to convince himself that it had nothing to do with the war in Europe. That the broken window at the Bay Ridge shop was only a coincidence, just bored boys making mischief. But it had happened on March 19th, the day after Mussolini and Hitler met in the mountains on the border of Italy and Austria—the meeting place itself a symbol of their union. This was worse than the Pact of Steel which had been signed the year earlier. That agreement formalized a friendship. But at the Brenner Pass conference, Mussolini agreed to join Germany's war against France and Britain, both allies of the United States. It was as good as declaring war on America.

After a telephone call to Vigorito, the glazier, Charles Mura helped Antonio clean the glass shards from the sidewalk, though Antonio insisted this was above and beyond the duty of an investor and business partner. "Nonsense," Charles assured him. "It's clearly part of the job."

"I just don't want to take someone off their machine," Antonio explained. "Business is finally picking up again and I can't spare them."

"No need to explain," Charles said. "You always do what's best for us."

'It's our own little Kristallnacht,' Antonio reflected but didn't dare verbalize this. He wrapped a triangle of broken glass in newspaper then carefully placed it into a large brown paper sack. "I'm afraid it will get worse before it gets better," Antonio told him. "I'm afraid of what *Il Duce's* actions will mean for the shop."

"People aren't that foolish," Charles insisted. "You and I, we're American citizens, not Italians. And we've got the papers to prove it, no?"

Antonio shrugged. "Did they ask if we were Americans before they broke the window?"

The following day, the storefront was egged, bleeding yellow blood across the brick and newly-installed glass. The men watched as Anna scrubbed. The cutter swore she knew the recipe for a solvent that would make frozen egg melt away like rain, and it did. She promised to be back at her table in "two shakes of a lamb's tail." And she was. *"Grazie,"* Antonio told her.

"Prego," Anna said, touching his arm for assurance. Then she returned to her scissors and patterns.

"Still think it's bored boys?" Antonio asked Charles.

"More likely bored men out of work with nothing better to do," Charles responded. "They're blaming us for the Olympics being cancelled last month," he tried to joke. But neither laughed.

Soon after, when the words "Guinea!" and "Dago!" were painted across the storefront in dripping black letters, Charles's brow furrowed in alarm. Antonio decided not to tell Luisa of this latest incident. It would only worry her. And what purpose would worry serve?

Chatonio's profits had already been slashed by the poor economy—fewer people were splurging on dressy clothing due to the war in Europe. It was clear America would join in, but when? In these uncertain times, people were making do with what they had, which was completely understandable. Antonio and Charles decided to take a salary reduction rather than cut their workers' pay. So much so that the DeMarcos had come to depend on Luisa's income from The Avid Reader. Previously, they banked her earnings, which had given them a little nest egg. Antonio didn't want to peck at their savings, however.

Almost a teenager, Gloria was now old enough to babysit the children of others. Trustworthy, caring and inventive, she was sought after by the other parents on the block. So, the girl had her own "mad money" and no longer received an allowance. Although Gloria did offer to contribute to the household expenses, Antonio and Luisa refused. Instead, they suggested Gloria open a savings account at Hamilton Federal on Eighty-Sixth Street. "It's good to save some and treat yourself with the rest," Luisa smiled. But more often than not, Gloria bought others trinkets rather than spend it on herself. It was just her nature. A toy airplane for Gio, a tube of lipstick for Siobhan, which they tried on in private then rubbed off because they weren't allowed to wear makeup yet.

When he was unable to sleep, tossing and turning with apprehension, Antonio tried to convince himself that they were fine, that they had enough, more than enough. That they were all healthy and happy, which was something money couldn't buy. But still, anxiety gnawed at Antonio until his heart beat hard in his chest and his breath became shallow. Those times, Antonio had no choice but to sit in his "worry chair" in the parlor, sometimes until dawn broke.

What if? What if? Antonio feared for the "what ifs."

Giuseppe offered to take the entire family to see *The Wizard of Oz* when it finally found its way to the Alpine Theater. It was a special showing for one night only. Luisa and Antonio thanked him but begged off, preferring to spend an evening at home alone. Gloria rolled her eyes at the very idea of her parents getting romantic, but she and Gianni gladly accompanied their Nonno to the movies. Especially when he tagged on, "Why not invite that nice girl, Siobash?" Nonno always managed to mangle Siobhan's lovely, lyrical Irish name, no matter how hard he tried not to, no matter how much he liked her.

They attended the six o'clock show so the girls would have enough time to do their homework beforehand and they'd be home early enough to get to bed at a decent time for school the next day. Their supper was hot, buttered popcorn and one candy of their choice from the showcase. ZiaVal smuggled in a sack of freshly-baked snickerdoodles in her purse. It had the makings of a perfect evening.

When the film switched from sepia to Technicolor as it jumped from Kansas to Munchkinland, the quintet gasped aloud with the rest of the crowded theater. And when those terrifying flying monkeys whisked Dorothy away, Gianni, Gloria and Siobhan sought each other's hands at the same time. (Nonno and ZiaVal had been furtively holding hands since the theater went dark.) Gianni let go to clap when Toto escaped but the girls kept right on clasping until after their hands got clammy.

Gloria turned to study her friend's profile in the semidarkness, Siobhan's dusting of freckles barely visible, her strawberry blonde braids appearing almost black, none of her hair's pretty sun streaks discernable. Then Gloria turned back to the screen, afraid her friend would catch her staring. But she couldn't help herself. So, she stared some more.

A moment later, Siobhan turned to see her friend's cocoa-colored eyes studying her. Gloria's halo of blue-black locks were shimmering, just like Lois Lane's in the comics. And then there was the tiny mole on Gloria's upper lip that Siobhan yearned to kiss. She squeezed Gloria's hand and Gloria squeezed back.

At first, ZiaVal considered it odd that the girls nibbled from the same snickerdoodle but then remembered her friend Gladys and how they used to squeeze into the same theater seat for scary silents like *The Cabinet of Dr. Caligari.* And they'd been married gals of almost thirty! But the closeness between Gloria and Siobhan seemed different. More intimate. Valerie's thoughts slipped away like smoke because now, onscreen, the Winkies were marching and chanting so chillingly that Gianni crept into his grandfather's lap and Giuseppe released Valerie's hand.

On the walk home, Gloria and Siobhan lagged, extolling the virtues of Judy Garland, from the ripe fullness of her lips to her rich singing voice. "Do you think she wears lip paint or Vaseline?" Siobhan posed.

"I bet Max Factor invented a special lipstick just for her," Gloria said with conviction.

"I think you're right," Siobhan told her. "His Tru-Color was the first smear-proof lipstick ever. I bet Judy was wearing it in this picture."

"And the silver paint on Jack Haley...do you think Max created that too?" Gloria wondered.

"I don't see why not," Siobhan said. "Don't forget, the Factors invented Pan-Cake makeup." The pair was fascinated with all things makeup, even though they couldn't wear it yet. There were many things they weren't permitted to do, yet still did.

Gloria and Siobahn surreptitiously held mittened hands against the cold and skipped to keep warm, humming, "We're off to see the wizard..." Valerie and Giuseppe passed a sleepy Gianni between them as they walked the chilly blocks back home.

April 1940

Booker T. Washington becomes the first Negro to be depicted on a United States postage stamp.

Germany invades the neutral countries of Denmark and Norway in Operation Weserübung, opening the Norwegian Campaign, as the British Royal Navy attempts to attack elements of the German fleet off Norway.

The Rhythm Club fire at a dance hall in Natchez, Mississippi kills 209 people and severely injures hundreds of others.

Antonio hated to have a fuss made for his birthday, but Luisa insisted that to be blessed with another year was reason enough to celebrate. "Especially in this crazy world," she tagged on for emphasis.

Luisa's birthday had been a month earlier and fell three days after Easter that year. So, her sisters rallied for a potluck supper which Luisa very much appreciated. Sitting at the table, taking in the parlor filled with her immediate family and Valerie, Luisa was stung by an odd brand of shame. 'How could it be that I am so happy and stuffed to the brim with delicious food, while others in the world suffer so?' she struggled.

Luisa looked at her brothers. What would their fate be if, God forbid, the United States entered the war. All three of them could be sent overseas.

But Luisa would not permit herself to feel sad, not on her birthday. She vowed to be happy for those who couldn't be.

And not three weeks after her own birthday, Luisa found herself gently parrying with Antonio about how to celebrate *his* birthday. "It's just cake!" she told him as she stirred the breakfast polenta.

"*Bella,* with your family, it's never just cake!" Antonio laughed.

"I love cake!" Gianni chimed in, hungry for his breakfast.

"And polenta too," Luisa told him.

"You love food. Period," Gloria said, then added, "Chubsy Ubsy" under her breath.

"I heard that," Antonio whispered into his daughter's ear. "No name calling." Then to Luisa he relented, "*Va bene*…okay. Just cake…and maybe coffee."

"Great!" Luisa said.

"Just family…" Antonio cautioned. "And maybe Valeria. And a couple of friends."

"Val *is* family," Luisa reminded him. "*Fantastico.* I'll make a few calls.*" Then she kissed his temple.

Days later, on a Tuesday evening, no less, the DeMarcos' small mock Tudor home was crammed with brothers, sisters, nieces, nephews, business associates and handfuls of friends. It was tiny compared to the year earlier, when Antonio turned forty, but it was a full house. Although they tried to steer the overlapping conversations clear of the war in Europe, it was unavoidable.

Serafino was afraid conscription would be reinstated—all the Tozzi brothers but Paolo were of draft age and had burgeoning families. In fact, Dominic's wife was expecting their second child. "I won't be eighteen until next year," Paolo said.

"So, you're safe," his beau Julianna sighed.

"For now," Dom reminded her.

"I was thinking of enlisting," Paolo told them. "I wouldn't mind crushing a few Nazi skulls."

"Shush," Mina said, then reminded him. "You'd have to get Papa to sign the papers."

Giuseppe piped up. "I ain't signing nothing," he said emphatically. "I won't. I will not have all three of my sons fighting in a war."

Valerie leaned forward and patted his hand beneath the tablecloth to calm him. "I don't think the government would do that, would they?" She squeezed his fingers, sensing his mounting tension.

But Giuseppe's boys could always ruffle his feathers; they had perfected it over the years. "Miss Val, they're the government." Serafino told her. "They could do whatever they like."

"Especially during wartime," Paolo weighed in.

Mina hated when her brothers triple-teamed their father. It reminded the scrappy teenager of the bullies over at Fontbonne Hall Academy, the toney, private all-girls school Giuseppe insisted she attend. But boys could be just as mean as girls, even more so. It wasn't that their Papa was slow-witted, but he thought first in Italian, then translated it into English. Her brothers took full advantage of the split seconds it took for their Papa to respond in English.

"Imagine, having to fight the Fascists," Dom tagged on. "The Italian fascists."

"That would be weird, fighting on Italian soil," Serafino agreed. Though neither of them had ever been to the country of their parents' and oldest sister's birth.

Again, Val worried aloud, "They wouldn't..."

Softly, Mina reminded her, "But my brothers speak the language, no? It would be smart to..."

Luisa, who had been hanging on the periphery as she delivered more of Val's crumb cake to one of the dessert platters, finally said, "Enough! *Basta!* You're as bad as washerwomen gossiping around a tub. There *is* no draft. America hasn't declared war. So, stop! Enjoy the party. You're scaring the children."

Gianni, upon hearing his mother raise her voice, clung to her leg and began to whimper. "See?" she told her brothers. "Enough." Then Luisa walked to the kitchen to tend to the coffee urn, Gianni suspended from her leg like an extra appendage.

The Tozzi brothers hung their heads, reluctantly listening to their big sister, just as they'd done since they were small. *"Brontolone,"* Serafino sighed. His hazel eyes, so much like his mother's, were bright with mischief.

"She is not a grouch," Barbara told him.

"And you're a *ficcanaso,"* Dom said.

"She isn't nosy," Mina defended her sister. "Someone's got to keep you knuckleheads in check. Or else you'd go wild in the streets like when you were kids."

"You were too young to remember," Dom snapped. "You were still pishing in your diaper."

"Luisa told me," Mina countered. "She said you two were incorrigible."

"Oooh, listen to Filomena and her five-dollar words," Sam said.

Their eldest sibling walked in carrying a platter of Siobhan's mother's sad, dry oat cookies and didn't miss a beat. "But you were!" Luisa shot back at Dom. "I always got in trouble for the things you did!" Serafino, otherwise known as Sam, laughed, a bit too heartily. "You too, Sam! *Maddona mia!* My bottom still smarts from the spankings I got because of you two *buffoni!"*

Luisa stabbed her fingers at them as she spoke, then rubbed her firm bottom for emphasis, grinning. The sip of blackberry brandy Antonio had coaxed her to take earlier had done Luisa a world of good. He cupped his hand over hers, still on her *culo*. She smiled, then pushed it away, squeezing it first.

An only child, Siobhan Reilly relished the harmless banter between siblings. She watched as though it were a spirited game of Hit the Penny on the Avenue. There was so much happiness, wrath, humor and love bopping about simultaneously under the DeMarco roof. Nothing resembling the cheerless existence behind the lace curtain Irish windows of her own home.

Gloria gave her friend a nudge with a copy of the latest *Modern Screen.* "Alice Faye!" Siobhan gushed. The yellow finger curls, the blue eyes unlike any sky that shone over Brooklyn, the red-apple cheeks, scarlet lips and creamy bare shoulders. Was Alice naked beneath that black lace fan? "Where'd you get the dime?" Siobhan asked.

"Babysitting that little brat," Gloria told her, pointing at her cousin Teo who was the unbearable age of eight. "But I know it will be worth every penny."

"I'll say!" Siobhan really didn't want to leave the party. But on the other hand, it was hard to pass up Alice Faye. Maybe she and Gloria would practice kissing again. After all, a girl had to know how to kiss.

They passed Luisa near the kitchen. "Cake soon," she told them. 'When had Mama gotten so annoying?' Gloria wondered. She tutted and sighed dramatically.

"We know, Mrs. DeMarco," Siobhan grinned. "Promise to call us?" Siobhan wished her mother cared enough to nag her—about anything—or made the effort to drag her drunken bottom out of bed or lift her head out of the cups. Let alone bake a birthday cake. It was a miracle she'd made those hockey-puck-hard cookies for Siobhan to bring over.

"Of course," Luisa chirped, ruffling the girl's bone straight red hair. It didn't feel clean to the touch but greasy, filmy. Didn't that lush next door teach her daughter proper hygiene? If Luisa could figure out a discreet way to hand Siobhan a bar of Ivory, she would. Maybe fibbing that it was on sale and she had bought too many bars would work. After all, Luisa didn't want to hurt the child's feelings. It wasn't her fault her parents were boozers. But first, the cake.

For a few moments, Antonio pretended he was a stranger in his own home. To do this occasionally gave him pleasure. He likened it to sitting in a music hall's comfortable velveteen seat and watching an opera. Except at Casa DeMarco, Antonio didn't sit; he moved about slowly, step by step, from one corner of the room to the next, observing with interest the vignettes transpiring in each. Together, the goings-on created a cohesive, masterful piece of "music."

For example, in one part of the parlor, his brothers-in-law politely bantered, a handful of Canios in *Pagliacci*—though none of them were contemplating murder. Sal, Dom and Paolo were simply contemplating the evil motives of *Il Duce*.

In the depths of the sofa, not far off, Giuseppe and Valerie sat listening, hands linked between the cushions, thinking no one would notice. (Antonio noticed, but did Luisa, bustling from room to room, serving dessert?) Maybe the older pair were Silvio and Nedda, *Pagliacci's* star-crossed couple. Antonio trusted these elders would come to a much better end than the couple in Leoncavallo's opera.

Then there were the ladies prancing in the kitchen with platters, cups and cutlery, providing background music as well as supplying the fretful voices in the Villagers' chorus. Now, Luisa, the lead, foraged through the catch-all drawer, in search of matches and candles.

Antonio caught slivers of the women's conversation: "...built like a stallion..." (to which the Villagers chortled) and "...if only he knew..." and "...that hussy down on Oliver Street..."

The younger children sat on the ground in the vestibule, the carpet folded back, playing marbles. And the girls were off in Gloria's room again, no doubt whispering about secret things only they found fascinating. Antonio caught blurs of words: "...Alice..." and "...that Tony Martin..." and "...positively dreamy..."

Perhaps these players were the Village Children, although Antonio couldn't recall any youngsters in the opera when he'd seen it performed by a local troupe at Regina Opera Company. Luisa had fallen asleep during Act II but he remained riveted. Yes, Antonio decided, there very well could have been children in *Pagliacci*. There are always children, as there are always clowns. Especially today.

Antonio spied Charles and his wife Antonella on the settee. His business partner smiled and raised his glass. *"Tanti auguri!"* Charles mouthed in the noisy room, then took a sip from his cordial cup.

Though Antonio did not want to think of unpleasantries, not on his birthday, not on any day, but regardless, his mind fluttered to Chatonio's dwindling sales, to Anna-Marie's tears when they had no choice but to lay her off, for she was the most recent hire. "I hope it's only temporary," Antonio had tried to console her with, though he doubted the truth of this statement. He and Charles knew that Anna-Marie had three kids, a sick husband and an ailing mother at home so they gave her a week's pay as severance, though they could ill afford it.

Between the Depression, the impending war and anti-Italian sentiments, Chatonio's orders had staggered almost to a halt, even among their more well-to-do clients. People were either making do with what they had or making clothing purchases in cheaper department stores. Chatonio's was forced to take in mending, hemming and such, anything to keep their small staff working, though these little jobs barely paid the employees, let alone showed a meagre profit for the owners.

Antonio's heart quickened with worry. He willed himself to think of pleasantries, like the operas he so loved. He circled back to *Pagliacci*. It was set in the Calabria of his youth, a place he doubted he would ever see again. His brother Franco had been back once years ago and vowed never to return, so profound was the poverty. "It makes Brooklyn seem like paradise," Franco said. Which it was to the DeMarco brothers: it was the promised land.

Franco passed Antonio en route to the powder room and clapped his elder sibling on the shoulder. *"Bella festa,"* he said.

"Grazie," Antonio called after him. "But it's not a party, it's just cake."

As if a stagehand were cued, the lights dimmed. Franco stopped dead in his tracks, turned and grinned at his brother's pained expression as the whole lot of them began to sing an off-key yet spirited version of "Happy Birthday to You!" first in English, then in Italian.

At the opening notes, Gloria and Siobhan were summoned from the bedroom, their faces flushed. They bumped shoulders in rhythm and sang, Gloria helping her friend with the cumbersome Italian.

Who was Antonio in this opera called life? Was he Canio, the actor and leader of the *commedia dell'arte* troupe? Or was he Tonio, the fool? (Such an appropriate name!) Or Beppe, the faithful friend? Perhaps Antonio was all three.

The cake was homemade by Luisa, of course, hazelnut cream, her husband's favorite. She waited to cut it until Antonio smeared his name for luck, as schooled

by Little Gio. Luisa handed the guest of honor the first
piece but hurriedly cut slices for the clamoring children.
The adults lined up as well, helping themselves to coffee
from the urn and tea from the china pot. Giuseppe,
Antonio noticed, poured a cup of Earl Grey for Valerie,
an Irish lass who favored tea.

Antonio ate and looked into the full room. Soon,
it would be empty and he would help his wife clean up,
reminiscing about how fine the evening had been and who
had said or done this or that.

Taking his plate into the kitchen, Antonio recalled
the last line of *Pagliacci*, after two murders had been
committed onstage.

"La commedia é finita!"

Yes, the comedy was finished. The curtain falls.

May 1940

Germany invades the Low Countries—the Netherlands, Belgium and Luxembourg. Ten days later, Auschwitz-Birkenau Concentration Camp opens in German-occupied Poland.

Winston Churchill is named British Prime Minister after Neville Chamberlain resigns. In his first address to the House of Commons, Churchill says, "I have nothing to offer you but blood, toil, tears and sweat."

On display at the 1939 World's Fair, nylon stockings are finally released for sale to the public. Almost five million pairs sell on the first day.

"I'm sorry but we have no choice but to close," Antonio said, his voice cracking. He was as gentle as possible when he told his workers at the Bay Ridge shop that he and Charles were shutting its doors at the end of the week. There were gasps, whimpers and muffled exclamations uttered under the breath. Announcing the shuttering of Chatonio's Bay Ridge location to his employees was possibly the most difficult thing Antonio ever had to do in his life.

Charles stood beside him, providing backup. He was a rock, a foundation, always. "Again, we're very sorry to have to do this but business has fallen off sharply in the past few months," Charles explained. "We can't float two shops any longer."

The workers stood in a ragged semicircle around their bosses: buttonholers, cutters, pressers and all the rest, expectant, afraid, angry. Antonio continued, "But we'll pay you until the end of the month." This would strap Chatonio Haberdashery's finances even more, but Antonio and Charles felt severance pay was important and necessary; these workers were like family.

"And after that?" piped Nunzio, the driver of their lone delivery truck.

Antonio shrugged. The words would not come. So, Charles stepped in, "After that it's in God's hands."

Nunzio snorted, "Tell that to my wife. Tell that to my five kids when they're hungry."

"Look, hopefully, it's not too long. When the economy is better, we..."

But Charles had already lost them. They began returning to their stations. Only Anna remained. Tears streamed down her face. "I've been working in factories since I was fifteen," she said. "But this place was different. This place felt like home."

"I know," Antonio told her. "For me as well."

"Why not split the work between the two?" she pressed.

Charles shook his head. "It's not possible. We ran the numbers. With two rents and two..."

"Ah, I see," Anna said. "So, we're numbers to you." She went back to her station, wiping her eyes as she sat. Then Anna began to work, dripping an occasional tear onto the polka dots.

Charles and Antonio looked at each other, sighed and shook their heads. "I'll see you tomorrow," Charles told him, retreating to his glass office. There was a great deal of paperwork to be done and bank business that needed tending.

Antonio grabbed his hat and light overcoat from the rack. He headed for the Bensonhurst shop. A brisk walk might clear his head.

"You have such great ideas," Valerie told Luisa as they gathered hardcovers for their latest venture. The young woman blushed, unaccustomed to fielding compliments. From her employer, there were many. Not a day went by when Valerie didn't utter a nicety about her star (and only!) employee—whether it be a new hairpin or the suggestion to start a lending library, as Luisa had done just now.

Like most businesses during the lean times of 1940, The Avid Reader had experienced a noticeable dip in sales. They were still in the green, but profit margins were slim and getting slimmer. Who could afford a few dollars for a hardcover except the affluent wives on Doctor's Row or the bankers whose stately homes lined Shore Road? Some were such voracious readers that they were running out of room in their wood-paneled private libraries. Others had even approached Valerie about donating their already-read books back to the shop. Valerie didn't have the space to become a used bookstore—nor did she want to—but Luisa had a solution.

"Why not have a shelf dedicated to book borrowing?" Luisa offered. "We could loan out books for a nickel apiece for a couple of weeks. It would be like the library, only better. We'd have more current books, a broader selection of bestsellers."

Valerie considered the idea for a moment. "That's an excellent proposition," she told Luisa. "Why, Mrs. Billings alone is good for a couple of books a week. I'll tell certain customers that they could donate books back to the shop when they're done reading them. I think they'd like that."

Within weeks, The Avid Reader had more than enough books to begin their lending library. On a late May morning before they opened, Luisa and Valerie pulled chairs up to the empty shelf and sorted through the pile, picking and choosing which titles to offer first. "Hemingway is always a sure bet," Luisa nodded, fingering the spine of *To Have and Have Not.* "I think Mr. Espinosa would enjoy this one."

"I think you're right," Valerie agreed and put it in the "yes" pile. "Luis's people are from Cuba." She took a sip from the mug of tea beside her on the floor. "You have a fine sense of our customers."

"Thank you," Luisa demurred. "I've learned a lot from you."

Valerie nodded her thanks as she examined *The Devil's Dirt.* "I hear this one's pretty racy."

"Sex, greed, murder...it's all packed into this slim little volume."

Valerie handed the book to Luisa. "Here, take it home. Give it a whirl before we put it out."

Luisa put *The Devil's Dirt* to the side then picked *Farewell, My Lovely* from the pile. "Why, it looks like it hasn't even been cracked."

"Mrs. Gelston read the first chapter and said it wasn't her cup of tea," Valerie explained. "Chandler is an acquired taste. Sparse writing style, short sentences. Mrs. G prefers the frilliness of Jane Austin. I tried to warn her, but..." Her voice trailed off.

They sorted through the stack of books, which had sprouted into three lesser heaps. Soon, there were only two. Their talk was of the titles, of the weather, of the coming summer when people seemed to read more. Valerie considered herself very lucky. The Depression hadn't struck her modest bookshop too hard, not with the wealthy clients who lined Shore Road and offerings like knitting circles, cooking lessons and children's crafts classes which brought in a steady stream of customers.

A large part of the shop's success was Luisa. She'd grown up in the neighborhood, seemed to know everyone and had a keen sense of what would pull them into The Avid Reader. For example, in warm weather, she suggested propping open the front door to be more welcoming. There was a dish of cool water outside for thirsty pups and the aroma of freshly-baked goods wafting out of the shop. Luisa sometimes baked in the evenings, said it calmed her, so The Avid Reader sold her creations for a very reasonable price—and offered free samples.

A small sign adorned with Luisa's neat handwriting announced the kick-off of Miss Val's Lending Library. They'd been talking it up to customers for weeks. "Alphabetical, by author, I think," was Valerie's suggestion to organize the collection. "It's the most familiar, no?" she proposed.

Luisa agreed and began handing Valerie the gently-used tomes to shelve, one by one. Something had been pressing upon the young woman's mind and this seemed an opportune moment to bring it up. As she passed her employer a copy of *Native Son,* with its attractive gray marbleized front cover and gold-leaf lettering, Luisa said, "I can't help but notice that you're getting very chummy with my father."

Richard Wright's novel slipped through Valerie's fingertips but didn't fall. She caught it with her left hand, then regained her composure. "Yes," Valerie admitted. "Joe is pleasant company." Luisa noted that Val used her father's Americanized nickname rather than his Italian given name.

"That he is," Luisa agreed.

"Where's the dust jacket?" Valerie asked, noticing that *Native Son*'s striking yellow and green wrapper was gone.

"Mrs. Cornacchio said that Jet had his way with Mr. Wright before she could rescue him," Luisa said, pointing out the almost imperceptible tooth marks on its green and gold spine.

"Hmmm," Valerie commented, shelving the book. "That dog has excellent taste."

Next, Luisa gave Valerie *The Story of Babar,* which Gloria had cherished until only recently. "I'm glad," Luisa said plainly. "About you and Papa, I mean. I'm glad you two…found one another."

Valerie exhaled deeply. She took Luisa's hand, squeezed it. "And I'm glad you're glad. Relieved, actually." She smiled with tears in her eyes. "Joe, uh, Giuseppe was so afraid you'd be upset."

"Upset? Why?" The topsy-turvy cover of *Brave New World* was slipped into place with the H's.

"Well, your mother, she…"

"It's been going on eight years, God rest her soul," Luisa said. "And for you, it's been even longer." She thought for a second. "Papa deserves to be happy. You do too," Luisa added with finality. "It's not good for people to be alone."

Valerie's face softened. "I agree. But mum's the word. I'll let you and Giuseppe discuss this when you're ready."

Luisa took away their empty mugs and unlocked the front door. She decided not to say anything to her father. He would tell her when he was ready, however long it might take.

Antonio was relieved that no one had spraypainted slurs on the Bensonhurst shop's windows or on its brick front for several weeks. Hatred of Italians had been replaced with hatred of Germans. This latest dislike would linger much longer and would become more profound as time passed. Only to be replaced by hatred for another nationality. The Japanese, for example, then another ethnic group.

The normally-buoyant mood of Chatonio's Haberdashery's flagship shop was notably quiet, somber even. There was only the chatter of the sewing machines, no laughter, no uplifted voices. It was such a great place to work that employees had even brought in family members. Their seamstress Raquel had recommended her sister Emma, who was a fine finisher at the other, soon-to-be-defunct location.

Word of the Bay Ridge shop's closing spread quickly at the Bensonhurst site. But there was no animosity toward the owners, only a sense of disappointment and fear; they couldn't help but wonder if their jobs were next.

Waiting for Antonio in Chatonio's vestibule was Mario Inzitari, accompanied by his burly companion. Some might call Rocco a bodyguard, but Antonio gave this man, a human four-by-eight, the benefit of the doubt. While it was suspected that Mr. Inzitari didn't earn his fortune from the import of quality Ligurian olive oil as he professed, Antonio chose not to ask questions he might not like the answers to.

"*Ciao,* Tony," Mr. Inzitari smiled, extending his hand. Antonio took it and shook it firmly. Mario Inzitari was one of those people who looked even more terrifying when he smiled, what with his scarecrow physique, buttonhole eyes, his pinched features and uneven, stained teeth. He resembled an Italian-American Ichabod Crane in that Sleepy Hollow story Luisa liked to frighten the children with around Halloween.

Antonio opted not to inform Mr. Inzitari that he didn't like being called "Tony." Inzitari was the sort of fellow you didn't correct; he gave the impression that he wouldn't take too well to being corrected.

"*Ciao, Signore* Inzitari," Antonio bowed his head.

"Please, call me 'Mario.'" Antonio would not. "So, it's ready?" Mr. Inzitari inquired. Of course, his suit was ready. This wasn't the sort of gentleman you kept waiting...for anything.

Again, Antonio nodded. Three days earlier, Rocco had come in to inform Antonio that Mr. Inzitari's daughter Elisabetta was getting married rather suddenly and that Mr. I would need a new black suit "ASAP." Could Antonio comply? With a man like Mario Inzitari, a humble haberdasher had no choice but to comply. As with most of his *primo* customers, Antonio kept Inzitari's measurements on hand. He chose his finest black wool serge for its luxurious feel, breathability and excellent drape. For Inzitari, comfort was as important as appearance.

Antonio measured and cut the cloth himself. He also sat at the helm of the Singer, though Raquel, his most skilled seamstress, told her employer that she would welcome the task. Antonio stayed late to see that the suit was completed in more than enough time. Mr. Inzitari was there now for a final fitting.

The telephone pole-slim man stood behind the dressing room curtain in his three-button undershirt and striped boxers, both sharply pressed. His black silk socks were held in place with garters. He slipped on the suit. "Fits like a glove," Mr. Inzitari grinned, a horrifying gaunt jack-o-lantern. "What you do with a needle and thread is magic. Just magic, Tony."

Antonio allowed himself to exhale. "Thank you kindly."

After Mr. Inzitari was dressed in his street clothes, the suit lovingly returned to its hanger and protective garment bag, he handed Antonio twice the amount he normally charged for a men's suit of clothing, even a rush job. "Congratulations on your daughter's nuptials," Antonio said after thanking him.

Mr. Inzitari made a sour face, which told Antonio he didn't approve of the union. Perhaps Elisabetta was in the family way. "*Grazie*," his customer managed. "Oh, and…" Mr. Inzitari motioned to Rocco, who dug into his waistcoat and came out with a small package that filled his beefy palm. "For the Mrs."

"Nylons!" Antonio exclaimed. "Where did you find..." But Antonio stopped himself, remembering that Mario Inzitari had the power to procure anything, no matter how impossible.

"Let's just say they fell off the truck," he winked.

Antonio accepted Mr. Inzitari's gift with a slight bow. "Thank you very much. Luisa will love them."

"I know she will. And I hope you get a little nookie tonight because of it." Antonio reddened as his customer elbowed his ribs. "You get me?"

"Uh, yes, I do." He tried to smile but it came out as more of a grimace.

Antonio carried the suit to the Packard as Rocco held open the back door for his *capo*. "Oh, and another thing..." Antonio held his breath. "I hear you're closing shop in Bay Ridge," Mr. Inzitari began. Bad news traveled quickly, didn't it?

"Yes," Antonio sighed in response.

"May I ask why?"

"We're a bit...overextended."

"I see," Mr. Inzitari growled. "Well, if there's anything I can do. And I mean *anything*. Just say the word." Antonio knew that he would never say "the word," even if his children were hungry, because that word would be the beginning of the end. "I'm serious, Tony," Mr. Inzitari tagged on. "Serious as a heart attack."

"I know you are," Antonio said. "Thank you."

Mr. Inzitari lowered himself onto the Packard's plush leather upholstery and tucked his long, broomstick legs inside. Antonio handed Rocco the suit which he lovingly laid in the trunk. "And if you ever decide to dump that clown Charlie Mura, let me know. I'd make a much better business partner."

Antonio felt a chill though the day was mild. He closed the car door and waved. Before Antonio turned to go back into the shop, Rocco stopped him and handed him another package of nylons. "Here," he said, shoving it into Antonio's hand. "For that cute little dish from Havana. Raquel, is it? And make sure to say it's from me."

"I will, "Antonio promised, though Raquel would likely toss the stockings into the trash. She was married, a good Catholic woman. Her husband Enrique was a merchant marine who was often at sea. Raising her stepdaughters practically single-handedly, Raquel had no patience for *basura* like Rocco.

"How could you be so *stunad*?" Gloria gasped at her brother. "Do you know how expensive the World's Fair is?" Immediately, Gianni began to cry, winding up like a fire engine siren.

"Gloria!" Luisa barked at her daughter. "Apologize to your brother!"

"Sorry," she whimpered, though she wasn't.

Luisa was livid. "He's not even five. He doesn't know how expensive things are! Go to your room. And don't stomp!"

But Gloria stomped anyhow. Luisa comforted her son, rubbing his head and assuring him that he wasn't stupid.

Antonio walked into their home amid this minor fracas— Gianni weeping into Luisa's apron, Luisa scolding their daughter, Gloria's door slam. "So, how was your day?" Antonio asked hesitantly.

"Great," she sighed. "Yours? How did they take it?"

He kissed the side of her head, smelling onions and lavender shampoo. "Remember when Churchill said something about toil and tears on the radio?" Luisa nodded. "Well, it was sort of like that."

Luisa squeezed his arm in support. "We'll talk later."

Antonio caressed his son's jet-black curls. Through Gianni's tears, Antonio deciphered, "...so mean...," "...World's Fair..." and "...hate her."

"Now, now, Gio, we must never hate anyone," Antonio corrected.

"Not even Hitler?"

"No, not even Hitler." Even though Antonio himself hated Hitler, and that sharp-chinned weasel Mussolini too.

"How does *pasta e ceci* for supper sound?" Luisa posed, deftly switching the subject from world dictators to dinner.

"It sounds perfect," Antonio told her.

While Gianni consoled himself with Superman on the parlor radio, Antonio stirred the pot in the kitchen, watching the chickpeas dance in the glistening tomato sauce. Luisa drained the ditalini in a colander and slowly spooned it into the sauce. "That's it, just keep stirring so the pasta doesn't stick," she encouraged Antonio.

When the ditalini was in the pot, he asked, "What's next?"

"You can grate the cheese if you'd like."

"*Va bene,*" he said and fetched the wedge of Peccorino-Romano from the icebox. They preferred its sharp tang to the milder Parmesan. No stranger in his own kitchen, Antonio knew where the grater was stored and grabbed that too. Though he enjoyed this hearty dish, he realized that Luisa turned to it whenever she fretted about finances. It was filling, satisfying and frugal. Comfort food from her youth when Mama Assunta had eight mouths to feed and a thin purse. "We'll do fine," Antonio told Luisa. "You don't need to worry."

"Ah," she told him, adding a sprig of fresh parsley to the pot. "But I always worry. Not just for us. How will Anna get by? She's like family. I came up with her through the sweatshops."

Antonio tapped the cheese against the metal grater. Already, he had a slight mountain of white, more than enough for tonight. He reached for a bowl. "Anna will be all right. We're paying them a small severance. She's a hard worker, she'll manage to get something."

"But there's no work," Luisa pointed out.

He slid the fluffy mound of cheese from cutting board to bowl. "So, what was the outburst about this time?" Antonio wondered, referring to his children.

"I think Glorina is worried too, concerned about money," Luisa told her husband.

"But we try not to talk of such things in front of her. We…"

Luisa took the dish from her husband and placed it in the center of the kitchen table. "She's a smart girl. She listens to the news. She sees the papers. So, she worries."

"Just like her mother," he smiled. Antonio wiped the cutting board with a damp rag. Then he slid the loaf of semolina bread from its paper sack and began slicing it into chunks. "I'll go talk to her."

Luisa nodded. "It all started with the World's Fair. It just reopened for the summer."

"We'll go," Antonio said emphatically.

Luisa rebuked, "But tickets are so dear. We can't…"

Antonio kissed her mouth to silence her and perhaps, to strengthen her. "We'll go. After all, how often is there a World's Fair in New York? And Queens at that, just a train ride away? Hmmm?"

"With all that's happening in Europe, we…"

"That's the very reason we *should* go. For all of those who can't," Antonio said. For this, Luisa had no response. Antonio cleaned his hands and left to tend to their daughter.

June 1940

Paris, bombed by the Luftwaffe, soon falls and is occupied by the Nazis.

The first annual Sturgis Motorcycle Rally is held in South Dakota.

Albert Einstein gives a public address in the "I'm an American" radio series on the day he takes his citizenship test.

Just so long as it didn't interfere with Superman, Gianni didn't mind listening to the guy with the funny accent talk on the radio. "Is that Doctor Rubinstein from around the corner," he wondered, half paying attention.

"No, stup..." Gloria glanced at her father, who'd recently reprimanded her for calling her brother names. "No, silly," she corrected. "It's some German scientist."

"It's Albert Einstein, maybe the most important German scientist in the world," Luisa offered. "A physicist. He's explaining why he left his homeland seven years ago."

"The bad men?" Gianni asked.

"Yes, the bad men chased him out," Antonio told him. "One very bad man in particular." On the National Broadcast Company radio program "I'm an American," Einstein was explaining why he had applied for citizenship that very day, when just four years in the future, he would have become a naturalized American citizen. The reason? Einstein was afraid.

"As long as I have any choice, I will only stay in a country where political liberty, toleration and equality of all citizens before the law is the rule," Einstein said.

"Do you understand what he's saying?" Luisa asked her daughter.

"I think so," Gloria told her.

Earlier that day, a camera crew had been on hand to capture photographs of Einstein as he took—and passed—his final citizenship test in New Jersey, not far from Princeton University where he taught. Antonio had a feeling that cameras would also bear witness to the humble scientist when he was sworn in as an American a few months later. Antonio himself had the good fortune to partake in this act a decade earlier, though his own citizenship ceremony had considerably less fanfare. Just Luisa and his American-born baby Gloria sat in the observation gallery, his wife beaming with pride. Luisa soon followed suit and became a U.S. citizen shortly afterwards.

As Einstein explained why he chose to become an American, Antonio presented Luisa with a booklet of orange and blue colored tickets. "The World's Fair of 1940 in New York" the top one read. "For Peace and Freedom." She fanned them between her fingers. "Where...where did you get these?" she gasped. "They're so hard to come by...and so dear. We can't afford..."

Antonio hesitated. "Let's just say they were a gift," he told Luisa.

Her face dropped. "Like the nylons?"

He shrugged, "Something like that. *Ma, bella...*"

"Don't *ma, bella* me," she said. Luisa tried to hand the tickets back to her husband, but he wouldn't take them. "What did you have to do this time?"

"Not much," Antonio said. "Just take out the seams of some dresses…in a hurry. And confidentially." Antonio recalled Mr. Inzitari's daughter Elisabetta standing in the dressing room, cowering behind the flimsy curtain, her bulging belly straining against the fabric of her full slip.

"Ah, so she *is*…how do you say…"

"Incinta," Antonio finished.

"Knocked up," Luisa corrected, quite crassly. Gloria turned at her mother's harsh words, then returned to reading *The Whispering Statue*. How she loved Nancy Drew; how she wished she and Siobhan could pal around with her. But alas, Gloria knew the girl detective wasn't real.

"Shush," Antonio told his wife.

"He's bribing you!"

"I prefer to think that it's a reward for my discretion, for my silence," Antonio explained. "Next week, Betta and her husband will go off to Palermo on an extended honeymoon…"

"Just before she starts to show," Luisa barged in.

Antonio ignored her. "…and when they return to Brooklyn many months later, Elisabetta will have given birth to a baby. Prematurely, of course."

"Of course."

"Mario says…"

"Ah, so now he's 'Mario." Luisa sighed, "Tonio, Mr. Inzitari is a very dangerous man."

"Not to me," he assured her. "Trust me, Lu. I know what I'm doing."

"First, little gifts, then he'll ask you to do something you're not comfortable with. Then you'll be…"

Antonio kissed Luisa on the forehead. "Trust me, *bella,"* he implored. Luisa would certainly try but would make no promises.

Groggy from the long subway ride which involved changes to several trains, the children immediately perked up when they caught a glimpse of the six-hundred-and-ten-foot high Trylon and the one-hundred-and-eighty foot in diameter Perisphere looming above the landscape. The tall, pointed tower and mammoth circle resembled a contraption from the *Flash Gordon* serial, they all agreed.

The DeMarco Family had risen before the sun because the journey would take many hours. For the momentous occasion, Siobhan had slept over the night before, snuggled up in Gloria's bed beside her. How could they not have taken the girl with the fifth ticket? 'At least I know she'll have a decent breakfast—or *some* breakfast at all—before we leave,' Luisa thought to herself as their weedy neighbor wolfed down her meal. She'd made sure the child bathed (a bubble bath!) and put her freshly-washed hair in pin curls as well.

The three children gasped in unison when they saw the splendor set out before them, and truthfully, the adults had to hold back their gasps as well. The Empire State Bridge led them past a stand of international flags as they joined scores of others to explore "The World of Tomorrow." And to think, just two years earlier, the twelve-hundred-acre plot of land had been an ash dump. Now it housed pavilions presented by sixty countries and thirty-three states plus the "Town of Tomorrow," with its futuristic model homes.

Of course, the family couldn't see every attraction (nor did they want to) but the DeMarcos and their little hitchhiker had pored over brochures and newspaper clippings at home before their Saturday sojourn to Flushing Meadows, so they had a proper plan of attack.

"Where first?" Gloria asked excitedly, though she knew the proposed route by heart. They were to hit the International Zone then choice pavilions like the Transportation Zone, where they would watch a 3D film of a Plymouth being built. In air conditioning, no less.

"What's air conditioning?" Gianni wondered.

"You'll see," Antonio told his son.

The day was a beautiful blur. They paused to examine the marker for the Westinghouse Time Capsule, which was buried at a depth of fifty feet, not to be opened for five thousand years. Siobhan counted on her fingers. "That's not until 6939!" she said incredulously. "Do you think they'll care about a bunch of seeds, a Mickey Mouse watch, a pack of cigarettes and stuff Albert Einstein wrote?" Siobhan pondered.

"I'm sick of Albert Einstein," Gianni sighed. "I wanna go on the roller coaster."

"You'd be surprised who'll care," Luisa told Siobhan. Then to Gianni, she said, "We'll get to the rides soon enough. But you may be too small for the bobsled coaster. No tears if you are. Promise?" Gianni nodded.

Antonio lobbied to visit the British Pavilion to see the replica of the Magna Carta. "It's the papa of the Declaration of Independence, of the Constitution," he explained. But the group was unmoved.

"Yawn," Gloria said in an exaggerated gesture.

Since war broke out in Europe the year before, some exhibits didn't reopen. Like those of Poland and Czechoslovakia, for example. Germany had never participated, citing budget pressures. The USSR Pavilion was dismantled after the Fair's first season, leaving in its wake an empty lot christened "The American Commons."

Luisa pointed out a splendid building complete with columns, a two-hundred-foot waterfall, a high tower and a slew of statues, including a topless woman nicknamed Mimi by fairgoers. "There it is!" Luisa said.

The abandoned Italian Pavilion was so grand that Luisa felt proud even though it had closed in May, after Italy invaded France.

Still, the Italian Pavilion was a monument to their heritage, so they paused to take in its opulence. The structure was dedicated to Marconi. "Here's a scientist even you would like," Antonio said, pointing out the placard.

"Macaroni?" Siobhan sounded out. "I like macaroni. Especially the way Mrs. D fixes it."

"No, *bella*," Antonio corrected tenderly. "I'm referring to Guglielmo Marconi. He invented the radio."

"You're right, papa, I like Marconi!" Gianni announced. "Let's go inside."

"Yes, let's!" the girls chimed in. Finally, there was something they could all agree upon.

"We can't," Luisa told them sadly. "They shut it down last month."

"Why?" all three children asked.

"The war... Mussolini," Antonio apologized.

The world's largest carillon trilled in the spire of the Florida Exhibition. "The Transportation Zone is next on the list," Luisa announced. There, General Motors had a sprawling Futurama exhibit depicting the unimaginable world of 1960. After a brief wait, the five joined more than five hundred others in a conveyor system ride which transported them over a huge diorama of a utopian realm. Propelled twenty years into the future, a network of expressways connected the nation, spreading across mountains, over rivers, and through cities and towns.

Afterwards, Antonio lingered at GM's auto dealership while Luisa was drawn to the Frigidaire products, imagining a kitchen without slabs of ice and endless pans to drain. Next door, on the roof of the Ford Pavilion, race car drivers circled in endless figure eights.

The massive Eastern Railroads Presidents' Conference building housed a primitive Tom Thumb engine and a locomotive that ran continuously at sixty miles per hour all the livelong day. These captured the males' attention while the females gravitated toward "Railroads on Parade," a stunning live drama depicting the birth and growth of the train system.

Stretched across two-hundred-and-thirty acres along the shores of Fountain Lake was the World's Fair's most popular area. It wasn't educational, scientific or high-minded, nor was it "creative, energetic or innovative," as the Fair's theme proclaimed. It was the Amusement Area, and was nothing but fun, pure and simple.

Gianni squealed with delight when he caught sight of the Life Savers Parachute Jump lording two-hundred-and-fifty feet above all, the riders' bodies drifting from the sky like autumn leaves. Brave souls were seated two-by-two on narrow wooden benches which were suspended beneath individual parachutes—and dropped. It was rumored that after the World's Fair, the Parachute Ride would be moved to a prominent spot on Coney Island, if not sold for scrap metal, as other rumors professed.

"Woooowwww!" Gianni marveled, while Gloria and Siobhan grabbed each other's hands, wide-eyed.

"Absolutely not," Luisa said. "Not any of you. That's just *pazzo*. Besides, it doesn't look very safe. Right, Papa?"

"Right," Antonio agreed. When Gianni began to whine, Antonio tagged on, "Listen to your mama. She knows what's best for you children." Siobhan, though disappointed, was secretly thrilled that she'd been forbidden to do something, anything. Her parents were rarely sober enough to dispense rules and regulations. That Gloria's father considered her one of his brood made her feel cared for.

Painted a bright cherry red like one of their candies, Life Savers Parachute Jump did look precarious. The

DeMarcos plus one stared at it in wonder until the littlest among them broke the spell. *"Guarda! Guarda!"* Gianni proclaimed, pointing. Looming just beyond the Clown Mural was a towering, white roller coaster, its highest track decorated with colorful flags. Luisa broke into a scowl. "But *bella*, they have to go on *something,* no?" Antonio coaxed in a whisper.

Reluctantly, Luisa agreed. As the long line approached the gate, they saw a painted sign depicting a clown bearing a measuring stick. Alas, Gianni didn't make the mark, although he puffed out his chest and tried to appear taller. "And them girls is too young to ride," the rough-voiced attendant barked. "Without an adult, that is."

"You go," Antonio smiled, knowing that his wife used to sneak off to ride Coney Island's Cyclone with her friend Anita when they were teenagers. So, it didn't take much convincing for Luisa to grab the young ladies' hands and saunter through the gate. As was her custom, Luisa charmed the operator into letting them wait until they could ride in the first car, for everyone knew it was *primo*.

It was the feeling of falling, falling, falling that Luisa liked most, the sensation of losing control, as the metal cars clattered across the tracks. This was one time when it was permissible to scream, and scream all three did, for bloody murder, at the top of their lungs. As they whipped through the sharp curves, Siobhan's slender body pressed into Gloria's fleshy one, thrilling her further. And as the roller coaster jolted the other way, Gloria's curvy frame pressed into her friend's angular one, stirring her as well. All three linked hands atop the front bar, which they held onto for dear life, as though Luisa clinging to the girls' hands could keep them safe.

Antonio watched from the ground below, swearing he could pick his wife's gleeful shouts from the other voices. He reveled in Luisa's joy as she returned to solid ground, rosy-cheeked and beaming. "Thanks for letting me go," Luisa told him, giving him a quick peck on the lips.

"Of course," he said. "I know how you love roller coasters."

"Well, it was no Cyclone," she gushed, "but it will do."

The narrow-gauge Gimbels Flyer was more Gianni's speed. Though it didn't have the peaks and dips of a roller coaster, the blue and white train traversed wood bridges and curved through the children's section of the Amusement Area. To a chorus of grumbling, Luisa had Gloria (the grumbler) and Siobhan (the non-grumbler) accompany the boy on the ride. She noticed that Siobhan instinctively took his hand to see that he safely navigated the big step onto the car. "It was all right," Gloria admitted afterwards with a smirk, clearly having enjoyed the kiddie ride.

"Again! Again!" Gianni begged, but there was no time to try any ride a second time. There was so much more to see and they'd barely scratched the surface.

At Luisa's insistence, they bypassed Morris Gest's Little Miracle Town, a pint-sized village inhabited by wee folks. Even though Gest was quoted as saying, "Midgets are gigantic, little in body but great in mind and heart," Luisa felt this attraction poked fun at its inhabitants. Her friend Daria was, in fact, a dwarf, and Luisa could never forget the hurt and anger she felt when people pointed at Daria on the street and laughed. This is why Luisa and her family walked on.

Frank Buck's Jungleland had rare birds, wild animals and exotic reptiles, performing elephants and Monkey Mountain, a chattering hillock dotted with six hundred primates. It was there they met the Mayor of Jungleland, Jiggs, a five-year-old trained orangutan. "He's your age," Gloria pointed out, "I bet Jiggs would be fun to play with. He's probably a lot smarter than your friend Kevin."

To which, Gianni began to protest. "Why are you so mean to him?" Siobhan whispered. "He's just a kid." Gloria thought her witty jibes might endear Siobhan to her, but they had the exact opposite effect. "I wish I had a little brother," Siobhan added, ruffling Gianni's hair. "It's lonely being an only child sometimes."

Gianni smiled and pressed his body into hers. "I can be your little brother too if you want," he said.

"I would like that," the freckle-faced beauty told him. "I'd like that a lot."

Dream of Venus was a wildly bizarre building designed by artist Salvadore Dalí, its skin bedecked with coral and sea creatures. Somehow, Luisa and Antonio missed the articles describing this controversial, surrealist funhouse which included unusual sculptures and statues. Inside, nearly-nude ladies posed as things like pianos and mermaids. Partially-clothed women swam in water tanks, enacting scenes from Dalí's bizarre dream.

This pavilion piqued the girls' interest as well as Antonio's, but Luisa was shocked. "Dream of Venus..." she stammered. "I thought it was about the *planet* Venus!" Several within earshot chuckled when Gianni announced, "Boobies!" and pointed at a woman feigning slumber beneath a purple satin bedsheet. Luisa covered Gianni's eyes and hustled their entourage out of the pavilion. Luckily, the "low-minded entertainment" wasn't raided by police on the day of their visit, as it had been on other occasions.

Also not intended for the eyes of children was the Bendix Lama Temple. Commissioned and brought back from Manchuria by explorer Vincent Bendix, this was a twenty-eight-thousand-piece, full-sized replica of a 1767 Potala temple. Since attendance was poor in 1939, a provocative show was added. It depicted "the erotic temptations of a young Buddhist priest" and featured a variety of naked women.

"You go," Luisa encouraged her husband. When Antonio hesitated, she pressed, "After all, you let me ride the roller coaster."

While Antonio explored the sprawling temple, its golden two-tiered roof supported by bright red columns, Luisa took the children to the restroom. When Antonio rejoined them at the meeting spot, slightly flushed, Luisa asked, "How was it?"

"I'll tell you about it later," he said.

Another star attraction was Billy Rose's Aquacade, a song, dance and swimming extravaganza in the style of Hollywood musicals. The colossal amphitheater, which held ten thousand spectators, ringed a swimming pool which contained nearly eighteen-hundred tons of water. "Please! Please!" the girls begged. "It has Johnny Weissmuller," Gloria tagged on, hoping this would be the clincher. "You love Johnny Weissmuller, mama."

"I don't care if it has Pope Pius himself," Luisa told them. "It's eighty cents apiece and that's too much."

Though the World's Fair tickets were free, the DeMarcos counted their pennies once inside. They skipped Schaefer's Diner and Childs Restaurant in favor of food stands. There, they dined on the cheapest eats— ten-cent hot dogs and knishes—and shared bottles of grape and orange Nehi. Plus, they indulged in the special treat of ice cream cones at the Sealtest Dairy Building.

Feeling magnanimous, Antonio permitted the children to choose a souvenir from the shop, even Siobhan. "Are you sure, Mr. D?" she asked. "It all seems awful expensive."

"How often does the World's Fair come to New York?" he responded. "I want you kids to have something to remember it by."

"Oh, I'll never forget this day," Siobhan told him.

Gianni chose a tin zeppelin. The SR-47 came complete with yellow back propellers and a miniscule key that sent the striped dirigible gliding across the ground. Gianni cradled it like a kitten, deeply enamored. The girls each chose a commemorative doll. For Siobhan, it was kerchiefed, dark-haired Gypsy Rose from Hungary, which

275

she said reminded her of Gloria, and for Gloria, it was red-haired Aino from Finland, who reminded Gloria of her ginger-tressed best friend.

After a long, full day, the sky began to darken and the children were beginning to tire. Antonio carried Gianni toward the exit, zeppelin clutched in the boy's fist. They left behind Borden's one-hundred-and-fifty pedigreed cows (including Elsie) and Vermeer's "The Milkmaid," endlessly pouring her pitcher of shimmering milk. They left behind the Frozen Alive Girl and the Temple of Religion's stained-glass tower. They left behind the Helicline which guided fairgoers from Democracity, the utopian city-of-the-future nestled in the Perisphere's belly. They left behind everything, but for a very long time, would remember it all.

That evening, as Luisa undressed, Antonio saw that she'd been wearing Mr. Inzitari's nylons. "Ah, so you caved in," Antonio smiled. She stood there in a short, silky chemise, garters and stockings.

"A gift is a gift," Luisa said. "I wear them in good faith. Whether or not they fell off the truck. Besides, they're so comfortable."

On Luisa's nightstand, *The Devil's Dirt* sat. "Any good?" Antonio gestured.

"Yes," she paused. "It's about a crazy family...crazier than ours...and they're obsessed with getting rich and s-e-x," she spelled. "But a lot of it is in a Southern dialect, which I find hard to follow. And it uses words I don't like. 'Darkie,' for instance. And the Walton Family is horrible. Oh, and there's a character named Black Jim instead of just 'Jim'..." she gushed.

Luisa cut herself off. She realized that she could ramble on too long when asked about a book. But her passion for reading was a quality Antonio loved about

his wife, her passion for life in general. "Go on," he
encouraged Luisa, sitting on the edge of the bed
beside her.

"But there are other parts, like when Pluto watches
Sweet Sue bathing in the backyard, stark naked..." Luisa
grabbed the book and flipped through it, trying to locate
the right place. She read aloud,

> *"Sweet Sue did not even run from Pluto's prying eyes,
> nor did she attempt to shield her nakedness with the
> washrag or her long, graceful hands. She just stood over
> the chipped, red-rimmed basin, glaring at Pluto, silently
> daring him to...'"*

Suddenly, from the depths of the house came Gianni's
plaintive wail. "Mama! Papa! My zeppelin!" Until that
moment no one had realized that the boy had left his
prized SR-47 on the BMT until it was too late.

July 1940

The Tacoma Narrows Bridge opens in Washington State, making it the third longest suspension bridge in the world.

As America celebrates its independence, two New York City police detectives are killed by a blast while investigating a time bomb left in the British Pavilion at the World's Fair.

In the Battle of Cape Spada, Australia's HMAS Sydney *and five destroyers sink the Italian cruiser* Bartolomeo Colleoni.

I n the July heat, there was nothing better than sitting in a cool, dark movie theater to while away the long, hot, lazy hours. There was only so much stick ball, stoop ball, games of tag and skellies a child could play. The Alpine Theater offered shelter from the thunderstorms predicted that day. Luisa packed meatball sandwiches made from her Sunday sauce leftovers. Following a "discussion" with Antonio, she finally agreed to permit the children to go to the theater alone. Gloria had been campaigning to do so for months but this was the first time her mother relented.

"It's only a few blocks," Antonio pressed as his wife prepared the heroes.

"There are bomb threats every day," Luisa stressed. "Why, last month, there was an explosion at that commie newspaper office. And that very same day, a time bomb ripped apart the German consulate. Oh, and what about that bomb threat at the Brooklyn Bridge? And don't forget the World's Fair. Those poor officers were killed and three were horribly wounded. I just..."

When Luisa was on a roll, there was no way to stop her. Perhaps with a hug, Antonio hoped. On impulse, he took his wife into his arms from behind. "But that was three weeks ago and nothing since," he reminded Luisa, nibbling on her ear.

"Too close for comfort...in our very city," she agonized, pulling forward slightly to wrap the sandwiches in waxed paper. "Besides, the children are too young to go alone."

"Gloria is already twelve..."

"Yes, her birthday was the day after the bombing," Luisa snapped.

"And what were you doing at twelve, hmmm?" Antonio asked. "Practically running a household, correct?" Luisa sighed. "Let them have some fun, some independence. We can't keep them in a bubble, Lu. Besides, there's nothing your father could do if something were to..."

Antonio squeezed Luisa tighter as she placed the sandwiches into a paper sack. He felt his wife's strong will softening.

"You're right, of course," Luisa admitted. She took the fourth sandwich out of the sack and handed it to Antonio. "Enjoy your lunch."

"Made by your hand, I know I will." For emphasis, he kissed her open palm.

Gloria listened to this exchange in the hallway and gave a quiet yelp of elation. Finally, she and Siobhan could choose their own seats and not sit practically on top of the screen so Nonno could see it better. Even with Gianni in tow, they could feel like big kids. They could even sit in the balcony if they chose.

Andy Hardy Meets Debutante starred that dreamy Judy Garland alongside Mickey Rooney, and it took place in New York City. But not the New York City native New Yorkers knew. It was a cleaner, neater, Hollywood version of Manhattan. Before that sappy romance got underway, the children were treated to a *Flash Gordon* serial and a handful of cartoons, one starring a zany gray bunny who terrorizes a hunter with a severe speech impediment.

No one loved *A Wild Hare* more than Gianni who laughed and clapped throughout the seven minutes it ran. "That stupid hunter sounds just like Gio," Gloria whispered into Siobhan's ear. "Wabbit, Wabbit…" She leaned forward to tease her brother.

Siobhan laid a light hand on Gloria's shoulder to stop her. "Try not to be so mean to him," she suggested. "Just this once. For me."

For Siobhan, Gloria would do anything. "Sure. But why?"

"Just because." Gloria settled back into her seat. "Confidentially," Siobhan continued, "I think the rabbit sounds like my Uncle Gavin from the Bronx, don't you?"

"Now that you mention it…" Gloria laughed.

Gianni began to sniffle when the rabbit pretended to die, coughing and sputtering. Gloria handed out the meatball heroes at that precise moment because there was nothing she hated more than her brother's tears. He couldn't cry and eat at the same time, she reasoned. Their mom had given Gloria enough money to get a box of candy to share between them, which they would save until the feature began, no matter how much Gianni begged. Chocolate Babies were Siobhan's favorite so that's what Gloria chose. Because Siobhan liked them, the candies became Gloria's favorite too. Jujubes be damned. They stuck to your fillings anyhow.

It was a busy day at The Avid Reader. Their books were a source of refuge amid the world's instability. They provided a life preserver when British destroyers were being torpedoed by Italian submarines. They provided safe harbor at a time when ships of refugees were being sent away, only to return to European shores and the certainty of death camps. They provided sumptuous meals of Proust's "short, plump little cakes" and perfectly-roasted chicken with "gold-embroidered" skin when one was hungry. They provided the shelter of strong castle walls when bombs rained from Parisian skies.

Luisa and Valerie hosted summer kids' reading circles, which Luisa's own children begged off from attending this July day in favor of Andy Hardy. The reading group was working through Laura Ingalls Wilder's *Little House* series, which both boys and girls seemed to enjoy. Or maybe it was the home-baked cookies Luisa passed around which they may have enjoyed more. Who could say?

After the reading was over, Valerie snuck off to the bank. Giuseppe stopped by, hat in hand. "Where is Miss Valerie?" he wondered.

"She should be back soon," Luisa told him, ringing out a customer.

"Actually, it's you I came to see, *figlia mia,*" he said. Luisa liked when Giuseppe called her his daughter in Italian, as he had when she was a girl and he was a bone-tired bricklayer. The years had mellowed him. The decades of loss had tempered him. First, his daughter Beatrice, buried across the sea in Longobucco, and decades later, his wife Assunta, buried several bridges away in Queens.

Luisa pulled up two folding chairs—she hadn't yet stowed the ring of seats she and Valerie had arranged for the story circle. Luisa set the kettle on the hotplate in the back room and put out the cookies she'd managed to hide from the group: Chinese-style almond with a sliver of nut dimpling the center.

Her father's face was furrowed with seriousness, causing him to appear older than his sixty years. Maybe it was his seasons of hard labor, the toll of his injuries which led to his disability leave. Maybe it was more. Giuseppe took the tea mug in hand, blew into it softly. "Valerie says hot tea on a hot day can be very cooling," Luisa said.

Giuseppe smiled at the mention of Valerie. "Yes," he agreed. Then out of the blue, he remarked, "I'm afraid I wasn't the best husband to your mother."

Luisa was startled by the starkness of her father's words. She paused, searching for an appropriate response. "You were the best husband you could be at the time," she ventured. "And times were hard."

"Ah," he nodded.

"But I suppose we could all do better, no?"

"Not your mother," Giuseppe said. "Assunta was a saint."

"A saint who yelled a lot," Luisa conceded.

"De mortuis nil nisi bonum dicendum est,"
Giuseppe quoted.

Luisa was surprised to hear her father speaking Latin, a language of the church (which he didn't attend) and scholars (which he clearly was not). "Of the dead nothing but good is to be said," Luisa translated. "But still, mama did yell."

"I could have been a better father also," he said. "I drank too much, smoked too much and perhaps, didn't hug enough."

Luisa took one cookie into her hand, cracked it in two and gave her father the half with the bit of almond. He accepted it with a dip of his head. "You had so many mouths to feed and a lot of worry," Luisa told him.

"Besides, you're making up for it now. You're a wonderful *nonno*." She tacked on, "And father,"

They chewed their cookies in the quietness. "These are very good," he finally said. *"Molto bene."*

"Grazie," she said.

"Prego," he responded.

She shook her head. "Why so formal? So serious?"

"Lulu," he said, reverting to her childhood nickname which no one called her anymore. His expression was grim. "I've got something to tell you."

Was he sick? Was he in trouble? Did he… "Yes, papa, what is it?" Luisa gulped.

He took a deep breath then spoke. "Miss Valerie and I…we've been keeping company."

Luisa burst out laughing, relieved.

"What's so funny?"

She laughed so hard tears streaked her cheeks. Then Luisa snorted. Her friend Maureen called it "the snort of sincerity," when you guffawed so heartily you grunted like a piglet. "Oh, Papa," Luisa stammered. "It's just that… that…it's no secret. Everyone knows about you and Val. Why, even a child could see it."

"And to you, this is funny?"

Luisa willed herself to stop chuckling, but it was no use. Titters snuck out from between her teeth. "Yes… no…but…if you could only see your face. You look like you're on the way to Death Row."

"In some ways, I feel like I am," Guiseppi said. "I can't eat, can't sleep…"

Luisa rested her hand on his arm. "Papa, you're in love!"

"Bah!" he shook off her hand then took a thoughtful drink of tea.

"I'm so happy for you."

"Ridicolo! I'm an old man and she is…"

"…wonderful," Luisa finished for him.

"Terribile," he corrected.

She leaned forward. "Tell me, what's so terrible about being in love?"

Giuseppe considered this for a moment. He took a pensive bite of cookie, chewed, then swallowed. "Well, your mother..."

"My mother died eight years ago," Luisa reminded him gently. Out of the corner of her eye, she noticed Valerie outside the door, ready to enter the shop. But when Val saw father and daughter engulfed in earnest conversation, she walked on.

"*Si, ma...*" Giuseppe began.

"Yes, but nothing..." There was silence, then, "My mama, she's not coming back. And you deserve to be happy. It's exactly what I told Valerie."

"So, she told you?" Giuseppe set down the mug.

Luisa nodded. "Months ago." She grasped both of his hands and realized how rare it was that the two of them touched. Giuseppe's skin was rough from years of bathing in cement and bearing chisels. Rough but agreeable to the touch. "I'm glad for you. For the two of you." Giuseppe didn't seem entirely convinced. "Mama liked Miss Valerie, and vice versa. I think Mama would want you to be happy."

"*Va bene,*" he smiled.

"*Va bene,*" Luisa agreed. "It's good."

At first, Antonio balked when Charles suggested they install a few speakers in the workroom. "Playing music will keep up morale," he explained. It was difficult to hear the serials or the news because of the sewing machines' clatter so these were rarely, if ever, played. On Fridays, a different individual got to choose the radio station they dialed up. Some favored jazz programs, others popular Tin Pan Alley tunes while still others chose classical music. Of course, Antonio played opera. It was a pleasant backdrop to the repetitive work.

The July swelter gave the room a languid feel as Scarpia made his lurid Act Two proposition to the beautiful, virtuous Tosca. In song, she prays, asking God why he has abandoned her in her hour of need, singing, *"Vissi d'arte! Vissi d'amore!"* As the heroine explains that she lived for art and love, Antonio's seamstress Daria interrupted his favorite aria with a grave look on her face. *"Scusi,"* she said with a bow. *"Ma, il Signor Inzitari é qui."*

Antonio could feel the entire mood of the factory floor change. All ears shifted from Tosca's troubles to their boss's pending encounter with Mario Inzitari. There was always a seemingly insurmountable problem, an unreasonable request that somehow had to be met. An impossible deadline, an entreaty which tap-danced on the edge of legality. The workers heard much but said nothing.

Waiting in Antonio's glass-fronted office was Mr. Inzitari. He always seemed impatient, in a bad humor, even when he smiled. Instead of looking friendly when he forced a grin, Mario Inzitari seemed more menacing. Antonio took a deep breath. What could the distasteful man possibly want now?

After brisk handshakes, he got right down to business. "Tony," Mr. Inzitari barked, "I'm wondering if you could do me a favor."

For this man, "wondering" meant "demanding." Antonio braced himself. "I'll do my best," he said.

"That's what I like about you, Tony. You always do your best."

No one called him "Tony," but Antonio wasn't about to correct the powerful mafioso. "What is it?" he wondered.

"Next month, I have a shipment coming in," Mr. Inzitari began. "I'd like you to...hold it for me."

"And what is the nature of this shipment, Mr. Inzitari? Olive oil?"

"I'm not at liberty to say. And do me a favor, call me 'Mario.'"

"Mario…" Antonio said, then faltered. The name felt acrid like battery acid on his tongue.

Mr. Inzitari put his hand on Antonio's forearm, squeezed harder than was necessary. "Look," he told the tailor. "You don't have to give me an answer right now. Mull it over. Chew on it for a while. I'll be back."

But for men like Mario Inzitari, there was only one answer. And Antonio wasn't prepared to give it.

August 1940

The armed British merchant cruiser **HMS** Transylvania *is torpedoed off the coast of Ireland by a German submarine.*

Russian revolutionary Leon Trotsky is assassinated in his Mexico home after being attacked with an ice axe.

Film stars Laurence Olivier and Vivien Leigh are married at the San Ysidro Ranch in California.

The kitchen table was spread with maps, books splayed open on their bellies and a palm-sized Italian phrase book. There was barely enough room for their coffee cups. In fact, Giuseppe and Valerie had to hold their cake plates in their laps. The dishes held generous slabs of Cookie Hinton's Irish soda bread slathered with butter. "Do you really think we could do it?" Valerie burbled.

"Move to Italy? *Certamente!*" Giuseppe told her. "Why not?"

"Well, there's the war...a *world* war and..." she pointed out. Valerie rose to get the percolator so she could top off their mugs. Since she'd began keeping company with Giuseppe, Valerie had begun to appreciate the virtues of robust Italian coffee and he, the subtle pleasure of fine Irish breakfast tea.

"Wars end. They always do," he reminded her.

"But this one…" she said and poured the hot, earthy espresso almost to the brim then returned the pot to the stovetop.

"What else is worrying you, *caro mio*?" Giuseppe wondered.

Valerie took a deep sip of coffee, burning her lips, her throat. "It's nothing. I…it's just that…we're old."

Giuseppe considered her words, weighed their heft in his mind. "Me, at sixty, yes. But you, you're barely fifty." This had no effect whatsoever on Valerie. Not even a smile flickered on her lips, so her beau tried a different tactic. "True," he began. "We're older than most but still, we're younger than some. We're not too old to have fun, though. Eh?" Giuseppe took a bite of soda bread, the perfect blend of flaky and sweet.

"No, but…"

Valerie's beloved took both of her hands in his. "For now, we can just chart it all out, huh? Collect more brochures. Make plans. Take notes." He held a ringed composition book for emphasis. "And in the meantime, you learn Italian. *Va bene*?"

"*È più che buono*," Valerie announced. To which her silver-haired honey chuckled. "Did I say something wrong, Joe?"

"No, you're absolutely right. It's better than good," Giuseppe agreed.

They felt a small gladness that each no longer thought was possible. Not for them, not anymore. The pair were silent for a time, taking sips of their strong, dark coffee, quietly rejoicing in contentedness.

Giuseppe fished the hard-covered phrase book from the pile. Threads peeked through the red cloth binding. Stamped onto the green cover were the words "Learn to Speak Italian." He told her, "I know it will help. *Pronta?*"

"Yes," Valerie told him. "Yes, I'm ready."
They began.

In the dog days of summer, Gloria and Luisa took the same pilgrimage every August: to purchase a uniform for the coming school year. This time, they went to a new store called Robert Hall Clothes. It lacked the opulence of Macy's or Abraham & Straus downtown, but since it was perched on the edge of Bay Ridge, Luisa didn't have to take off more than a couple of hours from work to shop there. These days, she was putting in longer hours at The Avid Reader, for which she was glad, because Chatonio's had seen better days.

With Gianni in tow, Luisa and Gloria walked along Third Avenue to Eighty-Sixth Street then took the seven long blocks to Battery Avenue. Gianni complained nearly every step until he was promised a slice at Paulie's if he behaved.

The little one was starting kindergarten at St. Anselm's next month and needed a proper uniform—gray slacks, white button-down shirt and a crisscross plaid tie secured with a pearl snap. Gloria, who was entering seventh grade, had graduated from a plaid jumper into a plaid, pleated skirt, blue vest, white blouse and tie. How she hated that pinchy white collar which the nuns made students button to the neck.

"Where's Gio?" Luisa asked as she flipped through the starched blouses, searching for Gloria's size.

"Shush," the girl told her mother. "If he's lost, at least we'll have some peace."

"Gloria!"

She nudged Luisa, pointing to her brother, who was crouched in the middle of a circular rack that held girdles, hiding. "He's not lost," Gloria whispered. "But he thinks he's invisible."

"We'll play along," Luisa agreed.

They put a blouse into their shopping cart then headed for the skirts. "If this fits then we'll get a few more," Luisa said.

"Can't Papa just make them?"

"Sister Gertrude Ramilda says they must be regulation. She wants you girls to look the same," Luisa explained.

"But we're not," Gloria protested. "We're not the same at all."

"I know."

"Those nuns don't know a thing about real life," the girl sighed.

Luisa slid the blue plaid skirts on the rack until she came to one or two that might do. "Don't forget, nuns were girls once too."

"Mean girls," Gloria scowled. "Mean girls who hit kids with rulers."

Ignoring her, Luisa suggested, "Let's try these on. Your invisible brother should be okay out here for a bit."

Instead of private curtained changing areas, Robert Hall had a communal dressing room where ladies and girls had to strip down to their unmentionables in each other's presence. Luisa saw her daughter's face pinken as she slipped out of her pedal pushers. With her body, Luisa tried to shield Gloria from the two other women in the far corner of the changing room. "I don't know why we can't wear trousers," Gloria moaned. "Skirts are so icky."

Luisa sighed. First, Gianni's whining, now Gloria's bellyaching. She gathered the extra skirt fabric in her fingers. "Almost perfect. I can take it in at the waist a smidge."

"Why is it so long? And itchy?"

It was easy to ignore such a cranky puss. "Now, the top," Luisa said.

Obediently, Gloria pulled off her peasant blouse. Luisa noticed that her child's breasts were budding beneath her eyelet lace-trimmed cotton undershirt. She helped Gloria button the blouse. When she got to the top button, Gloria dramatically feigned choking. "You're a real Bette Davis," Luisa told her daughter. Then, "This one will do."

As Gloria dressed, Luisa asked in a low voice so no one else could hear, "Is everything all right? You seem so out of sorts lately." To which Gloria simply shrugged. "I'll tell you what," Luisa proposed. "Let's go to the underwear section and get you some brassieres. How does that sound?"

"Real ones? With hooks?"

"Of course, real ones. And maybe even some silky knickers."

Gloria was beside herself with bliss. After she hugged Luisa, they embarked upon their next mission, walking with purpose toward Ladies' Lingerie. Gianni crept from rack to rack, shadowing them.

The sprawling, boxy store had no ambiance, but what Robert Hall did have was a sizable, reasonably-priced selection. The floor girl figured out Gloria's size with the help of a frayed cloth measuring tape. The 32 AA's were arranged within the basket of packaged Young Miss brassieres. They chose a couple of dressy underpants from a rack of grown-up bloomers nearby.

Before they left Intimates, Luisa suggested, "How about Siobhan? I doubt she has undershirts, let alone a bra." Gloria was dumbfounded at her mother's generosity. "I'd say she's a size or two below you, mmm?" Luisa grabbed another bra for Siobhan.

Again, Gloria flung herself into her mother's arms, this time hugging her longer, harder. "Thank you, mama," she murmured into Luisa's full chest.

"*Di niente, tesoro.* It's nothing, honey," Luisa told her, patting her head. "Come, now let's shop for Gianni."

Luisa needed Gloria's help wrangling the boy into the dressing room. It was like fitting a wriggly worm into slacks and a shirt, let alone a necktie, but together, they managed the frustrating feat. When they were done, Gianni bolted toward a revolving display of pocketbooks with a warning not to spin them too fast by the floor girl.

It seemed that half of Bay Ridge was shopping for school clothes that day. Luisa and Gloria stood in Robert Hall's long checkout line. As they waited, they discussed what they might have for lunch. Eating out, even pizza, as Luisa had promised Gianni, was a splurge. She and Gloria talked of things large and small, from the impending war to the coming school year. "I think Bryan Ciri is sweet on you," Luisa ventured.

To which Gloria gave a monumental eyeroll. "He's all right, I guess. If you like the type," the girl conceded.

"Why, I think he'd make a nice boyfriend, a fine husband, even," Luisa said. "He's handsome, smart, kind...and those eyes." (Bryan was of dark, Italian stock but had indigo eyes.)

Gloria took a deep breath as the line crept forward. "Mama, I don't think I want to get married."

"Why not?"

"I just don't like boys."

"That will change, *bella*. You'll see."

"I don't think so, mama. Not for me."

Luisa contemplated this for a moment as she fumbled for her change purse. They were next in line. She looked at Gloria who was looking at her, waiting for the impact of her words, for the heft of her admission, to sink in. "Ah," Luisa said. "Ah." She leaned in closer. "So, you're telling me that you like girls?"

Gloria bit her lower lip then admitted, "Not girls. Just one particular girl."

"Next!" the woman behind the cash register called. They pushed the shopping cart forward.

"Ah," Luisa told her daughter as they unpacked the cart's contents onto the counter. "*Va bene*. I like her too."

The grand total was more than Luisa had prepared for, but she'd put aside extra money from her bookshop salary to pay for school clothes. She peeled off the dollars from the modest roll in her purse, feeling the weight of each one.

As "Mindy" bagged their order, they heard a crash then a security guard's voice. "Who belongs to this one?" he barked, holding Gianni by the collar. The carousel of purses lay on the ground beside them. Luisa apologized as she and Gloria helped right the rack and restock the pocketbooks.

In the end, there would still be pizza at Paulie's. And maybe even a Coca-Cola in a waxed cup to share. For even bad boys had to eat.

Antonio had been expecting Mario Inzitari's visit all month. Whenever the shop's door opened, he anticipated seeing his strapping henchman's frame blocking the sunlight, soon to be followed by Inzitari himself. But thankfully, it hadn't happened yet. Perhaps Antonio was safe. August had almost melted into September and there was no sign of the heavies.

Then one day, as "Ride of the Valkyries" filled the stifling factory floor, it occurred. Antonio was on one knee, pinning the hem of a black taffeta gown when the corner of his vision darkened. Raquel, who was serving as his model, gasped audibly when she caught sight of the suited pair. Antonio felt her body stiffen beneath the thick folds of cloth. Everyone dreaded the racketeer's visits.

"You can go now," Antonio told Raquel, lightly tapping her calf to show the urgency of his request. She gathered her skirts as she stepped off the fitting platform. "And mind the pins, Raquel," he cautioned. "I don't want you to get hurt."

"Si, signore," she said, "I'll be careful," and bustled off.

Instead of retreating into Antonio's clear-walled office, which offered little privacy, Rocco hustled him through the nearest door, a storage room filled with bolts and rolls of cloth in every imaginable texture and shade. Rocco shut the door with a thud after his boss entered. Beyond the door, Chatonio's workers tried to focus on their tasks, concerned for their beloved *capo.*

Antonio pulled himself to his full height, but he barely came to Rocco's shoulder. His suit was of a cheap fabric, Antonio noted, poorly crafted, and not by him. "So," Mr. Inzitari began, "have you given any thought to my proposition?"

"Si, signore," Antonio responded. "I've given it a great deal of thought."

"And..." Mr. Inzitari said eagerly. He gave the impression that he was a very busy man with many places to go and many people to see.

Antonio hesitated. "Well, since you haven't told me what I'd be storing here, my answer would have to be 'no.'"

Mr. Inzitari pulled back, registering his surprise, as though he'd been lightly pushed. "No?" he yipped incredulously.

"That's right," Antonio nodded, then continued, "I'm sure you understand. I don't know if I'd be holding contraband or a substance that's dangerous to my workers. I have their safety to consider."

"And what about your own safety?" Rocco broke in.

"Pardon?"

Mr. Inzitari stepped closer to Antonio, the tips of their shoes almost touching. "What Rocco means is nobody says 'no' to me. Ever."

"I'm sorry but I can't..."

"How about all the stuff I gave you? The stockings? The tickets?"

Antonio cleared his throat. His mouth was bone dry. "I assumed they were to show your appreciation. Gratuities, if you will."

"I paid you good money," Mr. Inzitari reminded Antonio, his voice rising slightly with each word.

"Yes. And I gave you good work. Often at a moment's notice."

"I know what you gave me!" Mr. Inzitari said through gritted teeth. Then he took a deep breath in a futile attempt to calm himself. "Look, I think you're making a big mistake."

"Perhaps," Antonio admitted. "But I've made my decision." In a bold gesture, the tailor opened the door. "Thank you for understanding."

"Oh, I think it's you who don't understand," Mr. Inzitari fumed. "Maybe you don't realize who I am."

"I know exactly who you are, sir," Antonio told him. "A loyal customer, which I appreciate. But this, I cannot do."

The racketeer stalked off without another word, Rocco in his wake. Still in the doorway, the giant turned. "I'd watch my back if I were you," Rocco said, poking his branchlike finger into Antonio's chest. "We know where you live. We know where your kids go to school, where your wife works. Accidents happen all the time. Remember that, Tony."

How could Antonio possibly forget?

September 1940

Nazi Germany begins the Blitz, raining bombs on London for fifty-seven consecutive nights.

A group of young men hiking through Southern France discover seventeen-thousand-year-old cave paintings near Lascaux.

The Selective Training and Service Act of 1940 is signed into law by President Franklin Delano Roosevelt, creating the first peacetime draft in United States history.

Summer was taking its last stand. The mercury promised to crawl into the eighties. The three Tozzi sisters were on the telephone early that morning, planning a last-minute barbecue. Since most shops were closed on Sundays, they pooled their resources and planned the menu with what they had on hand.

Mina said that Papa had just bought a mess of greens the day before plus they had a sack of tomatoes from Mr. Pannullo's garden. Barbara had a couple of pounds of chopped meat intended for meatballs and a gravy, but her husband Kirk would mold them into hamburgers instead. She also had a couple of heads of broccoli which would be steamed and tossed in lemon and olive oil, then seasoned with cloves of fresh, peeled garlic. Combined with Luisa's sausages and head of cabbage (which would magically become cole slaw), they would have a feast. Val could whip up a banana cream pie in no time. They'd send Papa to the Golden Loaf for rolls and they'd be set.

Luisa helped Antonio carry the folding table up the basement steps. "What about Franco, Rosa and Teo? Maybe Zia Claudia is also free," Luisa suggested.

"Let's keep it small," Antonio told her. "But then again, there's no such thing as small when you've got five brothers and sisters."

Luisa smirked. "That's true. So, what's a few more?"

"How about we limit it to as many as can comfortably fit around this table?" he said, snapping the legs into place. It sounded reasonable to Luisa.

The guests began drifting in at two o'clock, handful by handful. When Antonio opened the front door to admit the first bunch, he noticed a large, black Packard idling several doors down. Mr. Inzitari's. Antonio felt a chill in the warm afternoon. Before he closed the door, the Packard sped off.

Antonio tried to focus on manning the charcoal grill, but his mind was elsewhere. He charred two sausages beyond recognition but managed to salvage the rest. His brothers-in-law were embroiled in a passionate exchange, as was their custom.

"I don't see how FDR expects to be voted in for a third term by bringing back the draft," Dom said, a moist cigar stub indenting his lower lip.

"He didn't have much choice, did he?" Sam countered. No matter what the subject, Sam felt the need to challenge his younger brother. Kirk, their brother-in-law (Barbara's husband of less than a year), had the sense to stay out of it. As did Giuseppe and Valerie. Letting the heated talk peter out on its own was a sensible choice.

"I mean, we're not even at war," Dom pointed out.

"Yet," Paolo added. Still in high school, the feisty teenager was looking for any excuse to get off the back step of Eagle Warehouse's delivery truck.

"That's right, you're just itching to kick Nazi butt," Sam laughed.

"I want to defend my country if it comes to that," Paolo said. "With what they're doing to the Jews in Europe, opening all those death camps, and not to mention, bombing London every night for..."

"Silencio, idioti!" Luisa reprimanded them, carrying a platter of sausage from the grill. "The children!"

"Are the Nazis coming here, mama?" Gianni worried, his voice trembling.

"No, *figlio mio,*" Luisa cooed to her son.

"At least not yet," Dom told him.

"And if the Krauts do come, your Uncle Paolo will kick their *culos*, so don't be scared, Gio," Sam said. This prompted a high-pitched scream from Gianni, because like his mother, he was a worrier.

Luisa sighed, "Look what you did! Again!"

Barbara put the tomato salad on the table beside the sausage, cole slaw and green salad that was simply dressed with olive oil and red wine vinegar. "They're the same as they were when they were kids. Frick and Frack. Always causing trouble."

"Mangiare," Luisa said. "Don't let the meat get cold."

"You sound like Mama," Dom teased.

"And you sound like a ten-year-old," Luisa told him, stabbing a sausage with vigor. "Hot or sweet?" She fixed Antonio a plate so he could have a bite while he flipped burgers. *"Mangia, amore mio,"* she said, setting the dish on the table beside him.

Antonio managed a couple of forkfuls of Mina's tomato salad before the vinegar turned to acid in his gut. He hadn't been able to eat lately. Since his storage-room meeting with Mr. Inzitari, Antonio's stomach had been in knots. He kept expecting to see Rocco appear at the most inopportune moments. For instance, when he was walking hand in hand with Gianni to Hinsch's or taking Gloria and Siobhan to Hoffman's for malteds. But even Antonio's abject fear didn't make him doubt that he'd made the right decision refusing the mobster's dubious proposition.

Although the apprehension gnawed at him like a rodent, Antonio was unable to eat more than a few mouthfuls before feeling queasy. He had lost weight. Luisa even noticed that Antonio's belt buckle was pulled one notch tighter.

"How many cheeseburgers?" he called out to his backyard guests. Luisa had left sliced American cheese on the prepping table beside him. One by one, Antonio flipped the burgers then topped half with American. He cooked them long enough to melt the cheese. One minute, no more. Antonio clocked the time with his pocket watch, cradling it in his palm. Yellow goo oozed from one patty onto the coals and hissed. They were ready.

Antonio was slipping the first patty onto a browned bun when a brick came flying into the backyard. The burger fell to the grass as the brick smashed into a window on the garden shed, shattering it with a loud crash. Everyone jumped in surprise. Gianni began to snuffle. "*Madonna mia,*" Luisa gasped, clutching her heart.

Sam and Dom were up in a flash, Paolo close behind. They tore down the alley after a quickly retreating figure. "Hey, *stronzo!*" Dom yelled. "We got women and kids back here!"

The slim, sneakered figure was no match for the two older Tozzi Brothers who had packed on the pounds from their wives' excellent cooking. They quickly gave up chase. However, Paolo continued pursuit, grabbing hold of the attacker's t-shirt and tugging as hard as he could. It ripped down the back as the kid hopped a fence and disappeared into a neighbor's areaway.

"And don't come back, you rat bastard!" Paolo shouted.

By the time the brothers returned to the DeMarco backyard, Gianni had been placated with a cheeseburger and the patty that had fallen to the ground had been whisked into the trash bin. Dom grasped the brick in his fist. Stamped onto its face was TERRY, indicating the factory on the Hudson River where it had been fired. "Who would do such a thing?" Barbara wondered.

Antonio and Luisa exchanged uneasy glances; they knew.

The family continued eating, gathered around the folding table. Their conversation flittered like late-season moths, from one topic to another. Giuseppe told them how he yearned to return to Italy one day. Valerie shared memories of childhood summers in Ireland. Dom and Sam thrilled the crew with tales of their boyish exploits, sneaking onto the Fort Hamilton army base and running amok—much to the horror of their father, wives and sisters. However, Paolo, Gianni and Valerie considered their shenanigans spectacular.

"Fredo asked me to watch the submarine races at Plumb Beach with him," Mina said thoughtlessly as she cleared the salad bowls. "I think I might go."

"*Testa de ferro!*" Paolo called her.

"In English," Gianni protested. He hated when he didn't understand these colorful Italian insults that flew across the table.

"I am not a knucklehead," Mina told her brother with a soft shove.

"Ow!" Paolo complained. "Think about it… submarine races…"

"Yeah, so what? Admit it, you just don't like Fredo Cavallo."

"That's beside the point," Paolo insisted. "He's a chooch."

Their brother-in-law Kirk tried to smooth over the situation. "As for the submarine races…" he explained. "Where do they travel? *Under* the water. Right?"

"Oh, yeah," Mina conceded. "So, you can't really see them…"

"Fredo Cavallo is just trying to get into your bloomers," Dom chimed in.

"Dominic!" his wife gasped. "Little children have big ears!"

"Ha! Uncle Dom said bloomers!" Gianni chuckled. So did Dom's little one.

Luisa shook her head. It was no use trying to tame these monkeys; they had taken over the zoo.

By the time dessert was laid out, it had grown dark and citronella candles were lit. Antonio was concerned that more mischief might transpire after night fell. Perhaps a pack of lit firecrackers might be tossed into the yard, but thankfully, all was tranquil. Only the crickets made comment.

Luisa noticed that any time a book concerning Italy came into The Avid Reader, Valerie snatched it up and took it home with her. It usually appeared on the shelves days later. "You reading all of these?" Luisa finally asked one day.

"Yes, why?" her friend wondered.

"No reason," Luisa told Valerie, putting *The Bay of Naples* back onto the shelf.

"I'm fascinated with the place Joe is from," Valerie explained.

"Longobucco is very different than Napoli."

"Yes, I know," Valerie qualified. "But it gives me a sense of the country, the culture. This is an excellent book, by the way. It's about a British woman's travels through Naples. The illustrations are lovely."

Luisa glanced at the plain brown book's spine. "By *Mrs.* Steuart Erskine. Doesn't she have her own name?" Luisa harumphed.

"It was published in 1926. People weren't so modern back then," Valerie conceded. "Besides, letters to you are addressed to 'Mrs. Antonio DeMarco,' are they not?"

Luisa permitted a tiny nod. She loved verbal a "touché" with her boss. "True, but if I ever write a book, it would be under my own name."

"Well, Luisa Tozzi DeMarco, perhaps you should." Valerie smiled, reveling in the challenging conversation as much as her employee and friend did. "You seem to have a lot to say!"

"I do. Maybe I will write that book someday."

Luisa turned to direct a customer to the consignment table where they displayed the work of ladies from their knitting circle. Mrs. Freglette was interested in purchasing a baby bonnet and maybe a pair of booties. The consignment table, another Luisa brainstorm, was almost as popular as the lending library. "Her name was Beatrice," Valerie whispered into Luisa's ear as the customer browsed the knitted wares.

"Hmmm?"

"Mrs. Steuart Erskine's given name was Beatrice, like your older sister, God rest her soul," Valerie said with a dip of her head, just as Catholics did when they uttered the name "Jesus." Yes, Valerie, who was raised a Protestant, had been attending Sunday mass at St. Anselm's.

Luisa sucked in her lower lip at the mention of her older sister, the child left behind in Longobucco when Luisa was just a babe in arms. "Beatrice Caroline Erskine. That's the writer of the Naples book's full name. Now, isn't it a swell name?"

"It does have a nice ring to it," Luisa admitted.

"Beatrice also wrote plays, novels and poetry. She was born in London, the daughter of a reverend. So, you see, there's hope for any of us to become writers, don't you think?"

Luisa valued her friend's sunny attitude, which had become even sunnier since she began keeping company with Giuseppe. And he, in turn, seemed happier as well.

"Are you a writer?" the customer asked Luisa as she wrapped the baby's hat the woman had selected.

"Not yet," Luisa blushed.

"But you never know," Valerie told the customer. "Our Luisa is full of surprises."

School was difficult to get used to after the freedom of summer. Spending time at the bookstore, at the beach...Gloria didn't know which she liked best. At The Avid Reader, she got to read to little kids who were so cute and excited. Plus, ZiaVal insisted the children call Gloria "Miss Gloria." ZiaVal even snuck her a few nickels for her efforts when Luisa wasn't looking.

But at Brighton Beach, Gloria could slather suntan lotion on Siobhan's soft, peaches-and-cream skin and no one thought anything of it. They could lie beside each other on an old bed sheet in the sand, hold hands in a divot they dug between them and no one was the wiser. They could scream and jump in the surf, falling into one another's arms and no one considered it odd.

Plus, this past summer, she and Siobhan were even permitted to go to the beach by themselves. At Thirty-Sixth Street, they'd take the West End Line to the Brighton Beach stop. Then they'd walk the half block to the long stretch of sand. They could pick their own spot and stay as long as they liked. If they had enough money between them, they'd buy a knish to share at Mrs. Stahl's shop kitty-cornered beneath the elevated tracks.

But by fall, for some reason, Papa was nervous about Gloria going anywhere on her own. It seemed he was always looking over his shoulder. Gloria didn't know why but her new-found freedom was taken away.

This seemed to coincide with the brick being thrown into their backyard.

During Catechism at St. Anselm's, Sister Gertrude Ramilda spouted rot regarding the evils of this or that, especially the sin of "illicit behavior." Gloria never pinpointed exactly what illicit behavior was, but the nun seemed to be staring directly at Gloria whenever she said it.

"No," Siobhan insisted. "I think she looks right at *me* when she says it." The meanest nun at St. Anselm's could make them feel as though she were staring into the depths of their souls, uncovering their deepest, darkest, dirtiest secrets.

Sister Gertrude Ramilda was partial to bellowing from the Book of Leviticus. Those crusty, old Levites were hopping mad and made rules for practically everything, especially s-e-x.

"Thou shalt not lie with a man as with a woman; it is an abomination."

Verses later, Leviticus goes into gory detail:

"They shall surely be put to death; their blood is upon them."

Walking home from school that day, Siobhan shivered, "Moses sure yapped a lot about laying down with people."

"And how," Gloria agreed. "His brother Aaron too."

"What's an abomination?" Siobhan asked.

"It isn't good."

Several days later, Sister GR paraphrased St. Paul from Romans:

"Homosexuality is contrary to God's natural order and results from rejecting God."

The heavy, hirsute nun became red in the face when she proclaimed this tidbit. To hammer in her message, she included her own summation: "Homosexuality is one of the multitude of sins that will prevent you from entering the kingdom of heaven...along with the sins of self-gratification and gluttony."

Upon hearing this, the boys gasped. Howard Simon sniffled. As if that weren't damning enough, Sister Gertrude Ramilda tagged on, "And nose-picking."

The conversation on Gloria and Siobhan's walks home became deeper and more serious after one of the nun's diatribes. "She's only talking about men with men, right?" Gloria worried.

"I think so," Siobhan said. "I hope so."

Sister Gertrude Ramilda's diatribes were the main reason school had become so troublesome for Gloria. But she couldn't mention this fear of burning in hell because of her feelings for Siobhan to anyone. Not to Father Kent on Saturdays behind the safety of the confessional's grill, bathed in incense smoke. She couldn't even voice her concerns to her mother, though Gloria had hinted at it that day shopping at Robert Hall.

Although Gloria did come close to confessing it one night as Luisa peeled carrots at the table and Gloria did her homework a foot away. Her mother was dear and sweet and innocent—when she wasn't being annoying. But maybe Gloria was the one who was annoying, angry and scared and confused at what the sisters at St. Anselm's had told her. She liked the idea of going to PS 104 better; no nuns. But her parents wouldn't let her switch to public school, and that was that.

"Glorina," Luisa began, using one of her many pet names. "Do you remember me telling you about that little journal my fourth-grade teacher gave me?"

Gloria looked up; that certainly came out of the blue. "Mrs. Fitzpatrick. Of course. How come?"

"No reason. I was just thinking about it."

"What happened to that book?" Gloria asked.

Luisa shrugged. "I don't know. I guess I lost it somewhere along the way." A beat, and a carrot, later. Luisa wondered. "Do you have a book like that?"

"A diary? Of course. It's almost full."

Luisa was impressed. "Ah. What do you write?"

Gloria shrugged. "Things I'm thinking about. Things I'm scared of. Private things. Things I can't say to anyone else. I don't know. Just things."

"You know you can tell me anything, don't you?" Luisa told her.

"Yes, I know," Gloria said. "But some things are...too personal."

"*Vedo, vedo*. I see," Luisa nodded. Then she chopped the carrots into golden medallions.

At that moment, Gloria knew exactly what she would get her mother for Christmas.

Antonio told the police officer that he had tripped on an uneven part of the pavement. Passersby swore that the unassuming man in the well-cut suit had been pushed, tripped, then kicked by two men walking in opposite directions. But Antonio politely said this wasn't so, that these supposed witnesses were mistaken. He said that he was tired from working all day and had taken a bad step on the irregular sidewalk. The cops, both of whom knew Luisa's brother Serafino, checked the condition of the pavement. It was smooth and unmarred.

Antonio refused an ambulance to Victory Memorial Hospital, instead permitting the policemen to drive him to Dr. Lewy's office, where the physician cleaned his cuts, palpated his bruised ribs and reset his broken nose with his fingers. It smarted so much that tears streaked

Antonio's cheeks. Dr. Lewy, Antonio surmised, didn't believe his story either.

Neither did Luisa, as she took his bloodied shirt from his hands and soaked it in bleach. Luisa cried as she wrung out the shirt in the sink and soaked it some more. She cried because she knew exactly what had happened to Antonio. She cried because she was afraid. For all of them.

October 1940

A section of the Pennsylvania Turnpike, the country's first long-distance, controlled-access highway, opens.

Carmen Miranda makes her American film debut in Down Argentine Way *while Charlie Chaplin's satirical, anti-fascist comedy* The Great Dictator *debuts in New York City.*

The Warsaw Ghetto is established in Poland, Italian troops invade Greece and 32 Allied ships are sunk.

"Pipe dreams," Valerie told Giuseppe when he suggested they sell their Brooklyn homes and move upstate New York. Their plans to relocate to Italy were temporarily on hold due to the war. "But wars don't last forever," Giuseppe told her with a dreamy grin.

"Neither do we," she reminded him.

Giuseppe ignored Valerie's fears. "Which is why we should do it sooner rather than later, *bella.*"

"Could you leave your children? Your grandchildren?" Valerie posed.

"They'll come visit," he said. "Could you leave the shop?"

"I could," she nodded, then smiled. "Joe, I have an idea."

"I have one too," Giuseppe confessed. In the middle of Valerie's kitchen, he struggled onto one knee, leaving her speechless as he rooted through his suit jacket pocket. Out of it, he drew a square blue box embossed with gold around the edges. Giuseppe opened the box, revealing an emerald bracketed by a tiny diamond on either side. He chose that particular ring because it reminded him of Val's eyes. "Valeria," Giuseppe began. "Will you do me the honor of becoming my wife?"

"Yes," she gasped. "Oh, yes. Yes." Giuseppe slipped the ring onto her finger, over her arthritic knuckle, a perfect fit. His friend Mike, who had a modest booth in the Diamond Exchange on Forty-Seventh Street, had helped him choose the small but flawless stones, then took him to Evelyn of Milson's Findings to pick the perfect setting. True love, and at wholesale prices.

"I'll make you my bride," Giuseppe said. "Then we can run away upstate. There's a town near Kingston called Stone Ridge that I like very much. I think you will too."

The next morning, Valerie and Giuseppe stole off to City Hall to exchange their wedding vows, telling no one. Luisa didn't think it strange when her boss asked her to open the bookstore the following day. Val did this when she wanted to sleep in or run errands. Although Luisa did become suspicious when Valerie said she would be gone for a few days. "Gone? Gone where?" Luisa pushed.

"On an adventure," Val smirked like a little girl with a big secret. "Don't worry, you'll do fine without me." Then she disappeared out the front door. Luisa hadn't even noticed the emerald on her finger or the simple wedding band.

Then, when Giuseppe told Luisa he was going to visit his friend Enrico in Port Chester for a few days. Luisa's curiosity grew but she said nothing.

Valerie packed a satchel and tossed it beside his suitcase in the back seat of Giuseppe's Ford Deluxe. Together, they stole off like Hansel and Gretel into the woods. Their honeymoon trip took them to the Elm Rock Inn, a charming brick saltbox nestled among the trees. The room was appointed with a four-poster bed that had a lace canopy and a fireplace which they didn't use. Pausing only to drop off their bags, they met with Maureen Collins, a jovial realtor with a British accent who was more than happy to show them the former lock tender's cottage with a creek rushing behind it.

The garden was magnificent, doted upon by Shoshana, the previous owner. Bright pink coneflowers, bluish-purple Russian sage, sunflowers, a rainbow of asters and chrysanthemums. The cottage itself needed a bit of work, TLC, mostly. But Valerie's former bricklayer husband pronounced that the place had good bones. Giuseppe was more than able to do the work it needed himself with a little help from his sons, if they were willing.

Valerie was speechless, marveling at how Giuseppe had spotted the ad for the cottage tucked in the back of the *Brooklyn Daily Eagle*, inquired about the home and corresponded with the realtor by mail over the space of several weeks, unbeknownst to anyone. Valerie was even more speechless when Giuseppe handed Miss Collins the downpayment for the cottage, in cash, first checking with his bride to see if this was all right. "Yes," Valerie stammered. "Yes, it is more than all right with me."

The cottage boasted five creekside acres and there was a farm across the way. It was so close, you could hear the cows lowing. Valerie pictured their grandchildren (yes, they were *her* grandchildren too now!) wading among the slick river rocks and climbing the gnarled apple trees that grew beside the cottage to pick ripe fruit. She imagined cooking with Luisa in the spacious country kitchen and serving meals to their large, bustling family in the adjoining dining room. Autumn sunlight streamed in through the house's plentiful windows.

Of course, there were details to iron out. Would they sell their Brooklyn homes? Or just one for the time being so Giuseppe could repair the White Elephant upstate that no one else seemed to want but them? There was time enough to figure this out. And they had all the time in the world. Or did they?

After Miss Collins left, Giuseppe took his wife for a stroll on the old Delaware and Hudson Canal towpath. Never had either of them seen such a brilliant October. The sugar maple leaves were a brighter gold, the oak leaves a more vivid red. It was even more beautiful than fall on Shore Road or in Green-Wood Cemetery. But perhaps the extraordinary beauty could be attributed to the newness of it all, of the Stone Ridge forest, of their clandestine marriage. Giuseppe's family would know soon enough, Valerie told herself. She hoped they'd be pleased for the couple.

Could these aging City Mice transform into Country Mice? Could they live in the forest year-round, through the long, cold, gray winters? 'Yes,' Valerie thought. 'Yes, I think we could.'

Over time, the bruises around Antonio's eyes healed, although his once-perfect Roman nose was now slightly crooked. Twice the police from the Sixty-Eighth Precinct came by the shop and asked him to recount the incident that had brought him to the pavement so brutally it had broken bones. And twice, Antonio said he didn't recall what had occurred. But he knew they didn't believe him.

"Mr. DeMarco, if someone has threatened you or you feel unsafe, we can protect you," Officer Napoli assured him. But Antonio knew there was nothing anyone could do. He had refused the wishes of a mafioso, and this had

angered the man, angered him to the point of violence.
Mario Inzitari could have Antonio removed with as much
care as one might flick away a gnat. Just to prove a point.
The words, 'Nobody says 'no' to me,' echoed in Antonio's
mind. And yet, he had said 'no' to Mr. Inzitari. The
mild-mannered tailor spent his time waiting for the
other shoe to drop.

Just as Valerie had predicted, Luisa *did* do a fine job
managing The Avid Reader on her own in the handful
of days her boss was gone. It was busy, what with
students scrambling to get paperbacks for assignments
and the usual autumn surge in reading. During that time
span, there was both a knitting circle and a children's
story hour, so Luisa enlisted the help of Gloria and
Siobhan for the latter. The girls chose to read aloud the
brand-new book, *Hats on Parade,* with its vibrant pictures
and simple, repetitive text. They traded off pages and held
up the book so the children could see the illustrations.

The story was about a silly street vendor who wore all
his wares on his head. The children, in a semi-circle before
Gloria and Siobhan, were quizzed about the order of the
hats in his pile. They chortled and repeated the words:

> *...black hats, yellow hats, green hats and at the
> very top...*

"Pink hats!" the kids shouted with glee. They were
aghast when a crew of unruly raccoons stole the vendor's
hats. Gianni actually fell out of his seat because he was
laughing so hard when Siobhan showed them the picture
of the raccoons in the tree wearing the vendor's hats.

"You raccoons, you!" Gloria and Siobhan yelled
together, shaking their fists. The children shook their fists
back at them just as the little brown raccoons did in the

book. Siobhan thought the mustachioed street vendor resembled Gloria's father with his natty suit jacket, tie and smart striped slacks that matched his hat.

Luisa looked on with delight as she rang out a customer. The listeners never had this sort of reaction when she or Valerie presided over Story Hour. Perhaps it was the novelty of having children not much older than themselves in charge of the event. The girls read with gusto and total abandon, adopting goofy voices for the vendor who scolded the raccoons. Luisa would talk to Valerie about asking Gloria and Siobhan to do this every week. It might bring in more customers if the kids chatted it up at school.

The sky was beginning to color. Next month, when daylight savings time began, it would be dark by now. The weather was so temperate that Luisa propped open the bookshop's front door. The sounds of Fifth Avenue sifted in: high heels on the pavement, voices immersed in conversation, the ting of the trolley. A newsboy's shrill call sliced through the air. "Extra! Extra! Read all about it! Shooting at Lorenzo's Clam House!"

Luisa's heart dropped. Lorenzo's was only blocks from Chatonio's. Had Inzitari's wrath finally come to a head? Did the spurned mobster off her husband in a fit of rage? Luisa willed herself to calmly walk behind the counter and dial the telephone. No answer. It was just after five and Chatonio's would be closed. Antonio would be on his way home, she prayed.

But the raccoons only stomped their paws...,
read Gloria.

Should Luisa buy *The Daily News* from the boy? She didn't want to know if her worst nightmare was true. Just a few more moments of ignorance, of uncertainty. Her insides turned to liquid as she perched her body onto the high stool behind the counter. That bastard Inzitari wouldn't be so bold as to...

At last, the vendor got so mad that he ripped off his own striped hat and hurled it to the grass, read Siobhan, mimicking the action.

As the children roared with laughter, Luisa held back her tears. How could she live without Antonio? How could she raise her family on her own? How... She looked to the ground, hunched over, as if she'd been struck. Luisa's breath came in quick bursts. Somehow her lungs weren't filling with air. She wrapped her arms around her waist to soothe herself but even this didn't work.

A heavy set of footsteps approached. "Sitting down on the job?" a voice said. Luisa looked up. Antonio!

He had the evening newspaper clutched in his fist. Luisa flew into her husband's arms. "There's been a shooting," she mumbled into his chest, breathing in the familiar musk of her husband.

Antonio held her close. "I know." They unfurled the newspaper and read.

Birthday Blast at Local Mob Hangout

It wasn't mussel shells that were flying this afternoon at Lorenzo's Clam House but shotgun shells! An otherwise peaceful autumn day was racked with the rat-a-tat-tat of gunfire at the popular mob haunt perched on the corner of Eighty-Sixth Street and Fourteenth Avenue in the Bensonhurst section of Brooklyn.

The victim, New York gangster Mario Inzitari, was the suspected crime boss of the Morrongiello Family. Inzitari was shot and killed at the restaurant as his party of family and friends, including his wife, daughter and bodyguard, were celebrating Inzitari's forty-third birthday with a late lunch at the eatery. A rival gangster eyeballed Inzitari and reportedly sent hitmen shortly after Inzitari was seated at a butcher block table in a back corner. He was shot five times before he stumbled onto the street and died.

Miraculously, no one else was injured in the shootout, which spilled out onto the busy avenue. Inzitari's bodyguard, Rocco Mancini, was apprehended in an unrelated charge for unlicensed firearms.

Lorenzo's proprietor, Matthew 'Matty the Horse' LoPresti, dove into the kitchen and lay on the floor with his hands over his head as two men entered the side door blasting. "He came in for the scungilli; he left on a stretcher," LoPresti remarked sadly.

'Madman Mario,' as he was known on the street, was legendary for his fiery temper. Inzitari had reportedly made his fair share of enemies in his bloody rise to the top of one of New York City's most notorious crime families. Racketeering, dealing in illegal wares, prostitution and drug sales are among the litany of illegal acts associated with Inzitari. Although arrested repeatedly, none of the charges stuck. "Nobody says 'no' to me," was his common refrain, according to the New York City Organized Crime Unit.

Well, today, somebody did, in the form of a bullet bouquet.

Luisa and Antonio looked at each other in shock. "It's over," he said, hugging his wife. The pages of the *Daily News* fluttered to the ground as Gloria began reading *The Five Chinese Brothers* to the children.

November 1940

Franklin Delano Roosevelt defeats Wendell Willkie and is reelected for a third presidential term.

The city center of Coventry, England is destroyed by 500 Luftwaffe bombers as 150,000 firebombs, 503 tons of high explosives and 130 parachute mines level 60,000 of the city's 75,000 buildings, including the cathedral, killing 568.

Comedy duo Abbott and Costello make their film debut in One Night in the Tropics.

Watching Luisa and her sisters flutter about the crowded Thanksgiving kitchen was a true thing of beauty. To Antonio, it was reminiscent of butterflies flickering through a garden, drifting here, landing there, then moving on. There was no rush or hurry. Every movement seemed effortless yet full of purpose. No motion was wasted.

It seemed as though Luisa, Barbara and Mina had been working together in kitchens like this forever when in reality, they had not. Perhaps it was the benevolent ghost of their mother, Assunta, who guided them with more gentle kindness than she had possessed in life. Perhaps it was the unspoken bond of females who, at different times, had inhabited the same womb. Perhaps it was their common blood. But Antonio hadn't witnessed other sisters who moved about the kitchen in such a manner.

Although Gloria and Valerie were present, they were mere handmaidens, helpers, retrieving a dish or washing a bowl. Siobhan tried hard to join the circle too. But these three existed on the periphery rather than pierced the inner sanctum. They cleared antipasto platters from the two large tables in the dining room while the trio of Tozzi sisters danced through Luisa's kitchen, checking the doneness of the turkey, stirring the gravy, mashing the potatoes, melting the marshmallows atop the candied yams casserole.

At last, Thanksgiving supper was ready. They each grabbed a dish and helped move this moveable feast to the tabletops so the food could be eaten hot. Platters and bowls were passed from table to table. For once, there was silence, only to be broken by the sound of cutlery on Luisa's good china as nineteen…or was it twenty?…ate their fill.

Antonio gazed up from his plate, pleased that Franco, Rosa and Teo could make the pilgrimage from Westchester, having graduated from their cramped Williamsburg apartment two years earlier. And there was old Zia Claudia, still sharp as a tack, still lovely. Luisa's father, brothers, their spouses (plus Paolo's sweetheart Julianna) and their brood rounded out the group. These women in the ensemble comprised the second wave of the cleanup committee.

Taking advantage of a comfortable lull in the conversing and supping, Giuseppe cleared his throat. First, he thanked God for the grace of bringing them all together yet another year. Then he toasted his wonderful daughters for bringing such a sumptuous meal to the table. Then he raised his glass to Antonio, their host, who opened the DeMarco home to them year after year.

"Maybe next year, though," Giuseppe tagged on, "we can celebrate in another place."

"Sam's isn't big enough but…" Luisa began, helping herself to a touch more of the yams.

"Ours isn't either," Dom's wife sighed.

"I was thinking of a different place," Giuseppe said. "A place in the country." The table began chattering all at once: "the country…" and "where in the world?…" and "is he losing his mind?…" Until the patriarch silenced them. "Valeria and I have purchased such a place, you see," Giuseppe said. "In a little town about one hundred miles north called Stony Ridge."

Valerie touched his hand. "Stone Ridge," she corrected gently.

"You *bought* a place," Paolo struggled to understand. "But how?"

"How does one usually buy a place?" Giuseppe laughed. "With money. *Con soldi*." With that, Giuseppe pulled the sales brochure from his suit jacket, unfolded it and showed them. It was passed around the table until Sam read out loud, "Colonial cottage…four bedrooms… two baths…ten bucolic acres… what the hell's 'bucolic'?" Sam asked. "It sounds like a disease."

"Language, Serafino," Luisa reminded him, then added, "Bucolic means relating to the pleasant aspects of country life." She glanced at the sheet. "Papa, it looks very nice."

"Thank you," he said. "It needs some work, though," he admitted.

"But it has good bones," Valerie tagged on.

"We could use help getting it up to snuff," Giuseppe said.

"You've got it, Pop," Paolo told him. "Say no more."

"Is it the best time, though?" Mina worried. "I mean, the war and the…"

"It's a fine time," her father assured her. "We aren't getting any younger. And if not now, when?"

The flurry of conversation continued. About the price of drywall, brass pipes and possibly a new oil burner. Giuseppe broke through the planning and postulating to drop another bombshell. "Oh, and Valeria and I got married," he told them.

There was a communal gasp. "When the hell did that happen?" Dom piped.

"Dominic, mind your tongue!" Luisa nudged her brother. The children giggled at yet another profanity. How had Luisa not noticed that glittering emerald on Valerie's finger, the wedding band?

"Last month," Giuseppe shrugged.

"October ninth, to be exact," Valerie said.

"We didn't want to…how do you call it…live in sin," Giuseppe explained. "So, say hello to your new stepmother."

"Oh, boy!" piped Gianni. "A stepmother! Just like in Cinderella."

"Except this one's not evil," Luisa pointed out.

Valerie became flustered as the family crowded around her, bathing her in hugs and poking gentle fun at the geriatric bride and groom. "I wanted to make an honest woman out of her," Giuseppe quipped.

They took a short break for dessert, first packing the leftovers into parcels that everyone could take home to enjoy the following day. The sisters-in-laws washed and dried the dishes while the sisters prepped and arranged the desserts: an array of pies, biscotti and cream cakes, all homemade. The coffee perked in the urn while the tea kettle warmed on the burner. The dining room tables were reset for dessert as the excited talk of Giuseppe and Valerie's home in the woods resumed.

But something troubled Luisa. She touched her stepmother's arm. "What about the bookshop?"

"Ah, I have an idea about that," Valerie admitted. "A proposition. I was wondering if you might want to buy it from me."

"Buy it?" Luisa repeated, in shock. She never thought she would own a home, let alone a business.

"Yes, buy it." Valerie told her.

"But I don't think I could afford..."

Valerie smiled. "The asking price is one dollar. Could you afford that?"

"Yes, I...I think I might," Luisa stammered. "Antonio?"

"It sounds fair," he consented. "More than fair."

"But there are some conditions," Valerie counted off on her fingers. "First, that you keep it for at least ten years."

"I could do that," Luisa agreed.

"And second," Valerie stressed. "That your father and I always have a place to stay when we come visit the family in Brooklyn."

"But of course!" Luisa said. "That goes without saying." Her face darkened. "But this seems too generous an offer. How could you afford..."

Valerie squeezed Luisa's hand. "That's not your concern, my girl. Besides, between the sale of both Giuseppe's and my homes, well, we'll be very comfortable."

"What about us?" Mina said, gesturing to herself and Paolo.

Giuseppe told his daughter, "It will take a while to get the house up and running and you'll both be on your own before you know it. But you and Paolo are welcome to come join us upstate."

"Thanks, but I ain't no country bumpkin," Paolo said with a glance at Julianna. "Besides, I got ties here."

"We understand," Valerie told him. "But please remember there's a place for you in Stone Ridge. For all of you."

Guiseppi chimed in. "But I expect you guys to put in...how do you call it? Sweat equality..."

"...equity," Valerie corrected.

"Sweat equity in our home," Giuseppe continued. "From making curtains to patching walls to stripping

323

floors. This way, you'll all be part of the place in Stony Ridge in some way."

"Stone Ridge," Gloria corrected this time. She liked the idea of a home in the country just like the City Mouse and the Country Mouse. Maybe Nonna would let Siobhan visit too.

Sitting beside Gloria, Siobhan laughed to herself at the Tozzis and DeMarcos, all animatedly speaking over one another in a mixture of English and Italian. There was always something exciting going on at Gloria's place. Not the same sort of excitement that occurred in the Reilly home several doors down—no fallen-down-drunk parents, no fight that's broken out because the last of the Four Roses has disappeared and no one would own up to it. This was good excitement, positive excitement. And you never knew what might happen next.

That evening, Antonio found it difficult to sleep. From his over-stuffed belly to Giuseppe's dual revelations. Not only was the old man moving upstate but he was married! And Luisa would soon be a business owner. Though The Avid Reader didn't pull in a ton of money, it showed comfortable, steady earnings thanks to his wife's dedication and ingenuity. He had no doubt that it would continue to flourish.

"It was nice wasn't it, Tonio," Luisa whispered dreamily from the other side of the bed, a slight smile on her face, tiredness tinging her words. "Especially the lasagna, eh?" It was a mystery why Italians insisted upon a pasta course, even in their American holidays, but the Tozzis were guilty of this overindulgence.

"Especially the lasagna," he agreed. "But the turkey was delicious too. And the stuffing. Everything was, Lu."

When no response came, Antonio realized that Luisa had drifted off to sleep, heavy as a stone, exhausted from the Thanksgiving Day preparations and its execution. Though his body ached slightly from all the table-assembling and chair-toting, Antonio still couldn't rest his beehive mind. So much had transpired in the past few days, the past few weeks. It was a relief to be free of dread, just to be busy and content and full.

Although Antonio told himself that he should stay far away, he couldn't help but attend Mario Inzitari's funeral the month earlier. It was almost as though Antonio needed one final confrontation with the bogeyman before he could rid himself of the monster. Perhaps he needed evidence that the Wicked Witch was dead and needed to watch her disintegrate into a puff of smoke before he would believe she was truly gone.

It wasn't enough for Antonio to visit Lorenzo's Clam House to witness a worker scrubbing Inzitari's blood from the sidewalk. Antonio needed more. So, he went to church.

Antonio considered it ironic that the funeral for such a sinister man was held at a church as exquisite as Our Lady of Perpetual Help. For clearly, there had been nothing helpful about Mario Inzitari. He seemed to take an unnatural thrill in doing just the opposite—in destroying people rather than aiding them.

The gray granite behemoth was perched between Fifth and Sixth Avenues between Fifty-Ninth and Sixtieth Streets. Romanesque with a limestone exterior, the most important citizens of Sunset Park and beyond were married, baptized and sent to their eternal rest at OLPH. Inzitari's glistening coffin was muscled by eight henchmen down the two-hundred-and-twenty-foot-long center aisle. One of them was Rocco Mancini, newly released from jail, his face ashen. Perhaps Rocco feared he would be next on the hit list.

The church yawned one-hundred-and-ninety feet wide and was full almost to capacity that day. It was said to hold eighteen-hundred souls. Antonio took a seat in the last row, hoping no one would notice him slip in. But there were some in attendance whose job it was to notice.

Inzitari's coffin came to rest on a platform before the altar, then was covered with a white and gold embroidered cloth. Black would have been a more appropriate color, Antonio ventured.

The dome above the altar depicted the Assumption of Mary. The altar itself was semicircular, surrounded by murals portraying Christ the King, Moses, David and John the Baptist. Above them, a host of angels presided. Encased in a marble cage was the crucifixion, the cross appearing to be hewn from real wood. How Assunta would have basked in a church this grand. Antonio wondered if she'd ever visited it.

Sunlight streamed in through OLPH's stained-glass windows on the second level. The rich reds were Antonio's favorite. So rare was he in church—he had many bones to pick about the opulence of Catholic churches and how the sect squeezed every penny possible from its poor parishioners. But Antonio observed this church not through the eyes of a true disciple but as someone who appreciated fine architecture, the artfulness of a structure, the craft, even if OLPH's design was a bit over the top.

To Antonio, the fact that a man as purely evil as Inzitari could be celebrated with a mass was the height of hypocrisy. He sat quietly, without comment, in the back row, impassively watching the gangster's sniffling wife, his grieving daughter. How many families had Mario Inzitari caused to grieve?

When the funeral was over, Antonio stood outside, leaning against a pillar, taking it all in. The exit procession was a march of Who's Who in the mob underworld. There were faces Antonio recognized from the newspapers, and, of course, Rocco, who glared at him but could do nothing as he helped carry his former *capo*'s coffin to the waiting hearse.

"Sorry about your friend," a voice rang out. Antonio recognized the man as Officer Napoli, the one who'd questioned him after his attack weeks earlier. Only now Napoli was out of his uniform and in an ill-fitting suit.

"Mario Inzitari wasn't my friend," Antonio corrected the officer.

"Then what was he?" the fellow accompanying Napoli asked. He was bulky, light-haired, Nordic-looking, also wearing a cheap suit.

"More of an acquaintance," Antonio said.

"Ah, a business acquaintance," the second cop huffed knowingly.

"I did business with him," Antonio qualified. "Tailoring. I made Mr. Inzitari suits of clothing."

When the larger cop opened his mouth to further torment Antonio, Officer Napoli nipped it in the bud. "Knock it off, Mikalsen," he told his partner. "Antonio is good people. He just had the misfortune of getting tangled up with 'Evil Inzi' and lived to tell the tale. No small feat."

"How do we know this WOP ain't a crook too?" Mikalsen asked. Antonio cringed at the word, an abbreviation, really, but it was still hurtful. Napoli winced at it too. The term WOP stood for "without papers." Both Napoli and Antonio had papers to prove their citizenship, yet the moniker stung.

"I can always tell," the Italian police officer assured the Norwegian. "If anything, Mr. DeMarco's a victim."

Officer Mikalsen wasn't so sure. "Ah, you WOPs always stick together," he admitted in defeat. Again, the other two men flinched at the word.

"And you Squareheads don't?" Napoli told him. "Knock it off, Per."

"Still, we could have the Dago deported," Mikalsen pushed.

"The Dago is a citizen," Antonio said proudly. "I'm an American, like you."

Napoli put a solid hand on Mikalsen's beefy shoulder. "Besides, he's married to Sam's sister, so he's a straight arrow in my book."

"Sam Tozzi?" Mikalsen gasped.

"The very same," Napoli confirmed. "And Sam will kick your sorry Weegie butt next time he sees you in Kelly's Tavern if he ever gets wind of this. Dom too."

Mikalsen's entire demeaner changed. He clapped Antonio on the back, nudging him forward. "Hey, no hard feelings, chief, huh?"

"No hard feelings," Antonio lied, his blood boiling to his ears.

Mikalsen walked off, leaving his partner to clean his mess. "Pay him no mind," Napoli told Antonio. "He's not a bad fellow, just a bit..."

"Ignorant?"

"Yeah, that too." Napoli adjusted his cap. "Hey, you still have that place on Eighteenth Avenue?"

"I do," Antonio said. "With my partner Charles." Antonio fit his fedora back onto his head, fixing it at a jaunty angle. "Come by sometime. I'll give you a fair price. A man like you deserves to look sharp."

Napoli laughed. "I might just do that."

Weeks later, on a quiet Thanksgiving evening, Antonio recalled his visit to Our Lady's church, his encounter with Officer Napoli and his boorish partner. Antonio remembered finally, resolutely, putting the ghost of Mario Inzitari to rest. The humble sartor was thankful for many things in his life—his home, his family, his health, his business (though floundering, it was slowly recovering). But most of all, he was grateful that the vengeful mafioso no longer darkened his doorstep.

December 1940

Captain America, a superhero born in Red Hook, Brooklyn, hits comic books for the very first time.

Mahatma Gandhi writes his second letter to Adolf Hitler, calling him "My friend" and asks him to stop the war Germany has begun.

In a fireside chat to the nation, Franklin Delano Roosevelt says that the United States must become "the great arsenal of democracy."

Christmastime was bittersweet. War was looming and no one was sure which of the Tozzi boys would be called to arms first. (Or would they all be foolish enough to enlist together?) Was Antonio too old to be drafted? These concerns plagued Gloria as she helped her mother and brother trim the tree two days before Christmas. A sad, little Scotch pine this year.

Antonio was still at work, determined to make a go of the struggling shop. There was a last-minute rush on gowns, dress coats and other finery for the holidays. Antonio hoped to capitalize on this surge and didn't refuse any job, no matter how small. He also didn't want to ruin his workers' holidays by making them stay late so close to Christmas, although he knew they would. They would do anything for Antonio.

He treasured the solitude, finally breaking the shop's silence with the strains of Schumann's *"Frauen-Liebe und Leben"* on the office Victrola. Occasionally, Antonio traded the Italians for the Teutons, but these days it was rare. True, the Germans could make violent and terrible war, but they could also make achingly-beautiful music.

Antonio didn't hear Luisa come in, so he was startled to see her standing before his sewing machine, shaking flakes of snow from her cloak, her hair. She carried a wicker picnic basket. Inside were chicken cutlets (leftover from the family's supper) pressed into a hunk of soft, split Italian bread and wrapped in waxed paper. She'd also tucked in a handful of the Christmas cookies she'd been making with the children the past few days, along with a Thermos of strong coffee. "I thought you were putting up the tree," he said.

"It's done," Luisa told him. "I thought you might be hungry."

"I am," he admitted.

"Then eat," she said, unpacking the contents of the basket onto Anna's vacant cutting table.

Luisa sat and watched her husband eat, chewing thoroughly and completely, as was his fashion. To this day, she liked the way Antonio ate—purposefully, neatly, taking his time between bites, savoring the food offered to him like a gift. Not like her brothers, who gobbled their meals like hungry strays. Antonio dabbed the corners of his mouth with his napkin. "Won't you join me?" he said after a couple of bites, remembering his manners.

She shook her head. After all this time—what was it…thirteen years? Fifteen? Luisa had lost count. But after all this time, she still loved him. Still liked him, even. "I already ate," Luisa told him.

"Of course, you did," Antonio said. "It's late."

"Gloria offered to put Gio to bed so I could bring you supper."

Antonio nodded. "She's a good girl."

Luisa nodded in return. "A young woman, almost."

"Almost."

Antonio folded the waxed paper neatly into squares then placed it into the basket. They shared the cookies, trading the jar of coffee back and forth between them, chatting about their days. Luisa saw the pile of sewing to be done. She offered to help, not waiting for a response, instead, taking her place at the machine that was usually Raquel's, if she remembered correctly. "Ah, it's like getting back on a bicycle," Luisa said.

"But you can't ride a bike," her husband reminded her.

"A mere technicality," she smiled. "But if I did ride a bike, it would be this familiar." They worked quietly for a number of minutes. "Who is this?" she wondered, pausing to take in the music, letting it surround her. "Wagner?"

"Close," he said. "Schumann."

"Ah, yes," Luisa told him, working her knee on the sewing machine's pedal. "The one about the woman's life: her one true love, the engagement, the haircut. And everything in between."

"That's the one," Antonio said.

More silence. They conquered garment after garment. The pile to be done grew smaller. "Do you remember when you worked from our railroad apartment above the sweets shop? When you were expecting Glorina?"

"Heffernan's. How could I forget?" Luisa said, above the machine's whir, above the music.

"Those were some of the happiest days of my life," Antonio admitted.

"Mine too," Luisa told him.

"Simple times. Uncomplicated times."

"Though we didn't realize it then," she conceded. "We worried so much."

"Is today any different?"

Luisa smiled. "Still, if I had it to do all over again, I would worry less."

Antonio laughed. "*Veramente?* You?"

"Yes. Truly. Me." Then Luisa became more serious. "So many changes will come this next year. In the world, in this family."

"There are always changes," Antonio reminded her, pausing to swap the thread on his machine from black to white. "Change is the very essence of life. We grow, we learn."

"Not all the time, though," she reminded him.

"If we are smart, we learn," he said. "And we are smart, *bella.*"

The neat, squat mock Tudor home on the corner of Ridge Boulevard and Eighty-Fourth Street was dark by the time Antonio and Luisa DeMarco returned home. Gloria had left the Christmas tree lights on in the parlor so her parents could enjoy it the moment they stepped through the front door. They welcomed the brief lull in their lives before holiday preparations began in earnest.

Before the Eve, before the day. Before the *frito misto* was breaded and fried. Before the *struffoli* was first boiled in oil then bathed in honey. Before the seven fishes were cooked. Before the gifts were wrapped then ripped open and gutted like mackerel. Before Gianni asked, "Is he here yet?" ("He" being Santa Claus.) Before the caroling and the card-playing. Before finally, finally coming home from supper at Giuseppe's on Christmas night. Before all of this, Luisa and Antonio took a moment to appreciate the silence. They sat on their worn, tufted, red velvet sofa and gazed at the lights of their Christmas tree.

Days later, after it was all over and it was officially the day *after* Christmas, Luisa went up to bed, wearing her new fuzzy slippers. (A gift from her sister Mina.) Luisa was surprised to see a crudely-wrapped present set on her pillow slightly after midnight on December 26th. Was this a gift Antonio had forgotten to give her during the day? No. The tag bore Gloria's neat, Catholic school handwriting.

"Merry Christmas, Mama. I think you need one of these," it read.

Inside the package was an indigo blue journal. A fountain pen was attached to the diary with a gilded ribbon. Luisa smiled. It reminded her of the red-covered journal her fourth-grade teacher, Mrs. Fitzpatrick, had given her when she was a girl. How could Gloria have remembered?

Luisa uncapped the pen, opened the book and started to write:

"Immigrant hearts…" she began, *"…are different than typical hearts…"*

1978

Epilogue

When my mother Luisa died two months ago, among her things I found the journal I'd given her for Christmas in 1940. It was stashed in her nightstand beside the bed she shared with my father Antonio for more than forty years.

In the beginning, she wrote in her diary religiously, daily. Sometimes, it was just a sentence or two. Others, she scrawled pages upon pages. Toward the end she didn't write in it often, just a few entries a year.

After I unearthed it, I read Mama's diary hungrily, from cover to cover. More than once. It contained almost forty years of her life.

Luisa's more recent journal entries tended to hinge upon important events: birthdays, holidays, births, deaths, the day John F. Kennedy was shot, the day Neil Armstrong walked on the moon... I was always struck by my mother's constant joy and amazement with life. At how she luxuriated in uncomplicated pleasures and deeply mourned losses.

Her baby brother Paolo was killed in the Battle of Anzio. In January 1944, she'd scrawled:

There are no words for this kind of grief...

The page is warped, the ink smeared, from where her tears stained the paper.

Thank God, this awful war is finally over… was her entry on September 2, 1945.

Not again… she scribbled when the Korean Conflict began in 1950.

What a great time to be alive… she wrote when Elizabeth became queen in 1953.

Also tucked into the pages of Luisa's journal was a photograph of my mom and dad holding Ji-a soon after I adopted her from Korea. To be clear, my daughter has two mommies: me and Siobhan. But in the 1950s, convent orphanages didn't permit two women to adopt an abandoned child. Even in the wake of war. So, I'm Ji-a's mother on paper and Siobhan is 100% Mother #2.

Ji-a (Americanized, or Italianized, to "Gina") roughly translates to "wise and beautiful." To see how my Italian immigrant parents opened their hearts to this scared, scrawny little Korean immigrant and to see Ji-a blossom under my family's love was unbelievably moving. Immigrants stick together, I guess. No matter where they're from.

Yes, Siobhan and I are still together. We've never actually been apart. Although sometimes throughout our decades together, we've had to pretend that we were sisters, cousins or really, really close friends. But it's all right. We know the truth. Our families know the truth. And that's good enough for the two of us.

Siobhan helps me with the bookstore. Bookstores, I should say. When ZiaVal—who became Nonna Val after

she married my grandfather—gave my mom The Avid
Reader for the grand sum of one dollar, my mother hired
me and Siobhan to help her run it. Even though we were
barely thirteen, she trusted us completely. And we were
great at it too! Siobhan and I brought in a whole new
clientele—kids—and teenage reading groups. Our first
teen book club selection was *Little Women* and we read
all the Alcott books in the series including *Good Wives*
which none of us seemed to enjoy. Too sexist, Siobhan
had grumbled.

My mom ran the bookstore until 1959, when she
turned it over to us. And two years ago, Siobhan and I
opened a little bookshop in Stone Ridge, where Nonno
Giuseppe bought that lock tender's cottage back in 1940.
Before he died, Nonno built upon it and built upon it
until it became more like the Tozzi Family Compound
with sheds, outbuildings and even a chicken coop.
When she passed, Nonna Val left the property to her
stepchildren as a legacy gift and enough money to keep it
going. And it's still in the family to this day.

When we opened the upstate bookstore, Siobhan
and I moved up here too. We bought a sweet cottage off
Binnewater Road in Rosendale, the town next door to
Stone Ridge. Siobhan and I called the bookshop "Luisa's
Lair." It's in a cozy spot off Main Street that occupies a
former dairy farmer's milking shed. My mother loved it.
Loved that we named the upstate bookstore for her.

After taking a break from school, Gina decided to
go back to college and is working toward her master's in
Asian studies at SUNY New Paltz, so she's close by.

My bratty little brother Gianni is still in Brooklyn
and manages The Avid Reader. He expanded into the
space next door and added an adorable coffee shop to the
works. It's a great place where people feel comfortable, a
spot to learn and convene and get caffeinated. He often
hosts reading events by local authors, not just famous
ones. Believe it or not, Gianni kept the old hot plate

my mother used to create simple meals for their hungry clientele. It's on display behind the coffee counter like a shrine, a homage to our mom.

I guess you're wondering about my father. Antonio and Uncle Charlie kept the tailor shop until just before my dad's sixty-fifth birthday, when he decided it was time to retire. Just like that, suddenly one day. Gradually over the years, his employees shifted from Italians to Asians. Again, immigrants, getting the job done. It was comical listening to my dad mangle the few words of Mandarin or Korean he managed to learn to communicate better with his staff.

Chatonio's never made a heap of money but that was all right; it made enough. And unlike most men of his day, my father never felt the need to compete with my mother to be the main breadwinner. As with most everything they did, they did it together. They shared the load. They supported the family equally. It was seamless and worked well for them.

Antonio was very content in his retirement, always busy. He still read the news in two languages every day. He still went for long walks along Shore Parkway, his coattails flying in the breeze like wings.

On November 21, 1964, the day the Verrazano-Narrows Bridge opened, he and my mom got dressed in their Sunday best and took Ji-a across the bridge on the bus. On the first stop in Staten Island, they got off, crossed the street and took the bus back to Bay Ridge. It was a momentous occasion for my folks, the longest suspension bridge in the world at the time, named for an Italian.

Four years later, Antonio was found sitting on a park bench on Shore Road, facing his treasured Verrazano-Narrows Bridge. A woman walking her dog thought he was napping but he still hadn't moved when she came back from Key Food two hours later. My dad hadn't fallen asleep; he was dead. This was in 1968; he was sixty-nine.

I didn't think my mother would be able to function without him. After all, they'd been together since she was a teenager. But like everything else thrown into her path, difficult as it was, Luisa managed to soldier through.

Antonio's funeral mass was held was at St. Patrick's Church, where they'd married in 1927. Where my Nonna Assunta had died in 1932. Where Gianni and I, and later, my daughter Gina, had been baptized. And where Luisa had her funeral mass ten years after my dad's.

At first glance, my parents' lives might look very small. They didn't accomplish big things. They didn't travel very often, except to Stone Ridge. Few besides the family and the Bay Ridge community knew who they were. But I think it's these supposedly tiny lives like theirs that make all the difference. It's these seemingly insignificant people who create the true fabric of our society. It's the immigrant hearts beating that make the world go on. And on. They always will.

Acknowledgements

After I finished my seventh novel, *Cry of Silence*, I spent time thinking about what my next book should be. At some point, I realized that except for flashes of *Better than Sisters*, I hadn't written much about my mother's side of the family. ("The El Trilogy" was all about my dad's side.) Growing up, I loved hearing the story of how my maternal grandparents met. They were two ordinary people who never did anything extraordinary and yet...

This is how *Immigrant Hearts* was born. I took the truth and ran with it.

I always find it challenging to christen my characters, so I borrow the names of friends and family. An avid reader and one of my biggest cheerleaders, I dubbed a major character after my friend Valerie Hodgson. I borrowed the beautiful, lyrical name Assunta from my friend Antonella's mother, who sadly passed away while I was writing this book. And one of Chatonio's star seamstresses, Raquel, was named for another grandmother who worked in the garment industry for much of her 101 years. Then there's the surname of my friend Scott Mura and the conglomeration of a buddy's wrestling name and real name. But unlike the novel's Mario Inzitari, Len is a sweetheart of a guy.

The idea of a multifaceted bookshop came from Bay Ridge's indie bookstore, The BookMark Shoppe, whose inventive owner Christine Freglette offers knitting classes and sells crafts from local artisans. I borrowed the setting of my friend Susan Einhorn's idyllic creekside cottage for the Tozzis' upstate home. And so on.

I'd like to thank my former classmate Maria Cornacchio-Kehoe for being an early reader and for not casting judgement upon my very raw second draft. Maria had excellent suggestions as well as an eagle eye. Kudos to my cousin Bobbi Wicks for being a devoted late reader, as she's been with so many of my books. And a huge thanks to my friend Jackie Castro for always being so encouraging. A shout out to Joy Rosenthal, Esq. for sharing her legal expertise. Much gratitude to my cousin Susanne for sharing with me the photos that grace the book's front and back covers

My publisher and friend Vinnie Corbo greets my projects with enthusiasm and offers a fresh, creative eye, personally designing outstanding covers and interiors, as well as picking perfect between-the-sections vectors.

Finally, appreciation goes out to my family for accepting the neglect that goes hand in hand with writing. A big thank-you to my husband Peter for his never-ending support and "patronizing the arts," as he so aptly phrases it.

And of course, I would be nothing without my readers, who continue to challenge me with, "What's next?"

About the Author

Catherine Gigante-Brown is a Brooklyn-born writer of fiction, nonfiction, poetry, scripts and plays. Her articles and essays have appeared in publications like *Time Out New York, Essence, Ravishly* and *Literary Hub*. Her poetry and fiction are included in several anthologies. A handful of her films and theatrical works have been produced. Catherine's novels *The El, The Bells of Brooklyn* and *Brooklyn Roses* (aka "The El Trilogy"), *Different Drummer* (which is also a musical), *Better than Sisters, Paul and Carol Go to Guatemala* and *Cry of Silence* are all published by Volossal. Catherine and her husband split their time between their hometown, Florida and Rosendale, New York. Together, they have one son.